PAU HANA

PARADISE CRIME COZY MYSTERIES
BOOK 5

TOBY NEAL
JOANN BASSETT

FOR ALL THOSE WHO SMILE AT CHILDREN AND ANIMALS

PAU HANA
A Paradise Crime Cozy Mystery #5
By
TOBY NEAL
and
JOANN BASSETT

1

THE FIRST REPORT of the girl in the window came in around noon
on Tuesday. It should have been straightforward: notify local
authorities, police show up and rescue the kidnapped child, bad
guy goes off to jail. But it didn't go that way. Not by a long shot.

I would've remembered that Tuesday even without the girl in
the window, because that was the day we got a new neighbor.
Leaving for my job as postmaster that morning, I spied a moving
van parked in the driveway of a cul-de-sac near the entrance to
what is now known as New Ohia State Park.

Aunt Fae and I lived in a former model home in the planned
subdivision that's now a state park. Terrazzo floors, ten-foot ceil-
ings, stainless steel everything in the kitchen—you get the idea. For
a while we were the only residents of the community and paid our
rent by caretaking the park on weekends and holidays. The other
model homes sat empty and sad, pretty seashells with no hermit
crab to live in them.

I really wanted to check out who was moving in, but I didn't
want to be late for work. In a government customer service job we
got major grief for the little things: being tardy, not smiling, or that

all-encompassing beef, "going postal." Now that people could rate us online, it was tough to keep the one-star ratings to a minimum.

I walked briskly out of the park and over to the postal building. Still fumbling with my keys to the back door, I called Aunt Fae on my cell. "Did you know someone was moving in down on Pikake Court?"

"No."

"There's a moving truck there."

"I'm on it," Aunt Fae said immediately. "Needed to take my morning pep step anyway."

Normally I'm the private eye in the family. As a former Secret Service agent, my daytime job is working as Ohia postmaster, and in my other time I keep busy with a part-time investigation gig for Security Solutions, a firm based in Honolulu. I also partner in K & K Investigations, my own little company. One "K" is for me, Kat Smith, and the other "K" is for my boyfriend, Pacific Wings pilot Keone Kaihale.

"Boyfriend" really isn't the right designation for Mr. K, as I affectionately call him. He's no "boy" and we're certainly more than friends, but I'm not sure what to call our relationship dance—two steps forward, one banana peel slip back? I'm new to the whole romance thing and am trying to take things slow due to a touch-phobia I developed as a child. Mr. K makes that tough, though, because he's so darn lovable and looks like someone in the "Men of Hawaii" calendar the ABC Stores publish every year.

I ended the call to Aunt Fae and began my usual routine once inside the postal building. Ohia is the epitome of rural Maui. We're located at the far east side of the island, with more mongooses than people per square mile, and no house-to-house mail delivery. Everyone must come to the post office to either pick up their mail from their box or get it through General Delivery if they don't have a mailbox. My job mostly consists of sorting the mail, filling boxes, selling postage, weighing packages, and generally wrangling the "talk story" crowd that gums up the line at four o'clock, the end of our postal day.

Today Chad, our mail driver from the main office in Kahului, showed up early in his delivery truck.

"Wow," I said. "You're early. You got a hot date later today?"

"No. I heard something weird from my friend the UPS guy." Chad wasn't chatty. Blemished complexion aside, his flushed cheeks and widened eyes signaled that whatever he'd heard from the driver in the brown truck was significant.

"You want to tell me about it?" We walked around to the back of the truck as I waited for Chad to lay this gem on me when he was ready. Chad unlocked the hasp, opening the back to reveal that the truck was piled high with boxes and bags of mail, per usual. Online ordering had hit us hard in remote areas like Ohia.

"He told me he saw a little girl in the window of the house where that hermit guy lives out at the end of Halepua'a Road. He was pretty shook up about it."

"So?" I was relatively new in town and didn't know "that hermit guy" nor the place in question.

Chad squinted. "You know. That nasty hermit guy out at the back end of nowhere?"

I shrugged in answer, raising my hands. "Not ringing a bell."

"He's kinda legendary. Dude comes to town like twice a year. His place is way back in the jungle. I mean, it's not that far from here, but getting there consists of twenty minutes of tire-sucking mud and foot-deep potholes."

"So, what was UPS doing out that way?"

"My friend got lost. Once you get back in there the road's too narrow to get out of, so he had to keep going and hoped to turn around at the end. He said when he got there, it was this old shack kind of place. As he turned his truck, he saw a girl in the window with her hands on the glass, like this." He put up flat palms like a mime doing the "in a box" routine.

"What's so strange about that?" A couple of customers had come to the locked front door and from the frowns on their faces, they didn't appreciate me gossiping when they wanted to check their boxes.

"Something about her expression worried him. A lot. It seemed like she wanted help, as if maybe she was trapped out there. He asked if I knew what the deal was with the hermit guy suddenly having a little girl."

"You're pretty sure the Halepua'a guy lives alone?"

"Yes. No doubt." Chad cracked his knuckles. "Do you think I should report it or something?"

"You just did. *Mahalo*, Chad. Give me your friend's phone number, and I'll take it from here."

I wear more hats than an *ohia* tree has *lehua* blossoms. In addition to my jobs as postmaster and part-time investigator, I'm also the unofficial eyes and ears of the Maui Police Department in our town.

Once Chad and I unloaded the truck and I took care of the impatient customers, I hurried to my office. The tidy space with its glass window was a haven filled with the puffing steam of an aromatherapy dispenser provided by my co-worker, Pua Chang. I flopped into my chair and called my contact, Lei Texeira, a sergeant in the Maui Police Department, as I changed the "Energizing Eucalyptus" scent cartridge to "Peaceful Peach." Hopefully that would set a tone for the day.

"Texeira," Lei answered. No embellishments. She must be in a meeting or at a crime scene. We were in each other's contacts, so she had to know it was me calling.

"Lei. Got a minute for something . . . weird?"

"I'm just wrapping up a meeting here at headquarters," she said. Her tone implied: *Can't talk right now. My boss is up in my grill.*

"Got it. Call me when you're free."

Pua rolled in from the back, her kitten heels clicking. My co-worker was petite, perfect, and dressed in something classy and expensive, as usual. We were friends after a bumpy start, but I often felt as if I were a sheepdog looming over a whippet. She stuck her shiny coiffed head into my office and sniffed. "Peach. Nice." Her sharp brown eyes assessed me. "You seem frazzled, Kat. Anything I can do to help?"

"You're here, and that's already a help." I smiled at her. "So glad you're back to work. Running this place alone was no picnic. I'm waiting on an important call, so any chance you could open the front desk for us?"

"No problem." Pua withdrew and closed my door. She had boundaries, another quality I liked about her. I booted up the company computer and checked my work email.

Lei called fifteen minutes later. "Hey, Kat. You said you had something weird for me?"

"I don't know what it is, exactly, but just in case, I wanted to check in and let you know there's static on the coconut wireless about a hermit guy who lives out at the end of Halepua'a Road."

"No crime to be a hermit. Especially out your way," Lei said. Hana and its environs were known to attract the "off-the-grid" crowd with all that implied.

"Well, since he IS a hermit . . ." I was having trouble putting into words the worried feeling that had begun to form a lead ball in my stomach. "Our mail truck driver reported that his friend the UPS guy who went out that way spotted a female child in the window of the house. She may have been signaling for help, and Chad swears the guy lives alone."

"I see where you might be going with this. What's the hermit's name? Address?"

"Don't have that. Sorry. But I know it's the last place on Halepua'a Road."

"I can work with that."

"Do you want K & K to take a drive out there? Keone's last flight comes in at two, and I'm off at four. We can go check on the situation."

Keys rattled. Lei was on her computer checking something. A few beats went by before she responded. "I don't like the sound of this. I researched that address, and the occupant is a single male named Hugh Dragoon, according to the records. That must be your hermit. But there's no Amber Alert or 'child missing' Be On the Look Out at the moment." She blew out a breath; in my mind's eye, a brown curl lifted off her forehead, as I'd often seen happen in real life. "Pono's got court this afternoon and I'm scheduled to be on the West Side of Maui, in Kapalua, in less than an hour. That's literally as far away from Ohia as it's possible to be. It could take up to four hours to get out to you." It was like listening in on her internal dialogue. "I don't have time."

"So, is that a 'yes' on us checking into it?"

"It's a qualified 'yes.'"

"What do you want us to do?"

Lei chuckled. "Knowing you, it's better I clarify what I *don't* want you to do," she said.

I deserved that; I'd been known to break down the door and then check to see if it was unlocked. "Okay, shoot."

"Yeah, that's the first thing. No firearms. Under no circumstances do I want shots fired if there's a possible child on scene. Leave your weapon at home."

"Got it."

"Go by the address. If there's anything indicating a child's presence, I'll come out as soon as I can, or I'll send someone."

"Okay."

"But don't approach this Hugh Dragoon. That's for us to do if it's warranted."

"But how will I know if it's warranted if I don't talk to the guy?"

"You'll know. You've got good instincts. If possible, get some photos. Call me as soon as you've left the area after your visit."

"Will do."

"And Kat?"

"Yeah?"

"If this turns out to be something ugly, promise me you'll back off quickly. Hostage situations are the worst."

Like that wasn't chiseled into every Secret Service agent's brain. "You got it. I'll let you know how it goes, ASAP."

I glanced at the clock; four p.m. couldn't get here fast enough.

2

I usually eat at my desk, but the question of the new neighbor beckoned even as I tried to stay distracted about the girl in the window situation. I could answer my curiosity about at least one of the issues, so I went home for lunch at noon.

When I got to our house, Aunt Fae was nowhere in sight, which was odd. She's no recluse, but she does tend to be a homebody. Unless she was working at the Ohia General Store with our friends Opal and Artie, she was usually either watching a British cooking/baking show ("everyone is so polite!") or resting her feet on the comfy ottoman in the living room, perusing a cookbook or novel.

I called her name and listened, but the only sound in the silence of the house came from my formerly feral cat, Tiki. That one-eared, kink-tailed non-beauty of a calico squalled a "welcome home" while beelining to check if I'd returned to fill the kibble bowl a few hours early. She'd been hungry since her reappearance after giving birth to a litter of kittens and was intent on regaining her pre-baby weight. She was still nursing little gray Misty on occasion, the kitten we'd decided to keep, and that might have added to her calorie deficit, too.

Letting out an assertive yowl, Tiki wound around my calves in a kitty version of a square dance. *Allemande* left, then *do-si-do* your partner to the right. It was all I could do not to trip over her sashaying body.

"Okay, okay. I'm glad to see you, too." I bent down and gave her a pet; her patchy coat was smooth and soft and her puttering purr motor revved. She'd come a long way from the battered, unhealthy wildcat she'd been when we met. "Where's Auntie Fae, Tiki?" I asked.

Yep, I was talking to a cat.

I'd just asked Tiki Auntie's whereabouts, as if I expected her to clear her throat and say in a plummy, fake English accent. *I believe you'll find her in the conservatory, with the candlestick, possibly doing Colonel Mustard.*

I chuckled at my own humor because Tiki didn't; she had gone to sit beside her food bowl and placed a paw on its rim so I'd get the hint. "All right, all right."

I went to the pantry and opened the plastic cat food bin. Little Misty must have heard the sound; she came romping from the living room, tail held high, and pounced on her mother just as Tiki put her nose into the now-full bowl of food. Tiki's tail lashed in annoyance and she growled at her offspring. Misty was undeterred. She leapt repeatedly on Tiki's thrashing tail.

Watching Misty's antics, I mulled it over. Aunt Fae was allowed personal space, of course. Since she'd arrived in Ohia from her home in Maine, we'd done almost everything together, or with friends of mine.

Perhaps she needed a little "me time" away from... me?

I threw together a quick sandwich and, standing at the counter eating it, contemplated what I should take down to Pikake Court to welcome the new neighbors. Fruit? No, the pineapple on our counter was starting to emit an odor reminiscent of bad home brew. Sweets? Maybe. I went back to the pantry and dug through the shelves until I found the Hawaiian Host chocolate covered macadamia nuts we'd bought a week ago in Kahului. We'd picked up a bundled package of four boxes, because nothing says "Costco" like too much of a good thing—but now I frowned. There was only one box left.

Aunt Fae must have a taste for chocolate mac nuts—but then, who didn't love them? Surely our new neighbor would, too. I tucked the slim brown and yellow box under my arm and headed out.

THE UPSCALE PLANNED community of New Ohia had been laid out like a jacaranda tree, with the main road as the trunk and cul-de-sacs splitting off like so many clustered branches. The main road "trunk" ended at what used to be a swanky community center, with a sparkling blue topaz-colored pool and state-of-the-art fitness room. Our house was near the top, on a slight rise above the rest of the neighborhood. Pikake Court was one of the lower branches, close to the entrance.

The chichi community center was now open to the public. The pool hosted *keiki* (Hawaiian for "kiddos") swimming lessons, and at their morning aqua fitness classes, the local Red Hat Society ladies giggled and shrieked louder than the kids when they were in session.

The fitness center equipment had been sold to an aging Hollywood celebrity who had a vacation home in Hana, leaving that space available for arts and crafts classes and drop-in party use.

I stepped out on the warm asphalt in my favorite size eleven Nikes, box of chocolates under my arm. As I walked toward Pikake Court, I realized I was irritated and apprehensive, as well as excited, to be meeting the latest occupants of New Ohia State Park.

Aunt Fae and I had been tasked with watching over the park premises and picking up litter on weekends in return for next-to-nothing rent, so why hadn't we been apprised about new folks moving in?

But to be fair, the whole "park employee" designation was sort of a wink-wink, nod-nod thing, and there was no clear person to ask about park issues. That had probably led to the oversight in notifying us.

I vowed to keep my miffed attitude to myself, in spite of also having to give up the last box of chocolate mac nuts; it might be fun having other "New Ohians" nearby.

I pictured us bonding over a *pau hana* post-work drink, or a weekend barbecue. Neither Aunt Fae nor I had the skills necessary to bury a whole pig in the ground or harvest, cook, peel and pound *kalo* for *poi* to create a *luau*—but throwing a few shrimp on the barbie? Definitely a possibility.

I reached the area as the movers were hauling a massive metal trunk out of the truck. The guy who appeared to be in charge bellowed into the shadowy garage, "Where's this go?"

A feminine voice replied, "In here is good."

The two solidly built men wrestling the trunk shot each other glances suggesting the quicker they could set it down, the better. "Whoa. What you got in here? Rocks?"

The woman inside the garage gave a tinkly, girlish laugh. "Sorry it's so heavy."

I'm over six feet tall with firearms skills and the ability to bench-press my body weight. If I attempted a girly girl laugh like that, Aunt Fae would put a hand on my forehead to check for a fever.

"*Aloha*. Welcome to New Ohia State Park." I held out the box of mac nuts as I entered the dim confines of the garage, and as my eyes adjusted, I took in a woman around my age (thirtyish, give or take) standing next to Aunt Fae.

Skin the golden color of a caramel apple set off her pretty face. Her long black hair was pulled up in a high ponytail. In the low light of the garage, it was impossible to determine what box she might check in the "Ethnicity" section of a census form: Black? Asian? Native American? All of the above?

But what really caught my attention was that this woman was nearly my height. Probably not quite six feet, but darn close.

"You must be Kat," she said. "Fae has been telling me about you."

"And there you are, Auntie. I was wondering where you were," I said. "And yes. I'm Kat."

Aunt Fae took over. "And this is Elle."

Elle stepped forward and stuck out her hand. Thank goodness she wasn't one of those huggers. Many folks I'd met since landing in Hawaii insisted on embracing complete strangers. We shook, brief and firm. "Welcome to the neighborhood."

"And as your aunt said, I'm Elle Beane."

I paused, raising my brows.

"Yeah," she went on. "I hear you're both from Maine, originally. I'm only going to give you one guess what my middle initial is."

"L?"

"You got it."

"Your name is Elle L. Beane?"

"I've got parents with a sense of humor."

"Apparently."

"Oh, but I got off easy. I have two brothers and a sister. You ready for this?"

My mouth was somewhat ajar. I nodded.

"My twin brothers are Pinto and Navy, and my baby sister's name is Garbanzo."

"Seriously?"

"Yes. She goes by 'Gabby.' She's only seventeen but she swears the only thing she wants for her eighteenth birthday is her day in court."

"To change her name."

"You got it."

I remembered hospitality and held out the box. "I've got no follow-up to that. My full name is Katherine Smith. Here's your consolation prize, Elle L. Beane."

"Chocolate macadamia nuts. How thoughtful." Elle took the box and shot a quick glance at Aunt Fae. My aunt rolled her eyes and pointed her chin toward a credenza by the door that led into the house. The two missing boxes from our kitchen rested there.

"Oops. I see you've already got the candy thing handled."

"Thanks anyway. Why don't I return your kind welcome by offering you a box to take home? I can't maintain a healthy lifestyle with this much temptation around." Elle didn't appear to be a woman who'd succumbed to the siren song of sugar even once in the last year. She was lithe and toned, with calves that hinted she knew her way around an uphill climb. She handed Aunt Fae the box I'd just given her.

"That reminds me," Aunt Fae said. "I need to get to the grocery store before they close. Would you like to come to dinner with us this evening, Elle?"

"Thanks, but I'll have to take a rain check. I've been hired on at the Hotel Hana and I've got orientation at five."

"New job, huh? Is that why you're here?" I was curious as to how she'd been able to nab one of the model houses in the park.

Elle caught my gaze and glanced away. "Yeah. It's a long story."

"Well, we'll wait until next time to get that," Aunt Fae said. "Glad to have you as our neighbor, Elle."

"And I've got to run back to work, but the sentiment holds for me as well," I said. "Catch you later, Elle, Auntie."

I waved and set off, jogging back to work and putting our new neighbor out of my mind.

Since Chad had alerted me to a possibly dire situation in which time was of the essence, I needed to leave promptly after the post office closed. I ordered my steps mentally as I washed up a bit in the restroom before going to relieve Pua at the front desk.

First, I'd try to speak to Chad's mystery friend Doug Beachum, the UPS guy. Get info from the source. Then, I'd get directions to the hermit's place on my cell's GPS. Then, I'd drive out and take a look around, after which I'd call Lei and file my report.

I felt the thrum in my chest I get when my investigator's "spidey sense" signals something's up.

Just three more hours of postal work, and I'd be hightailing it out to spy on a hermit and maybe rescue a little girl.

I'd never served on a child's protective detail during my Secret Service career but, to my mind, the stakes with kids were always higher.

3

ASIDE FROM HIS part-time duties as my partner at K & K Investigations, Keone Kaihale's primary job was as a pilot. He flew small planes on short routes, currently Kahului to Hana and back, and occasionally a quick jaunt over to Moloka'i or down to Hilo. Mr. K takes his job seriously and is all business when he's in his tailored white uniform, but the only thing I can think of when I see him in that uniform is peeling it off. I mean, *dang* is he cute.

Mr. K called me on the post office landline a few minutes after two o'clock. "Sorry, Kat. I picked up another flight this afternoon. One of the Moloka'i guys came down with something and they need me to do a hop over there."

I told him about the girl in the window.

"I don't like the idea of you going out there by yourself," he said.

"I promised Lei I wouldn't do anything but check it out. Maybe shoot a couple of pics if there's anything that seems to be off. But no other shooting. She made me promise no firearms."

"You sure you're okay to handle this alone?"

"I got this. I'll tell you all about it when you get back."

"That's my Kitty Kat. More qualified to kick butt than any guy I know."

I felt a warm fuzzy as I said goodbye. One of my favorite things about Mr. K (besides how awesome he looked in his uniform) was that he wasn't threatened by my height, my sharpshooter skills, or the fact that I could lift him as easily as he could lift me.

FOUR P.M. CAME AT LAST, and I locked up the Post Office and walked across the road after waving goodbye to Pua. The sweet half-moon of sand, jetty, and aqua waves just across from the post office, bounded by the Hana Highway, was the nearest spot where I could get a good cell phone signal outside of New Ohia.

No matter how long I lived here I'd never tire of the zing of pleasure I got when the ocean, or more specifically, Ohia Bay, came into view. Every day the water looked different, with as many moods as a teenager has hormones. Today, the water was the color of antique Chinese jade—an intense deep green.

Palms beside the pier waved. Off in the distance, a great black 'iwa frigate bird soared; it was paradise all right.

I took off my Nikes, peeled off my socks, and walked down to the gently foaming surf. I sighed with pleasure as the cool water lapped around my feet, massaging my tired toes in the wet sand, enjoying the gentle waves as they played around my feet.

I took out my phone and tapped in "Halepua'a Road" on the directions app. Nothing came up. I tried various versions of the word; my Hawaiian spelling was still goofy half the time, so maybe that was the problem.

Still nothing.

"Darn it." I got out of the water reluctantly, put my shoes back on, and crossed back over the road heading toward the Ohia General Store. Grandiosely named Hana Highway was barely a two-lane road with not much in the way of shoulders and a faded-out center line, but it was the only way to get anywhere on this side of the island.

Opal and Artie Pahinui owned and operated the store beside the post office which functioned not only as a repository of daily needs such as food and basic housewares, but as the nerve center for the community. If you needed to buy something, they probably had it. If you needed information about local life, they probably knew it, and that included the latest gossip.

What would they know about the hermit?

"Hey, Kitty Kat," said Artie as I came up onto the porch. He was the one who'd nicknamed me that until Mr. K had adopted it too.

"I'm amazed at how you can tell who's coming," I said. Artie was blind. He could play stunning Hawaiian music on ukulele and guitar, though he could no longer see his own reflection in a mirror.

"I recognize your walk," he said. "And I feel your presence. You'd be surprised at how much you miss by relying on eyes only."

Opal, his wife of many decades, came outside onto the porch and joined us. She wore an emerald flowing muumuu with a pale pink, loosely knit shawl secured with a silver pin depicting a plumeria blossom. I didn't know how many scarves and shawls Opal had, but it must've been dozens. The closet of their attached home behind the grocery business must be as crammed with garments as a shopping mall stocked up for the Christmas rush.

"Hey there, Kat," she said. "What brings you over? Haven't seen you in a while."

Since I'd moved from the shack behind the post office to New Ohia, I'd been a bit neglectful of my former neighbors. They'd been beyond helpful when I'd first come to town, second parents almost, and I felt the sting of abandonment guilt. "I'm sorry, Opal. I've just been so busy with work and the move, and the kittens and—

She laughed and cut me off. "No worries. We miss seeing your beautiful smile, that's all." That made me feel even more negligent. "And speaking of kittens . . ." The two rambunctious boys from Tiki's litter that Aunt Fae and I had given Opal and Artie came bouncing out through the rubber flap the Pahinuis had installed in the screen door of the store. Ben and Jerry were growing even faster than their sister Misty, and they ran over and pounced on my loose shoelaces.

We all laughed at their antics; it was good to see Opal and Artie smiling so hard. I was relieved the kittens were working out for the elderly couple.

"I hate to cut this visit short, but I've got to ask you something and then get on the road," I said. "It's a case."

"What's going on?" Opal tugged her shawl tighter as though she felt a chill.

I told them about the UPS driver's report of the girl he'd seen in the window at the hermit's place.

"I'm surprised that guy even has glass in his windows," she said. "I heard he put that shack together using old pallet lumber and stuff he dragged out of the landfill."

"Do you know him?"

"Nobody 'knows' him, but we're aware of him. He comes into the store every few months. Doesn't talk to anyone. Real sour attitude. Most folks steer clear. I heard he was stationed in the Middle East and he got that PTSD or some such thing. In any case, if he's got a child out there, I'd be worried."

Artie gave a dramatic strum on the ukulele balanced on his knee. "Me too. That man carries darkness."

"Do you know how to get to his place?"

Opal said she wasn't entirely sure. "I don't think his road is far from here. But his place is real isolated, way deep in the jungle. If I was going out that way, I'd try turning off the highway at the big white rock and then I'd keep an eye out for the next turnoff after the little clearing with the coconut tree. The road out there is to the right. I don't think it's possible to go left at that point. Anyway, I think that's it, but like I said, I can't be sure."

That was about as clear as mud, but I asked her for a pen and paper, made notes, thanked her and agreed to come by the next day and tell them about what I found.

"You want me to read the runes before you go?" Opal shook the small bag of *kukui* nut shells she carried deep in a pocket of her tentlike dress. The sound reminded me of shaking a kitty treats container to bring Tiki out of hiding. Opal used her homemade runes to get a "read" on situations and the results were always interesting.

"I'd love that, but I don't have time. I want to get out and surveil the place before it gets too dark."

"The sun leaves that area earlier than here," Artie said on an ominous note.

I waved goodbye, jogging home to get my car. How did Artie differentiate between daylight and dark? He hadn't always been blind, but now that he was, he must sense the change in temperature to recognize that night was coming—or maybe Opal kept him on track.

In any case, his comment wasn't about the literal daylight but a spiritual darkness he sensed. Opal wasn't the only one with a touch of the psychic. He could tell things about people and so far, he'd been a hundred percent right in his perceptions on my previous cases.

His warning didn't make me feel a whole lot better about my urgent solo quest into the jungle.

I jogged home and grabbed a bottled water and my pepper spray. Yeah, I had to leave my former service weapon at home, but between my hands, feet, and the thumb-sized canister of spray, I was likely to be the winner in any confrontation that didn't involve a bullet. Hopefully the hermit wouldn't be packing one.

Happy to have good signal, I took a minute to call Doug Beachum, the UPS guy. He confirmed his story to me. "There's a front window visible when you drive up. She was standing there, and when she saw me, she put her hands up against the glass."

"What did she look like? How old?"

"I don't have kids, so I'm not good at guessing—but elementary school age at least. Brown hair. Couldn't tell much else."

"Was she asking for help? Like, trying to get your attention?"

He paused; I heard him swallow. "I'm not sure. It was just . . . sad and spooky. Something was wrong."

The hair rose on my neck; I could picture it. "Okay, thanks. I've passed this on to the police, just so you know."

He whooshed out a breath of relief. "Oh, good. That guy is a real piece of work and shouldn't have a kid out there."

I thanked him and ended the call.

I got into the big white Ford Explorer my gig at Security Solutions provided me and drove out of New Ohia. I took a left and followed Opal's directions; I soon found the white rock and finally, the road that only went to the right.

The big SUV I drove took the ruts in stride, but I wasn't looking forward to seeing the rust red mud that was no doubt coating the undercarriage and side panels of the vehicle like a frosted birthday cake. After a half-mile of barely passable dirt road, I understood why the UPS guy had had to go all the way to the end to turn around. The potholed lane was so narrow in spots that bushes and vines scraped both sides of the SUV at the same time.

I was sure I'd come the right way when I started seeing a profusion of "No Trespassing" and "Private Property" signs nailed to tree trunks in positions both high and low. As I rolled past the first sets of signs, the warnings became more ominous. "Violators Will Be Shot, Survivors Shot Again" and "If You Can Read This, You're In Range," along with a couple of signs so faded I couldn't make out the message. By that point I was pretty sure the unreadable ones didn't say things like *"E Komo Mai means Welcome"* or *"Aloha!"*

My odometer signaled that I'd traveled nearly a mile down the narrow road when I spotted an ancient gray Jeep Wrangler parked at the edge of a grassy cleared area; in the middle of the clearing was a house.

Calling it a "house" was generous. The structure was more like a larger version of the shack I'd lived in behind the post office before I moved to New Ohia. Mismatched pieces of different sized lumber had been nailed together to form the rough, unpainted dwelling. A rectangular front opening in the building threw off a shimmer from the leaf-filtered late afternoon sunlight that indicated it probably did, indeed, contain glass.

I put Sharkey, my pet name for my "Great White Shark" of an SUV, in Reverse. I backed up a few yards so the vehicle couldn't be spotted from the house. Even coated in mud, the white vehicle probably looked like an alien spacecraft in the midst of all that jungle greenery.

I got out and stepped into ankle-deep mud. "Oh crab on a cracker," I whispered, prying my foot out and hopping to dry ground. I had taken off my Nikes in anticipation of mud, but the slippers weren't a great second choice—too flimsy, and now slippery. I wiped the rubber sandal on the grass and my foot too—good enough for now. The one great thing about wearing flip-flops, or what the locals called "rubbah slippahs," is that they could be hosed off in a minute, along with feet.

Shoe dilemma solved for the moment, I stood beside Sharkey, listening. The dark recesses of the native forest were alive with birdsong and *skritching* noises I imagined were either lizards or some kind of tropical insects. But after about half a minute, I heard something else.

A rhythmic sound.

It was like someone beating a large wet towel against a wall, or maybe throwing an axe into a tree trunk. *Thwap*, pause. *Thwap*.

It didn't sound like chopping wood, and the noise raised my neck hairs, which had been happening a lot today.

I stealthily made my way down the rutted track, keeping to the side so I could dive for cover if necessary. This kind of surveillance brought out my primal fight-or-flight instinct; I hated doing it unarmed.

But I didn't have to like it. Not one bit.

When I got within recon distance of the dwelling, I pulled out my phone and snapped a few photos. The outside walls of the shack were a patchwork of rough wood, and the nearly flat roof consisted of various sizes of corrugated metal sheets slapped together in no discernible pattern. In addition to a small paned window, the front of the place had a weathered, unfinished front door that didn't fit properly in the frame, although it did sport various locks and deadbolts festooned above a tarnished brass handle.

On closer inspection, I noticed the window frame was bent, as if it had been salvaged from a junkyard or pulled from an abandoned property. The casing was corroded metal, probably aluminum, and whoever had fitted it into the hole had slapped white caulk around the edges as a sealant, but they hadn't bothered to wipe away the excess.

There was no front porch or any effort at making an entryway for visitors. The door opened directly onto a two-by-two-foot patch of packed red earth, surrounded by an approximately thirty-by-ten-foot "yard" of knee-high grass and brush.

Who knows what lurked in that grass in the way of critters, or maybe even booby traps? But then, maybe that was the point. The dwelling was not, in any way, designed to be welcoming.

The strange *thwap* noise I'd heard was still coming from behind the house.

What should I do first: peer in the window and risk getting my head blown off? Or go behind the house to check out the noise, and risk getting my head blown off?

I could also announce my presence and be highly likely to get my head blown off.

I drew a mental line through the last option; Lei had forbidden me from engaging the target.

But what if the noise turned out to be the guy doing some unspeakable act to his captive? There was no way I could live with myself if I didn't at least attempt the other two options and see if I could find the little girl.

I crept through the grass toward the window, carefully placing one foot in front of the other, fiercely aware that my rubber-slipper-clad feet were as vulnerable as if they were bare. I should have taken the time to put on my rubber ankle boots . . .

As I inched forward, I searched for metal animal traps, hidden trip wires, or deep holes camouflaged to swallow up unsuspecting delivery drivers or religious folks hoping to convert an unrepentant sinner to everlasting life.

I cupped my hands at the sides of my face and peered in when I reached the window. It was darker inside, making it hard to see into the interior of the shack. All I could discern was a sparsely furnished room with an unpainted wood floor, two straight-backed chairs, a small table, and what appeared to be some kind of wash-stand or workbench with a bucket at the base of it. To the left was a rough wall dividing the room from the rest of the shack. A doorway led to that area of the dwelling, but from my angle, it was hard to see into that space.

I backed away from the window and considered my next move.

So far, I hadn't seen the girl, nor any evidence of one. Maybe the UPS driver had been hitting the *pakalolo*, or happy weed, and after a mile of shifting jungle shadows and teeth-jarring ruts, he'd fanta-sized the face of a little girl who didn't exist.

But he'd been so clear about it. She had to be hidden here, somewhere.

Thwack. There was that sound again.

My last option—to go around back—was no longer a choice, but a necessity.

4

I CREPT around what I was pretty sure was the north side of the shack, pressing myself flat against the outside wall as best I could. There were no windows or doors on that side of the building, so my progress was unimpeded; no one could see me or pop out and confront me. When I got to the corner, I cautiously angled my head sideways using a move I'd learned in surveillance training that allowed me to glimpse as much as possible of what lay beyond—without providing a target for Mr. Smith or Mr. Wesson.

A quick survey of the backyard caused me to zip my head back and flatten my body against the wall again, my spine tingling with shock; I bit my lip to avoid crying out.

The cleared area behind the shack was awash in blood. The dirty penny stench of it was overpowering, causing me to swallow bile that'd sneaked up my esophagus. I concentrated on controlling my breathing.

Had I come too late? What kind of madman would murder someone right out in the open like that? Then I recalled the twenty-plus minutes of nearly impassable road. A guy who knew he'd get away with it, that's who. What were the odds that the UPS guy would've unknowingly stumbled out this way this morning? And had his showing up led to this atrocity?

I had to know. Curiosity may have killed the cat—but for this Kat, allowing someone to get away with murder was worse.

I stepped forward from the shadow of the shack, peering around the corner to get a better view of what I'd glimpsed.

A man, likely Hugh Dragoon, stood next to a low tree stump about three feet in diameter, his body blocking my view of whatever horror lay atop it. In his right hand he held a short, wide machete, the blade stained with blood. He appeared to be late thirties, maybe forty, with a full reddish-brown beard and messy Albert Einstein hair. He wore baggy camo military style pants and a T-shirt which had probably been tan or khaki green at one point but was now so saturated in blood I wouldn't take bets on the original color. His feet were protected by black leather boots which seemed as if they'd come from an Army surplus store.

He must have seen my movement because he spun and glared at me. He raised the machete threateningly. "You can't be here," he said. His voice had the froggy quality of a guy who'd just woken up. "Git, or I'll shoot."

I held up my hands like a teller caught in a bank robbery. "I mean no harm."

I scanned instinctively for a firearm, but saw none: instead, my mind focused on details. The man had a tattoo on his neck, a blue diamond-shaped design. Bad ink surrounded three numbers or letters that I couldn't make out. Was it a gang symbol? Maybe a military insignia? It was impossible to tell in the lengthening shadows of the afternoon.

"I said, *git*."

I tried to recall various training scenarios we'd practiced at the JJRTC, the Secret Service's James J. Rowley Training Center outside Washington, D.C. I couldn't remember a single instance that dealt with how to de-escalate a situation in which a madman is merrily chopping up something macabre in his backyard.

"I'm hoping you can help me," I said. "I'm lost and need directions."

"What're you talkin' about? You on foot?"

"Yes," I lied. "I was trying to find that famous bamboo forest trailhead and ended up here."

He squinted warily at me and lowered the machete. "Bamboo trail's miles from here."

"Is it?" While I played for time, I surveyed my surroundings. The amount of blood on the ground, on his clothes and machete, and on the stump in front of him was overwhelming. There were bloody chunks stacked a foot high on a tarp just to the left of where he stood, but he appeared unconcerned about me seeing them.

Then it hit me.

I said, "Are you a hunter?"

"Yeah. Got me a good-sized wild pig this very mornin'. This'll keep us for the better part of a month." He gestured toward the pile of unrecognizable pieces of freshly butchered flesh. I recalled the older commercials touting pork as "the other white meat."

Ugh. Didn't look appetizing at all.

"My name's Kat Smith," I said. "As I told you, I'm trying to find that hiking trail. If you need proof . . ." I slid a business card from the post office out of a pocket and held it out.

"I know'd who you are," he replied, ignoring the card. "You're that new gal at the post office."

I must've shown my surprise because he went on, "You dumb civilians. You don't never see me, but I seen you all. I know'd all about what goes on down there, too."

"You know my name. Now what's yours?" I took a step forward and stuck out my hand as if to shake with him. The thought of touching that ghastly blood-caked palm caused my touchphobia to kick in, big-time. My brain was screaming *run!* but I forced my feet to keep moving forward. I glanced toward the shack, hoping to spot the girl.

"Stop right there," the hermit said, brandishing the grisly blade like a pirate in a Disney movie. "I tol' you to git, and I mean *git*."

"Do you live here alone?" I ventured. There's nothing quite like the adrenaline rush of trying to interview a suspect while he's threatening to behead you. "You said the meat would keep 'us' for a week."

"What's it to you?"

"I was just wondering if you had a wife or kids or anyone here who could show me the way back to the main road." I gestured to the pile of pig parts. "Since you're obviously busy."

His eyes widened as if I'd accused him of something. "There's nobody here but me. Now, you start movin' or I swear I'll put you down faster'n I did this pig."

He took a step toward me. We locked gazes. The man's blood-shot gray eyes had the flat, distant appearance of someone who'd given up long ago and had nothing to lose.

As we say in the Secret Service, "Beware of an adversary with nothing to lose."

It was time for me to "git" as he'd told me to. I backed up a step, but while doing so, managed one last scan of the environs of the backyard: bloody tree stump, wild boar parts piled on a tarp, filthy machete scabbard lying a few feet away from the back door.

And then I saw something that made me forget all of that: a pair of small pink rubber slippers, tucked up next to the back door.

5

HUGH DRAGOON TOOK another step forward, waving the huge blade like a battle flag. "If you don't git in the next two seconds, I'm not gonna be 'sponsible for what happens to you."

The man meant business, and while I felt confident that I could take him, I remembered my promises to Lei with a sinking sensation.

I shouldn't escalate things with this guy with a vulnerable child somewhere on the premises.

I whirled around. "I'm sorry to have bothered you. I'll just retrace my steps and get out of your hair." In my haste to leave I dropped the business card, but I didn't take time to bend down and retrieve it.

When I got back to Sharkey, dread twisted my guts again: I'd have to drive forward, right up to the hermit's shack, to get enough room to turn around. "Dang it," I muttered.

Mr. Congeniality would see my ride and be able to identify it. He could run me off the road at his first available opportunity. There was no choice though—I couldn't back up all the way down the impossibly narrow track.

I gunned the engine and made it to the turnaround area in

seconds flat. I was so focused on executing a nearly three-sixty turn without slamming into the hermit's rusty Jeep I didn't notice if he'd come around from back to watch me leave.

Sharkey bucked through the ruts as I mentally rehearsed: I'd give my report to Lei. Once alerted to the situation, the next people heading out this way to visit the "pig whisperer" would be armed and badged. I'd done what I'd agreed to do, and now it was up to the proper authorities to ride in on their white horses to investigate those little pink slippers and save the day.

I finally reached the white rock and exhaled a big whoosh of breath, sighing in relief that my back window hadn't been shattered by a shotgun blast.

That's when I remembered I hadn't had time to take a photo of the slippers. All I had to prove what I'd seen was my word, and it might not be enough to get those white horses moving.

My abs tightened with worry.

I'd lived in the area long enough to know there was no cell service in the area except in parts of New Ohia and out by the beach, but that didn't keep me from trying. With one hand on the wheel and the SUV bucking in and out of potholes like an irritated bull, it was dicey trying to phone Lei to report what I'd found. And though I'd expected to fail connecting, it was still disheartening when my frantic call didn't go through.

I finally got back to the K & K Investigations office, which was housed in the shack behind the post office. I unlocked the door and dashed inside to use the landline. I threw myself into one of the two chairs at the old Formica table and punched Lei's digits into the cordless phone.

"Hi Kat," Lei said. "How'd it go? I'm in a cruiser and you're on speaker."

"You need to get out to Halepuaʻa Road ASAP. The guy's armed and hostile, and he—"

She cut me off. "Hold on, I need to pull over."

I waited while she negotiated whatever situation she was in.

"Sorry about that," she said coming back on the line. "I want to take notes and I'm alone in the car."

"Notes aren't going to be necessary," I said. "There's nothing to say except you absolutely need to get out there and rescue that girl."

"What's this about the target being 'hostile?' I thought I made it clear I didn't want you to engage."

"Circumstances dictated the need for a more direct approach."

Lei's tone was chilly. "I'm listening."

"The man who lives there was outside, behind his dwelling. At first, I did what you said and just peeked in the windows and checked around. But I heard him chopping back there, and when I peeked around the corner there was blood everywhere. My adrenaline kicked in and, well, I had to get to the bottom of what was going on."

Another pause. "Go on."

"Turns out, Hugh Dragoon was butchering a wild boar. That's where the blood came from. He told me to leave, then got aggressive when I asked if he lived alone. And there's definitely a child on the premises."

"You saw a child? What'd she look like? How old? What condition did she appear to be in?" Lei's questions peppered me like buckshot.

"Yeah, well. Unfortunately I didn't see her."

I heard a sigh, followed by, "Are you going to make me say it? Go *on*."

"I suspect a child is there because there were rubber slippers by the back door."

Another pause.

"Yes, pink rubber slippers," I said. "They didn't seem like they belonged to the hermit. They were child-size and pink. Like a little girl would wear."

"At any time did you have eyes on the girl?" Lei rapped out in her 'cop' voice.

"Um." Now it was my turn to pause. "No. But I saw her shoes. And remember, the UPS driver saw a little girl in the window this morning. I called him before I went out and confirmed it."

"So. What we have here is a delivery driver who *thinks* he may have seen a child through a window, and a pair of pink rubber slippers seen on the premises."

"Correct. But don't you think it should be investigated? The guy threatened me with a machete. And so far, everyone I've talked to is certain the guy is a hermit who lives alone."

"Is the property marked 'No Trespassing?'"

I admitted it was.

"Then work with me here. I can't investigate an individual who acts hostile toward trespassers on his own property. The UPS driver's account is hearsay. And as far as the pink rubber slippers, what am I supposed to do with that?"

"Are you telling me you're not going to do anything?" My voice rose an octave or two; I was ready to howl like an opera singer.

"No. I'm saying I'll put in a call to Child Welfare Services and let them take it from there. Police get involved when there is a clear need for safety, and we don't have enough for that." She sighed. "You know how it works, Kat. I need probable cause to go out and hassle a guy who hasn't broken any laws and is likely to escalate the minute he feels threatened."

She was right. But it certainly didn't *feel* right. "Please, Lei. There must be something more you can do."

Silence stretched between us. "I have a contact in the Hana PD. I'll see if he can cook up some reason to go out there. And I'll make that call to Child Welfare."

"I wish I'd been able to get a photo of the slippers; a picture tells a thousand words, and the sight of them is something . . ." I choked up, then coughed. "Geez. This is bothering me more than it should."

"Not if there really is a child in danger," Lei said softly. "Thanks for caring, Kat. Never lose that." She ended the call.

I leaned forward and rested my head on my folded arms.

That poor little girl.

I pictured a ghostly pale face in the window, palms pressed against the filthy glass, brown hair bedraggled. I pictured her tiptoeing through those bare rooms, maybe locked up in the area I couldn't see into.

A tiny chirp sounded from above me, and I glanced up to see what it was. Tweedledum and Tweedledee, the two brown spotted house geckos who lived above the stove, pumped their bodies up and down in greeting. One of them chirped again.

"Well, hey guys. Get any good bugs lately?" My voice sounded hoarse, rusty.

Further back in the corner, her eight long hairy legs spread for balance, squatted Miss Prissy the cane spider. She was at least half an inch bigger than when I'd seen her last. Though I'd been told these big brown arachnids were harmless, I tolerated rather than liked her—after all, her favorite place was way up high in the shower. Relaxing under the water while she watched . . . well, that was just creepy.

"Speaking of creepy." I stood up and addressed my menagerie. "That should be Hugh Dragoon's middle name. If you critters don't mind, I think I'll go for a swim and wash the smell of that place off me."

6

I NEEDED to cleanse myself of both my bloody encounter with the hermit and the nagging sense that I should've done more for the child.

I kept a bathing suit in the shack, so I grabbed it out of the drawer and took it into the bathroom. I changed out of view of the prying eyes of my "pets," and then slipped into the terry cloth robe I kept in the closet and headed across the parking lot toward the beach.

Noticing Artie sitting out on the front porch of the Ohia Store with his ukulele in hand, I made a wide arc to avoid catching his attention or engaging with him. I'd promised to check in with the Pahinuis when I had more information, but I didn't want to worry them further when I didn't know where things were going with the situation.

I tiptoed across the two-lane road as if trying to avoid waking a sleeping baby.

The water of Ohia Bay was now dark navy blue, and though this was Hawaii, the wind had gone chilly with the exit of the sun behind clouds. In the evening gloom I picked my way down the beach, mindful of the ever-present possibility of a wayward

Portuguese man-o'-war who'd washed ashore and might be waiting to sting anyone reckless enough to run into it.

I shimmied out of my robe and waded into the water up to my chest, skimming my hands along the surface. Once I got used to it, the silky salt water was warm for a winter afternoon. I dove forward, exhaling bubbles. As I swam laps parallel to the shoreline, exerting myself and releasing my cares to the sea, my stress settled back into the normal range.

Lei's offer to report the situation to Child Welfare Services was frustrating, and there was no great assurance that the Hana PD would send out an officer, either.

I'm not a patient person. Loathing inactivity had worked for me as a Secret Service agent. No one who's any good at the job embraces "wait and see" as an option. We had a saying that I'd lived by until recently: "To delay is to invite defeat."

This situation, so far, felt like defeat.

I got out and made my way back to where my terry robe "towel" lay folded up on the sand. The sun had set when suddenly, the sky shimmered with the apricot-hued golden afterglow unique to Maui. "Ah, just what I needed," I said aloud. "Thanks, universe."

I dabbed seawater off my body and was about to slip into the welcome softness of the robe when my phone began chiming in its pocket. Who could be calling me this late in the day?

I checked the ID window before I answered for Lei. "Hey lady," I said. "Tell me something good."

"I wasn't expecting you to pick up," Lei said. "I've contacted CWS. They verified they have no reports of children missing, but they're going to send someone out that way. My cop contact wants to wait until they do."

"When?"

"I didn't get a solid 'when.' As you probably know, they're understaffed. But the social worker I spoke to seemed to take it seriously, even though I had little to give her."

"Okay. Thanks for the update."

"You didn't get a photo of the slippers, but did you take any other photos while you were out there?" Lei asked.

"I did. But I don't know how much help they'll be. I just got a few shots of the house and surroundings. I couldn't get a photo of the rubber slippers with the guy waving his machete at me like a Benihana chef."

"Send the pics to me anyway," she said. "It will give CWS a positive ID on the dwelling. There's no address to reference and they don't want to show up at the wrong place."

"Yeah, the sign for Halepua'a Road is down. I got directions from Opal at the store." I promised to send Lei the photos as soon as we hung up.

"The Child Welfare folks will keep me in the loop," she said. "And I'll let you know how it goes. I'm uneasy too, Kat. Hopefully this will just turn out to be a misunderstanding, so we need to stand down for the moment. It's in other hands now."

Anyone who knows me knows that along with being impatient, I'm not a big fan of handing things off. I'm a control freak. "I hear you, Lei. Loud and clear. Thanks for the call."

I made my way back, crossing the road to the K & K office, and was delighted to see Keone's green Toyota truck parked out front. I flipped my head down and shook out my hair, hoping for a sexy windblown—rather than drowned rat—look. I flung the long, tangled brown length back over my shoulders, tightened the belt of the robe, and opened the door quietly.

I peeked inside.

Mr. K was sitting at the table, his back to me, and he was on the phone. He was still in his uniform, and I enjoyed the way his back and rear view looked in it. Catching Keone unawares was a treat; it gave me a chance to ogle him without having to admit that's what I was up to.

". . . we can. Kat's out right now, but I'll run it by her," he said. "Talk soon." The person on the other end of the call said something, then he punched the button and put the phone in its cradle.

"What are you going to run by me?" I said.

Keone started. "Oh good. I figured you'd gone for a swim." He got up and came over to me, sweeping me from wet hair to sandy toes with an appreciative once-over. "Good to see you, Trouble. How about a hug?"

We have a close relationship emotionally, but I'm skittish physically, dealing with my leftover childhood touchphobia. Sometimes I unwittingly lash out if someone touches me, even affectionately, when I'm not ready for it. Keone learned that the hard way. Once, he crept in to wake me with a kiss, and I laid him out. And by "laid," I'm not talking the fun kind.

"Yes, please. I could use one." I opened my arms and accepted his warm embrace, twining my hands around his shoulders to play with the jet-black curls at his nape. His solid warm body felt especially good after the chilly walk back from the beach.

"Do I dare tempt fate with a kiss?"

I said nothing to that, instead wrapping my arms around his broad shoulders and pressing my lips to his. We're almost exactly the same height, so kissing is an eye-to-eye, well-choreographed maneuver. In fact it's so easy, it was tough to stop. Being in his arms was as satisfying and fulfilling as falling into a soft bed after a grueling hike. All my cares slipped away.

After a few minutes our need for oxygen superseded passion. Keone raised his head, his eyes a little glazed as they met mine. "You taste like the ocean. Yum."

"Thanks. I guess. Who were you talking to?"

Keone shook his head as if clearing away a cobweb I'd spun with our kiss. "That was your friend, Sophie Smithson. She's got a little surveillance job for us. You up for it?"

It really wasn't my call whether I wanted to do it or not. My ride, the Ford Explorer SUV I'd nicknamed "Sharkey," belonged to Security Solutions, Sophie's company based in Honolulu. She'd offered me a stipend and use of the company car in return for being on call to help out whenever she had a situation that needed to be handled on Maui.

Keone described the job: a few hours watching a wealthy client's house while contractors did some work on it for the absentee owner.

"What's the concern?" I asked.

"I guess the last time the guy had work done, he claims items went missing. He's on the continent right now and wants this work finished before he gets back, but he doesn't want to deal with sticky fingers."

The folks who live out on the East Side of Maui generally fall into two groups: local people who want to "live aloha" without the constant incursion of a tourist-driven economy, and rich non-residents who own second (or third or fourth) homes out here. Those "snowbirds" showed up every now and then to brag to the people back home about how much they adored "roughing it" in the wilds of Hawaii.

Meanwhile, the locals resented the off-islanders for flashing cash and paying exorbitant prices for a piece of paradise, pushing up prices of homes in the area until they were out of reach for the next generation.

In the months I'd lived in Ohia, I'd witnessed the friction between the two sides. Generally everyone kept to their corners, but occasionally some incident sparked a fire.

"What's this guy got that he feels requires our attention?"

"Sophie says he's got a few mil in artwork. Matisse, de Kooning, even a Picasso pencil sketch that he's especially fond of."

"That's legit," I said, revising initial skepticism. "What's the timeframe?"

"She'll get back to us on the exact dates once the guy's firmed up the construction contract."

"Okay." I sat down in the chair I'd used before. "You want to hear how it went out at the hermit's place?"

"I'm all ears, Trouble." That was Keone's pet name for me. I didn't like or dislike it. Truth was, if he'd called me "Baby," or "Snookums" or anything of that ilk, I'd have pushed back. No one over six feet tall can seriously accept being called, "Cutie Pie" or "Doll."

But "Trouble?" It kinda fit.

I gave Keone my full report: leaving my weapon in the car and sneaking around. Seeing all the blood and attempting to extract information from Dragoon. His threats and demands that I leave his property, and, finally, a fleeting glimpse of pink rubber slippers.

"You never saw the girl?"

"No. But I know she's there."

"What happens now?"

"Lei called Child Welfare Services. They've promised to get out there when they can. Currently, there's no missing child report."

"Huh. Seems there's not much more we can do."

"I know," I said. "But I have a bad feeling about this. Why is there no report? Someone must know who this kid is. They don't just appear out of thin air."

"True," he said. "But maybe the UPS driver imagined it. It's pretty thick jungle out that way. Maybe what he saw was just his eyes playing tricks on him."

"I talked to him. Doug Beachum seemed pretty certain."

Mr. K frowned and pushed out his plump lower lip thoughtfully. He looked so adorable that I was distracted. "Speaking of playing tricks . . ." I reached over to stroke a sensitive spot behind his ear. Our eyes wandered to the Murphy bed strapped to the side of the wall, and then back to each other.

Mr. K quirked a brow in inquiry, a suggestive smile curving his lips. My touchphobia had limited our physical relationship to what I could handle on any given day.

The adrenaline crash I'd pushed through with my swim had left me more mellow than usual, and after today's traumatic events, I craved more of how it felt to be close, held, caressed.

Keone sauntered over and pulled down the little bed. He sat on it, bouncing a little, then lifted one foot to rest on the bed and reclined, striking a pose with a wink. He unbuttoned the top buttons of his tight polyester uniform shirt, revealing a widening triangle of muscular golden chest.

I watched this, mesmerized. "Keep going, Mr. K. I'm enjoying the show."

"Nope. You're going to have to help me with the rest." He patted the mattress, covered in a sheet I had washed not long ago. "Come here, Kitty Kat."

"Don't mind if I do," I purred, and shed the terry cloth robe on my way.

7

THE NEXT MORNING I was jolted awake by what felt like someone shoving me—it was Tiki, giving me a kick. After a romp with Keone, we'd taken showers, then gone to my house for a meal with Aunt Fae, after which Keone drove home to his place in Hana, much closer to the airport for his morning flight.

I'd gone to bed almost alone. But not quite.

From the moment I'd arrived in Ohia, I'd had an intruder sleeping with me: *Tiki*.

I'd fashioned a nifty cat bed for her to share with her offspring, which she'd reluctantly used as long as her kittens were small. Now that four of the five had been adopted, the scruffy calico had reinstated herself next to me. Although I think she was a bit relieved we'd not offloaded them all, Tiki was doing her best to wean the last kitten and get back her pre-mom mojo.

Barely awake, the *boom* that came next shook my bed with the force of a seven-point earthquake.

The state of Hawaii is earthquake-prone in general, with five active volcanoes threatening to do their thing at any given time. The closest one to us is Haleakala, or "House of the Sun," only a dozen or so miles inland, or *mauka*, from Ohia. Haleakala hadn't erupted for over two hundred years, but maybe its day had come again.

I lay panting after the shock of being so rudely awakened as Tiki jumped off the bed and scuttled over to her basket, where Misty cringed and mewed in fright. She jumped in like a good parent, throwing her body over her endangered young. From the basket, she yowled for me to "do something."

"I would if I knew what it was," I said. "Give it a minute."

I waited for a second jolt, or boom, but none came.

I glanced over to the nightstand. The clock read five forty-three a.m. Almost light outside, but not quite.

"I'm not going back to sleep," I told Tiki. "Might as well get up." I tossed aside the covers and dressed for work, all the while prepared to hit the deck if necessary.

Downstairs in the kitchen, I put on coffee. Aunt Fae showed up before it stopped perking.

"What was that noise?" she exclaimed. She'd cut her hair shorter recently, and it stood up around her head in tufts. Her brown eyes were wide, her cheeks pale. "It shook the whole house!"

"I think maybe an earthquake?" I voiced my private worry. "Or maybe a plane crashed at the airport."

"My stars. Whatever it was, I'm sure the whole town's up and at 'em trying to figure it out by now."

She was right about that.

THE POST OFFICE didn't open until nine, but by six-thirty a.m. when I arrived, a small crowd had gathered in the dirt parking lot between the building and the Ohia General Store. It appeared that Opal and Artie were doing a gangbuster business selling hot coffee and their famous cinnamon coffeecake to the milling, worried crowd.

I'd taken Sharkey to work in case I needed to follow up with the little girl situation. I parked behind the post office in my official spot, unmarked but honored by the tradition of leaving the postmaster the space closest to the back door. This was fine because we already had two handicap spots out front, where the customers entered.

I crossed the lot, weaving my way through the gathering of early risers, greeting a familiar face here and there.

"Hey, Kitty Kat," said Artie, detecting me as he usually did and reaching out for my hand. I took his and patted his shoulder in greeting. "We just sold the last of the coffeecake. Can I get you something else? A banana? Some yogurt?"

"Thanks, Artie, but I'm good. Did you and Opal hear that boom this morning?"

"Sure did. Maybe Pele's trying to tell us something."

"Pele?" I was still unfamiliar with Hawaiian lore.

"She's the Hawaiian goddess of fire and volcanoes. We love and respect her, but when she's not happy, she lets us know it. Sounds to me like someone got on her bad side."

"You think it was an event up on Haleakala?"

"That seems to be the consensus."

I peeked inside the store. Opal was six-deep in customers, so I opted to linger in the doorway.

I craved another cup of coffee before heading over to work, and I hadn't taken time to eat anything either, but I didn't want to add to the chaos. With my lofty advantage of being nearly a head taller than almost everyone else in there, Opal spied me and waved me over.

"Kat, good morning. Did you hear it?"

"Sure did. Why else would I be down here so early? I'm hoping to find out what happened, like everyone is."

"Can you stick around for a few minutes? I'm out of nearly everything so I'm going to close up for a bit. I'll reopen when the next batch of coffee's ready." She rang up the last customer and asked me to flip the sign to *Closed! Be right back.*

Artie came inside. He locked the door behind us. Opal swiftly pulled the used filter and damp coffee grounds from the big coffee machine and replaced them, moving with the practiced ease of a Starbucks Employee of the Month. She wiped her hands on a tea towel and shoved a bowl of ripe bananas toward me. I grabbed one and peeled it.

"Whew," she said. "We haven't gone through that much coffee since the last time it flooded out here. Seems everyone got shook out of bed and came over here to talk story and try to see what's what."

"Does anyone know what that boom was?"

"Lots of speculation, but not much information. I think the big money's on it being an earthquake. The coconut wireless is tossing around all sorts of theories—plane crash, meteor coming down, sonic boom."

"Well, whatever it was—no aftershocks," I said.

Artie mumbled something. Opal put a comforting hand on his forearm. "Now, let's not get ahead of ourselves. We can't be sure about any of it."

I leaned in. "What was that you said, Artie?"

"I said, Kaho'olawe. They've been bombing that little island for my entire lifetime. They stopped some years ago and cleaned up the island, but that boom sounded like a bomb to me."

"Bombing an island? Here in Hawaii? Who would do that?" I said.

"No one's bombing it these days," said Opal. "If the blast was from Kaho'olawe, it's likely it was just an old, unexploded shell that went off."

"That sounded too big and nearby to be an old shell," Artie rebutted. "And I kinda know my explosions."

Artie proceeded to explain how the U.S. military began using the small island off the southwest coast of Maui for bomb practice after the attack on Pearl Harbor. The targeting and bombing continued much longer than Hawaiians thought was right.

"Nobody talks about it anymore," he said. "Hawaiians have been replanting and reclaiming the island since the military turned it back over to us. But Kahoʻolawe's just another example of a long string of abuses our people have had to put up with."

The coffee machine beeped, and Opal popped up and started pouring freshly brewed Kona coffee into big thermal pots. "Enough about that. We've got customers waiting."

I grabbed a to-go cup, filled it, and trudged back to the post office. It was too early to open for business, so I went in through the back and kept the lights off as I navigated to my office. I booted up my computer—maybe I could find out something online.

My co-worker, Pua, entered a few minutes later.

"You hear that huge noise?" she said.

"I heard it, but no one seems to know what it was."

"I know what it was." She took off a powder-blue cardigan with pearl buttons to reveal a sheath dress worn with low cream-colored heels. Pua is the queen of one-upmanship. She does it without even trying or intending to, I've come to believe.

She's the polished yin to my careless yang. I'm tall; she's short. I wear plain, movement-friendly clothes in neutral colors; Pua dresses as if she's giving a fashion show for Ann Taylor. I allow my desk to get cluttered; hers seems as if she's just disinfected it for a surgical procedure.

"My niece's cousin's neighbor is married to a Maui firefighter," she said. "They were called out to an explosion not far from here a little after five thirty this morning. They brought in aid from all over the island to deal with the fire that followed."

"Huh. What blew up?" Some primitive, psychic alarm signal tripped inside me; my heart began to pound. This was going to be bad. *Very bad.*

Pua lifted a perfectly arched brow. "I'm trying to tell you—the house of that recluse guy out on Halepuaʻa Road blew up. I doubt you know about him because he hardly ever comes to town. We almost never see him."

Shock made my knees go weak; I grabbed the doorjamb for support.

I hadn't told Pua anything yesterday about the girl or my errand out there, nor did I want to now. It wasn't that I didn't trust her . . . well, maybe it was, a little . . . more that I knew she'd want me to stay out of it. "Wow, Pua. That's awful. Was anyone hurt?"

"That I don't know. I heard the house was completely obliterated, though, and burned so hot it set the area around it on fire." She hung the cardigan on a padded satin hanger and hooked it on the back door. "They have to wait for things to cool off. They aren't able to search for remains yet."

I gulped; my coffee was threatening to make a reappearance as I pictured Hugh Dragoon and the unknown little girl, blown to ashes. "Yikes. Okay. I'll be out of my office soon. I've got some calls to make and computer work to do first," I said. "It's still early, and Opal has a new pot of coffee done. Why don't you go get some and pass on the news?"

Opal and Pua were friends, and Pua could gossip to the next link in the chain. Opal might even tell Pua about my "case" out there, and save me the trouble. Yeah, Pua would likely be miffed I hadn't scooped her in, but we could add my omission to our list of past relationship snafus.

In the meantime, I needed to hear what Lei had to say about this latest development. There was no doubt she'd have heard of the disaster.

8

I WAS REHEARSING a possible voicemail message when Lei picked up.

"Kat. I guess you heard about Dragoon's place blowing up," she said.

"Yes." My lips felt numb. I was having a hard time keeping my voice steady. The memory of the little pink sandals at the hermit's back door swam in my vision like a scene from a horror movie. "I'm ... in shock."

"I know. It's awful." A beat went by as we both thought about my visit to the shack. "If it's any comfort, my contact at Child Welfare Services reconfirmed that they have no unaccounted-for clients, and I checked the database again—no runaways reported. As far as we know, there are no missing children on this island."

"But I definitely saw a pair of rubber slippers out there. Pink. Like a little girl would wear." I was a robot, repeating it.

"I know. You said that before and I believe you. But I don't know what else can be done."

"What if the girl wasn't in the system? What if she was a neglected kid who wasn't on their radar? Or maybe she was related to Dragoon, and somehow he had custody ..."

"I checked for that last thing. No papers filed for that related to him. I searched for family, relatives already. None. The man was alone."

"What if she was a runaway from another island? Or maybe she was here with a tourist family, and he lured her away?"

"Again, unlikely. First off, the only way on or off this island is by air or sea. An unaccompanied minor would never make it past the authorities. And how would a youngster be able to sneak off a cruise ship or even a private boat without being confronted, and her loss reported?" Lei did that thing with blowing her forehead curl again. "Finally, if a tourist family was missing a child, it'd be all over the news and we'd have an Amber Alert."

"You still haven't addressed the UPS driver's report of seeing her."

"Would it make you feel better if I talked with him?"

"I hate to waste your time, but this is killing me. He was so certain when I talked to him. Maybe he remembered more about her than elementary age with brown hair."

"Tell you what, you help me out by giving me this guy's contact info, I'll talk to him today."

"I appreciate it, Lei. Sending his contact info now." I forwarded Beachum's number.

"Got it. Now, I need to ask you a favor."

"Okay."

"You were probably the last person out at that property. I need to get an official statement from you of what you saw and your assessment of the occupant's behavior and state of mind." She paused. "Of course, the fire investigation team will be checking for remains, and more than the fire department will be called in if the explosion was some kind of IED."

"Of course I'll give a statement. Whatever you need. I'm here at the post office until four. Let me know how you want to do it."

Lei said she'd come by after we closed; that would work best for her schedule and the long drive. We ended the call.

Pua returned, bearing warm coffeecake from Artie's second batch, and we opened on time.

I went through my postmaster duties strictly by muscle memory, dissociated from my body. I sorted mail, handled parcels, stuffed boxes, and sold stamps. People asked me about the "big boom" and I said "no comment."

If you had asked me who I waited on, or how many packages I processed, I'd have come up blank: details didn't register.

But every time I closed my eyes for more than a second, those pink rubber slippers appeared. They were a haunting memory—a glimpse of a crime scene that had no resolution.

Lei arrived at the post office door as I was about to lock up for the day. Her lightly freckled, tanned skin was sallow. Her big brown eyes were ringed in violet circles of fatigue. Her frizzing curls had been scraped into a ball, and her jeans and polo shirt were crumpled. "Is now an okay time to give your statement?"

"Perfect, actually. Come inside." I pulled down the shade that had "Closed" emblazoned across it in about 150-point black type. Seems the post office powers-that-be wanted patrons to see the "Go Away" message from about a block away.

"How are you holding up?" she asked, trailing me to my office. Pua gave a finger wave goodbye as she retrieved her cardigan and headed out.

"Not so good." I closed the office door behind us. Lei took one of the chairs in front of my desk. I sat behind it. I swept an assortment of pens and other detritus into a pile, then opened the desk drawer and scooped. The junk tumbled into the metal container with a satisfying clatter. I shut the drawer and leaned forward to meet Lei's gaze, lacing my fingers together to stop their trembling. Peaceful Peach fragrance surrounded us. Silence descended, a welcome respite as we sat for a long moment.

"I know you're skeptical, but I saw those sandals. There was a little girl out there." I swallowed. "And now there isn't."

"Not to mention a man named Hugh Dragoon," she said softly.

"So they found him?"

"No. Not a trace. The debris is too hot to search right now. The area around the house caught fire after the explosion." Lei stared at me. Her expressive brown eyes told me that she was struggling with the likelihood of me being correct about the child, but her tightly pursed lips said that she was still squarely on the side of waiting for evidence. "I'm hoping that what I have to say may help in some way."

"You talked to the UPS guy?"

"I did. As you know, his name is Doug Beachum, and although he's sticking to his story that he believes he saw *someone* in the window, he's now saying that in his confusion and haste to get out and get back on schedule he may have been mistaken. Who he saw may have been a man, not a girl."

"That's ridiculous." I frowned. "I talked to Beachum and he was certain it was a girl just a day ago. Don't forget, I spoke to Hugh Dragoon, too. He wasn't one to stare forlornly out a window. If anything, he probably would've run outside and started taking potshots at the UPS driver. And, what about appearance? Dragoon's a grizzled dude with a full beard. If Beachum mistook him for a young girl, he shouldn't be driving until he gets his eyes checked."

"In any case, that's what Beachum said. He couldn't swear that the person he saw in the window was a young child."

I clamped my hand over my mouth to keep from saying something I'd later regret. When I could speak without swearing, I went on. "We both know witnesses are prone to equivocate when pressed for absolutes. So Beachum said he may have been mistaken. I get why he's changing his story now when there might have been a tragedy. What's the upside for him? There is none."

Lei leaned forward, sincerity etched in the lines of her body, the intensity of her gaze. "Kat, I need to ask you to let this go. I'm here to get your official statement on what transpired out there yesterday. That's it. You okay with that?"

I closed my eyes for a good thirty seconds, gathering my thoughts and setting aside my frustration. "Okay."

Lei took out her phone and thumbed to a recording app. I retold the series of events that had occurred when I drove out to Hugh Dragoon's shack. She pressed me for additional details after my tale was done, and I answered her questions until I couldn't provide anything further.

"Thanks, Kat. I'll let you know any new information when I get it," Lei said when she'd turned off the recorder. She scooped the phone into her backpack and slung it on. "Get some rest, girl. You look done in." I followed Lei and locked the post office's back door behind her.

I wasn't ready to go home yet and have to talk to Aunt Fae, Mr. K, or anyone else.

I went back into my office, sat down, and pulled over the box of tissues Pua had thoughtfully supplied me with. I tugged out a handful or two, put the wads of tissue against my eyes, and didn't get up until they'd stopped leaking.

Truth was, this situation activated all my childhood issues.

I'd been in a terrible car accident with my parents on an icy road at age nine. They'd died on impact; I'd spent the night in the car with their bodies. The good news was, I didn't remember any of that. The bad news was, they'd been gone, I'd developed severe touchphobia, abandonment issues and PTSD. I'd been left alone in the world.

Thankfully, I was sent to live with Aunt Fae, the best thing that could have happened to me under the circumstances. I was doing better than ever now that I'd left the Secret Service and really embraced a new life on Maui, surrounded by loving friends, family in the form of Aunt Fae, and even a romance with Mr. K.

But what about that little girl? She'd had no chance for anything better, and I might have been able to do something about that.

9

I'D RUN across the beach for a swim, taken a shower, rubbed some lotion on my face and run a comb through my hair, but my reflection in the bathroom mirror confirmed my worst fears: I looked like what Aunt Fae referred to as "ten miles of bad road."

Though I told him I'd had a bad day and needed space, Keone came to the K & K office after his last flight anyway. He didn't knock —just opened the door of the shack and frowned, framed in the doorway. "You okay?"

"In a word, no." I sat hunched over my laptop at the old Formica table, going over notes I'd made from the recording of my interview with Lei.

"Need a hug?"

I checked in with myself. "I'm sorry. I can't. I feel . . ." I struggled to describe what was going on.

"Fragile?"

"More like . . . frozen."

"And a hug wouldn't help?"

"I'm sorry, no." I smiled, trying to take the sting out of it, but my lips wobbled.

"You want me to leave?" His voice was low, husky.

I mentally crawled out of the hole I'd been hiding in since I'd heard about the explosion, and really studied the man.

Keone was still wearing his "leave little to the imagination" white polyester pilot's uniform with the gold braid and blue stripes. His coffee brown eyes reflected sympathy and tenderness.

How could I push away the one person who'd, brick by brick, helped me tear down the wall I'd been living behind for the past two decades? "No, I want you to stay. But I'm probably not the best company right now."

He came inside and closed the door. "That's okay. You want to talk about it?"

I paused. *Did* I want to talk about it? Or had I wallowed in guilt and remorse already enough that day and I'd much prefer to talk about anything *other* than the tragedy out on Halepua'a Road?

I didn't know, so I changed the subject. "I didn't call Sophie this afternoon about the surveillance gig," I said. "I'm sorry."

"No worries. She didn't seem to think the homeowner guy was in a big hurry. I think she mostly wanted to see if we were interested in doing the job when it came up."

"Good," I said. "I'll deal with it in the morning."

We stared at each other for a moment. I'd run out of words. Just twenty-four hours ago we were snuggling on the bed a few feet from where I was sitting, and now I couldn't come up with a single thing to say.

"You want me to start?" he said.

I nodded.

"You had nothing to do with what happened out there. With all your years in law enforcement, I know you know this. But just in case you need reminding, I'm reminding you. You can't stop all the bad that happens in the world."

I nodded, swallowing an enormous frog in my throat. I'd thought I'd cried every tear my body could produce for the foreseeable future, but lo and behold, I felt something trickling down my cheek.

"A little girl is gone," I said in a barely audible voice. "A child, like I was after my parents' accident—afraid and alone. Maybe that barbarian blew them up because I showed up out there. Maybe my being there was the match that lit the flame that went 'boom.' Dragoon was a weird, scary dude, Keone. I mean, I'm trained to recognize unstable behavior and signs of criminal intention. This guy had both written all over him."

Keone approached and took the chair across from me. "You talked to Lei, right?"

"Yes. I had to give a statement because I was the last person—" I stuttered to a halt and covered my face with my hands.

Keone cleared his throat. "I get that. But what did she say about it?"

"About what?"

"About the possibility of a child being there?"

"I don't know where you're going with this." I lowered my hands and gazed at my boyfriend. "She was there. I know she was."

Mr. K shook his head and reached out as if he was about to take my hand, then put his back in his pocket. "I talked with Pono. He and Lei are on the same page on this. There's a very good chance no child was ever on the premises."

Lei's partner at MPD was Pono Kaihale, Keone's cousin. Of course, Keone would've done his homework about the situation before coming to see me. He went on. "There's no report of a child missing anywhere on Maui. *Keiki* are valued here, Kat. Even kids with lousy parents are watched over by neighbors, teachers, and especially *'ohana*—extended family. If there's no report, you can be pretty sure there was no kid."

"But the UPS guy saw her. And I saw her little sandals."

"Pono says the UPS guy isn't sure."

I swiped my cheek. The tickle from the tear track was beginning to bug me, but that wasn't the only annoying thing going on here. "It's been a rough day and I'm done talking about this. I should get going. It's getting past dinnertime and Aunt Fae's probably wondering where I am."

"Okay, Trouble. But if later on tonight you want to talk, you've got my number. Don't worry about the time. I don't have a flight scheduled until tomorrow afternoon." He got up and left. Clearly, I wasn't the only one frustrated.

I closed up the office, got in Sharkey and drove back to New Ohia. I wanted to veg out with the cats. Thankfully, Aunt Fae wasn't a chatty woman. I'd give her the quick version of events and she'd take it at face value. If she'd been in the Secret Service, she probably would've been known for her surveillance work but would've proved to be not so great at interrogation, and tonight, that was a good thing.

She'd likely ask where Keone was; she liked him almost as much as I did. But when I told her I needed space, she'd understand. I loved that about her. She had always accepted me the way I was, at any given moment.

I parked the car in the turnaround, reached the pretty double door and opened it. Unlocked, as usual. Our area was generally crime-free, now that we'd driven the gangsters out of town. I took off my Nikes, setting them on the shoe rack inside the entry foyer, frowning. There was an extra pair of slippers on the mat, an unfamiliar kind made of ropey material, like espadrilles.

Laughter greeted me as I stepped inside. I'd spent the whole day weeping and gnashing my teeth. Maybe a little levity would be a welcome respite if I could switch gears.

"Hey, Kat," said Aunt Fae. "Look who's here!" She threw an arm around Elle's shoulders and pulled her in, grinning like they were frat boys at a kegger. Elle, wearing cutoff jeans and a skimpy top, had cheeks as pink as Aunt Fae's. "Elle joined us for dinner after all."

What had happened to my stolid Aunt Fae? As she liked to remind me, "You can take the woman out of Maine, but you can't take Maine out of the woman." And Mainers were likely to look a gift horse in the mouth and check its fillings, for good measure.

"Get over here, Katty Whompuss," Auntie said.

Katty Whompuss? "Are you two drunk?" I put my hands on my hips.

"No, no, we're just having a bit of fun. Elle made this lovely libation for us." Aunt Fae lifted a blender half-full of pale green slush. To my knowledge, we didn't have a blender. And if we did, Aunt Fae would've used it to make kale protein smoothies, not whatever it was that had turned her eyes glassy.

"I hope you don't mind," Elle said. "Fae invited me over for dinner." She held up a hand and burped delicately.

"Yeah. I was there for that part," I said.

"I tried to call but you must've been out of cell range. I left a message that Elle was coming over," said Aunt Fae.

"Sorry. I didn't check my messages. I've had a tough day."

"I can imagine," said Elle. "Fae filled me in. You were out at that property yesterday, the one that blew up this morning. That's got to be really shocking. One day the place is fine and the next, it blows sky high."

I nodded but stayed silent. Maybe our new neighbor would get the memo that I wasn't in the mood to talk about it.

Aunt Fae picked up on it immediately. "Of course it was shocking. Clearly, Kat's in need of distraction and something to eat. Now, let's have some dinner and put all of that behind us for a while. I made a Mexican-ish food thing I saw on TV today. Chicken burrito casserole with black beans and red rice." She clapped her hands together with a smile. "Come on, girls. Who's hungry?"

As Aunt Fae had said, I really was in need of food and a distraction ... but it wasn't the casserole, the beans, or the red rice that ended my obsession about the tragedy that'd unfolded that morning. No, it was the margaritas. Turns out the tequila-fueled green beverage, favorite of Jimmy Buffett's fans, was a temporary antidote to heartbreak.

10

By my second and Aunt Fae's third margarita, we'd given Elle abbreviated versions of how we'd both ended up in New Ohia. She, in turn, told us about her new job as Events Coordinator for the Hotel Hana.

"How'd you come to get that job?" I asked. "Were you in the hospitality industry before?"

She smiled and shook her head; her shiny black ponytail swished. "Not at all. In fact, right out of college I joined the Army. I've been stationed at Schofield Barracks on O'ahu for the past couple of years."

"And you just decided to up and leave?" Aunt Fae said.

"Something like that." Elle pressed her lips together as if signaling she wasn't keen on defending her decision or getting into the details of her departure.

But Aunt Fae leaned back in her chair as if settling in. "What did you do at Schofield?"

I rethought my assessment of Aunt Fae not being much of an interrogator.

"I worked in the medical lab. You know, there are two sides to the Army. There's the side that tosses grenades and then the side that patches up our people after the enemy tosses 'em back. I was on the patching-up side."

"Medical, eh. What department?"

"Research. I was a project manager for a lab. Mostly blood and tropical disease work."

"So, how does that translate to being an Events Coordinator?" said Aunt Fae.

Elle snorted a chuckle. "It doesn't. But I was ready for a change. Like I told the woman at Hotel Hana who interviewed me, I'm a detail person. My strengths are in seeing what needs to be done and then managing the people and material to get it done. More importantly, I make sure nothing falls through the cracks. Event coordination seems easy, but when you think about it, most nasty reviews of wedding planners and event hosts have one thing in common—somebody dropped the ball on some important detail."

"Well, good for you." Aunt Fae smacked down the heavy tiki-shaped glass Elle had brought to serve the drinks in. "You've got my vote."

"Seems I've been doing all the talking here," Elle said. "What about you, Fae? What did you do before coming to paradise?"

Aunt Fae opened up more than I expected she would with a relative stranger. "As you may have heard, this amazing woman right here was pretty much my whole life for the better part of twenty years. I'd worked various jobs, never really finding anything that fed my soul, until Kat became my ward. Then, everything changed."

"You were orphaned, is that correct?" Elle said, turning to me.

I nodded. After the day I'd had, I didn't want to get into the nitty-gritty of my parents' fatal accident.

Aunt Fae went on. "For me, Kat moving in was like turning on a light in a dark room. Everything became more important, more meaningful. I had a new appreciation for my job at the water district." She held up a hand and ticked off items. "It was reliable, had benefits, and I was allowed to adjust my hours to fit with her school schedule. Plus I spent my days outdoors. We lived out in the country where winters are long, but the summers are glorious. We'd go camping and hiking and this sweet girl was the best company an old maid could ever hope for. I was crushed by the circumstances that brought her to me in losing my brother, her dad . . . but equally blessed that I was given such a wonderful companion to raise and spend life with after we lost him."

Aunt Fae's eyes were damp as we gazed at each other. It was hard to not start up the waterworks again myself, but I kept it in check by blinking rapidly while doing some mental times tables. I probably appeared to be having a seizure.

"Well, and this isn't the booze talking . . ." I said. "I was the fortunate one. I don't know what my life would've been like if you hadn't been willing to take me in, Aunt Fae."

She reached out and took my hand. I squeezed hers; I was finally ready for some physical contact. "Love you, Auntie."

"Love you more. Now, anyone up for a rousing chorus of 'Kumbaya'? Aunt Fae said. The three of us chuckled.

Aunt Fae got up to pour the last of the margaritas. Her hand slipped and the blender jar tipped over, spilling the last of the sticky green liquid. "Oops. That's gonna have to do. I'd make more, but I don't think we have tequila. Or margarita mix. Or even a blender."

We agreed what we'd had was more than enough. Elle got up to leave and reached out to touch my shoulder. "Great to get to know you better, Kat," she said.

"Thanks. You too." I meant it. I was well on my way to liking her.

She leaned over and gave Aunt Fae a hug. "Thanks for dinner. It was delicious."

I walked Elle to the door and waved goodbye. She swung the empty blender container back and forth in one hand and the canvas bag holding the tiki glasses in the other as she loped down the rise from our driveway toward her house on Pikake Court. I waited until she was out of sight before turning off the porch light.

How did Elle know I was averse to hugging?

And why did she really leave the Army?

I had a feeling, although it might've been a bit warped by tequila, that there was more to Elle Beane's story than just a woman who'd suddenly decided she'd rather plan weddings than save soldiers' lives.

11

THE TEQUILA HAD ENVELOPED my brain in a cottony fog, allowing me to drift off only a few minutes after my head hit the pillow, so I had no trouble getting to sleep at first.

Three hours later, however, I was startled awake by a dream that included a wild boar with a machete clamped in its teeth and flames consuming a pair of pink rubber slippers. I lashed out as I attempted to grab the huge knife from the pig's bloody mouth and swept Tiki off the bed.

"*Roh-awr!*" Tiki protested as she thumped onto the floor. Luckily, the bedroom floors in this swanky model home were covered in soft carpet, unlike the rough wood floor of my previous dwelling. Carpet or not, Tiki glared at me with an enraged expression of betrayal.

"I'm sorry," I said. "I had a bad dream."

She narrowed her eyes in a "you're gonna have to do better than that" squint and pranced over to the kitty bed. Little Misty mewed a welcome. Tiki paid her no mind, sitting down and squashing her kitten under her ample rump.

I flopped back onto my pillow, but I couldn't get back to sleep. I tried both sides, front and back, and nothing worked.

What is it about the dead of night that makes everything seem worse? After an hour of imagining all the ways I'd messed up when I'd gone out to the hermit's house, I rose and grabbed a robe.

Tiki followed me into the kitchen. She peered up at me with a little "merp" as if signaling that a treat would go a long way toward a pardon for knocking her off the bed.

I obliged. In fact, I gave her three or more treats before I remembered that although she loved them, they tended to give her fishy-smelling gas of eye-watering proportions.

"You know if you stink up my bedroom we'll be even."

Tiki yowled a "says you," stuck her back leg straight up, and began a self-cleaning ritual of her lady bits.

I rummaged through the refrigerator hoping to find something so tasty it would take my mind off my role in triggering yesterday morning's blast. Nope, nothing groundbreaking in there.

I would make tea. The electric teapot was way in the back of the cupboard. I winced as pots and pans clattered in my effort to wrestle the pot out of the narrow space.

By the time the tea water started boiling, Aunt Fae appeared in the doorway. "What brings you out here at this time of night?"

"Couldn't sleep."

"You still thinking about that explosion?" I nodded and gestured at the teapot. She smiled and nodded, letting me know she'd like to join me in a cuppa. "Want to talk about it?"

"I wish talking could make me feel better, but I don't think it will."

"You know, there's a whole profession that would disagree," she said.

"Counseling? Psychiatry? Those kinds of things?"

She nodded.

"I know. I remember when you took me to counseling after my parents died."

"You told me it helped."

"If you'd taken me to a witch doctor, I would've told you it helped. I didn't want to disappoint you."

"But you're grown now. Thinking back, how do you feel about it? Did talking to Annie make a difference?"

"It did. But this is different."

"How is it different?"

"Last time I was the victim of horrible circumstances. Now, I'm the instigator of horrible circumstances."

"You don't really believe that, do you?"

"It's hard not to."

"Well, I'm no expert on these things, but from what you've told me, I'd say that man was unstable. He was the instigator, not you."

"You're right. But that's what makes me feel responsible. I'm trained to recognize a potentially volatile situation, and I just bulled my way through. If I were still an agent, I'd be written up for my unprofessional behavior out there."

"Exactly what about your behavior was unprofessional?"

"First of all, I disobeyed a direct order from Lei not to engage with the hermit. And then, I provoked him by asking questions. Even though I knew when I first laid eyes on him that he was potentially dangerous, I went ahead and tried to probe for information."

"Oh, honey, you had no idea he'd go off like that."

"That's the problem, Aunt Fae. I suspected he was violent and unstable, but I did it anyway." I clapped a hand over my mouth as if to take the words back, but they were out there, hanging in the air between us.

"You wanted to help." Aunt Fae tightened her old terry cloth robe around her slim body; I remembered that robe. I'd given it to her one Christmas at least ten years ago. It had been a sunny yellow, but repeated washings had rendered it the color of sand. Clearly, it was well-loved.

"I guess I'm not sure what I mean." I folded my arms across my chest. "But I can't shrug off the fact that my visit to that house might have been a catalyst for the explosion."

Aunt Fae seemed to have run out of responses. Finally she asked, "Can I give you a hug?"

"Yes, please," I whispered. I closed my eyes as my aunt's arms encircled me and tightened. I was much taller, but she drew my head down to her shoulder. I relaxed at last, letting go of stress as I had when I'd been a child and was finally worn down enough to allow such affection.

Once again, I was grateful she'd chosen to come and live with me here in Ohia. We were a family, the two of us and our cats. Knowing that was a great comfort, no matter what came next.

12

A PALE GLIMMER in the eastern sky gave me permission to get up from a restless sleep the next morning. Tiki grumbled as I tugged on my bikini and robe. "You can come if you like," I told her. I slid my feet into slippers and hustled out of New Ohia, stumbling down the road to the beach. Tiki trotted behind me, sniffing for prey in the damp grass as we went.

Tequila hangover and lack of sleep aside, the velvety air, redolent with the scent of newly budded plumeria trees, soothed me as if recognizing an old friend in a crowd of strangers as we walked. At Ohia Bay, I shed my towel and robe, eyes on the dark blue horizon as salmon-pink, puffy clouds floated by.

The memory of yesterday morning's disaster seemed as unreal as the machete-pig nightmare from before. Tiki sat on my towel and kept watch as I slipped into the chilly water and swam hard and fast, goggles protecting my eyes from the salt water. I was mindful that this was feeding time for the few tiger sharks in the area, but today, I didn't care.

There were no sea turtles in view this time, but with the way I was churning through the waves, I'd no doubt sent them gliding off to calmer waters.

I eventually got back to shore and toweled dry. Tiki had disappeared—probably off chasing some field mice.

I had hours to go before I had to open the post office. I weighed my options: go home and take a nice hot shower, go to the K & K office and take a lukewarm shower in the tiny bathroom, or just wrap the robe around my saltwater sticky body and grab some coffee at the general store.

The store's promise of coffee won out. I needed that Elixir of Life after my long fitful night, and Artie and Opal's camaraderie was like applying balm to a wound.

I piled my hair on my head and tightly tucked my towel around it. In my white robe and towel-wrapped head I must've appeared to be an extra taking a break from filming a mummy movie as I padded across the empty road in my slippers.

Artie once again recognized me as I approached.

"Kitty Kat," he said from his usual spot on the porch. "We were hoping you'd come by today. Opal has been itching to get out her runes."

Ah, the runes. I could only imagine what they'd have to say about my current predicament.

"Before we get to any of that, I could sure use a cup of your fabulous coffee."

"Got it right here." Opal glided out of the store carrying a steaming mug for me; she must have seen me coming. This morning, she wore an aloha print muumuu and a velvet wrap. This one was purple with a fist-sized pin of lavender rhinestones depicting an octopus. She set the coffee down and opened her arms. "May I get a hug?"

I couldn't refuse Opal, but it took some deep breaths and force of will to endure. Thankfully, she kept it short.

"And how about a breakfast burrito, on the house?" Artie said. "I've been branching out on the store's breakfast offerings. Today I made a spicy scrambled egg and chorizo concoction and wrapped it in a spinach tortilla. You can be my guinea pig and let me know what you think."

"Very daring for East Maui," I said. "Yes, please."

"Folks out here might appreciate a little international flair now and then." He bustled off, navigating through the store's dim interior with the confidence of the sighted.

From what I'd seen, folks out here liked things to stay the same. Nothing brought out the stink eye like something Aunt Fae would call "newfangled."

Opal sat down next to me and handed me the mug of coffee. "How are you doing, Kat?" she said. "We've been worried about you ever since we got word of what happened out there. I hope you're not blaming any of this on yourself."

"I wish that were true, auntie. But it's not a matter of choice. I just can't stop thinking about it."

"Then let's see what the runes have to say."

The *kukui* nut shells rattled in her pocket as she took them out of the small pouch. She'd inscribed the nearly black shells with symbols only she could interpret. The past few rune readings she'd done while I was present tended to be enigmatic, similar to inquiring about your chances of finding true love by reading your horoscope in the newspaper or seeking financial advice from a fortune cookie.

She took off her shawl and smoothed it out on the little side table that was a fixture on the store's deck. "First, you must consider your intention. Bring to mind, with as much detail as you can, what you'd like to know."

I thought about the hermit blowing up his place and my role in it. I also recalled the pink sandals. I mentally requested clarity on who the little rubber slippers belonged to. Even as I did this, I felt foolish. Magical thinking was not going to bring back the dead, nor clear my guilty conscience.

"You ready?" Opal asked.

"I guess."

She blew on the shells and tossed them onto the purple fabric. Two skittered to the edge and dropped off.

"We won't bother with those," she said. "If they don't want to reveal themselves, then so be it."

Artie returned with a plate holding the warmed burrito under a clear plastic warming cover. He'd cut it in half and provided a fork, which I appreciated, because as hungry as I was, I might've been tempted to stuff the entire thing into my mouth at once. It smelled heavenly. I detected cumin and chili and the tang of fresh tomato salsa.

He sat down without saying anything, holding the burrito on his lap. Blind or not, Artie could always pick up the mood of the moment, and when Opal was reading her runes, the mood was somber.

Opal peered at the black *kukui* shells remaining on the velvet like a Russian chess master in a grand champion tournament. Artie and I remained silent. I glanced at his cloudy eyes and recalled that he was equally gifted in seeing the unseen. Whereas Opal's runes offered vague predictions, Artie's prognostications were pinpoint accurate and specific.

"See this one?" She pointed to one of the shiny black shells. "That's the center rune. The rune below it indicates the problem. The one above it presents an answer."

If only it were that simple.

Opal brought out her little notebook and sketched the placement of the runes. "I need some time with this," she said.

As far I was concerned, she could take all the time in the world. I wasn't holding my breath expecting scratched-up *kukui* nut shells to lift my heavy burden.

"I've got to run home and get ready for work," I said. "But I'd love to try that burrito now."

Artie removed the cover and handed it to me. I gulped down the burrito quickly, and thanked Artie for the opportunity to try it.

"What did you think?" he said.

"It's wonderful. But everything you make is great, so I'm probably not the best taste tester."

Opal smiled. "No, you're the very best taste tester. Artie doesn't need critics. He needs a fan who supports his efforts."

She offered me a second cup of to-go coffee, but I declined; I'd grab a cup at home with Aunt Fae. I still had more than an hour before I had to open the post office and I was looking forward to comparing hangovers with my housemate.

My body had dried during my visit with Opal and Artie, so I slipped out of the robe and towel and walked back to New Ohia wearing only my bikini. The bay winked with sparkles from the fully risen sun, and the sun's soft heat on my back was as welcoming as the feel of freshly baked cookies.

How could I be glum and guilt-ridden in the midst of all this beauty and warmth?

Then it hit me: the little girl in the window would never experience any of this again.

13

"Good morning," Aunt Fae asked as I came into the kitchen. "How's your head?"

"I needed a swim to clear it and a cup of Opal's coffee, but I'm okay now." Tiki narrowed her eyes at me from where she sat beside Auntie. Her bowl was licked clean, and she made no attempt to guilt-trip me into refilling it. But she also didn't make any "glad to see you're back" noises either. "You fed Tiki already?"

"I did. She was yowling like a hyena with her tail in a trap. I hope you don't mind, but I gave her extra. She seemed distraught that you'd left without feeding her."

"It was barely light when I went out, and she came with me. Hunted all the way to the beach and back; she must have worked up an appetite."

"Maybe so, but it hurt her feelings you didn't fill her dish first."

Tiki pranced out of the kitchen with her bent tail held high—the kitty version of a middle finger salute.

I'd been dealing with Tiki for months before Aunt Fae showed up. My one-eared, kink-tailed, formerly feral feline could've snatched an Oscar for her performance as a damsel in distress. I kept it to myself, though. Auntie would learn soon enough.

"I'm going to grab another coffee and then get ready for work," I said. "How are *you* doing this morning?"

Auntie yawned and stretched her arms over her head. Her iron gray hair stood up in spikes; she combed it with her fingers. "I'm fine. I had a bit of a headache earlier, but I took an aspirin. The bigger question is . . . are *you* okay? Are you feeling any better about that hermit situation than you were last night?"

"No, but I've got to move forward." I tightened the belt on my robe, heading for the coffee machine.

Aunt Fae's mouth twisted into a concerned frown. "I forgot to ask earlier, have you talked with Keone about this?"

"We tried to discuss it. But he agrees with Lei and Pono. They've all decided that since we can't be sure there was a little girl out there, I need to let it go. That's easier said than done."

Aunt Fae folded her arms and gave me her truthiest stare. "How is any of this helping?"

"What?"

"Not letting it go. How is holding on to it making it better?"

"I appreciate your concern, Aunt Fae, but it's too soon." I poured the coffee too fast into my mug, and some of it splashed on my hand. I hissed at the pain and turned away. "It's too raw. I'm going to get ready for work now and go do my job. That's the best place for me." I turned away and hurried up the stairs.

I showered and put on my usual postmaster outfit of black jeans and a white polo shirt. The bags under my eyes could've used a little concealer, but I chose to forgo it. Maybe subconsciously I wanted to appear as lousy as I felt—a sackcloth-and-ashes look.

When I got to the post office building, Pua had already unlocked the back door and turned on the lights. She eyed me like a judge at the Westminster Kennel Club zeroing in on a golden retriever with mud in its fur.

"You look horrible," she said. "Are you sick?"

"No. I'm fine. I just didn't get much sleep last night."

She put two fingers to her lips and whistled. "Ooh, care to dish?

And don't skimp on the details. I read a lot of romance novels so I'm not easily shocked."

"It's not like that. Aunt Fae and I had a guest over for dinner last night and she brought margaritas. I think the alcohol interrupted my sleep cycle." I proceeded inside, opened my office and set my travel mug on my desk. The coffee could kick in any time now.

Pua pushed out her lower lip. "Well, I wrote down a couple of phone messages for you from the office voicemail. You want me to open up this morning so you can deal with them?"

I thanked her and said I'd be out in a few minutes.

Keone had called the post office line twice.

Frowning, I called him back.

"Hey, Trouble," Keone answered in his bedroom voice. Normally, that rumbling, sexy tone would make me want to chuck my postmaster duties for the day and summon up a fake cough so I could play sick and go surfing with him. But not this time.

"I'm at work," I said. Like that was news.

"I know. I'm checking in to see how you're doing."

"I'm okay."

"You don't sound okay. You want to catch a quick lunch with me later this morning? I've got to head out to the airport a little after twelve, but I could pick you up at say, eleven?"

It was nine and since I'd eaten Artie's breakfast burrito, I doubted I'd be hungry by then, but Keone's invitation wasn't about food; it was an offer of support. I'd had issues with recognizing relationship dynamics before, so I gave myself a little mental pat on the back for spotting this one so quickly. But as I'd told Aunt Fae, I was tired of hashing over the events of yesterday.

Could I ask Pua to take over for an hour? While I dithered, he went on. "Okay, here's what I'm thinking," he said. "I'll plan on coming for you at eleven. If you change your mind, give me a call on my cell."

The likelihood of me calling to cancel and him getting the message was remote. There's spotty, meaning pretty much nonexistent, cell service between Ohia and Hana where Keone lived. He knew I wouldn't leave him hanging if he showed up and I'd changed my mind but hadn't been able to reach him.

Clever man.

But I could be clever, too. And I was about to prove it.

14

KEONE SHOWED up at eleven dressed for work in his splendiferous uniform. My black jeans and polo shirt were a sad contrast to his spiffy white getup. If clothes made the man, in that outfit, Mr. K was definitely *the man*.

We decided that lunch would need to be premade sandwiches and root beers from Artie and Opal's store, eaten in the K & K office. We could've gone to Hana and grabbed something from the food trucks, but that would've required us to drive separately, since Keone would need to leave for the airport in less than an hour. We returned to the shack and settled our meager repast on the slightly rickety table.

"I'm worried about you, Kat," he said by way of jumping right into it.

"I'm a wreck because I didn't sleep well last night," I said. "Margaritas with the new neighbor."

"I'm not talking about appearance. That's one of the things I like about you. You hardly pay attention to your clothes or hair—or makeup for that matter."

Was that the proverbial left-handed compliment? I don't know how left-handed people feel about that phrase, but from where I was sitting (and I'm unequivocally right-handed) it seems like a "dis."

"Like I said, I didn't sleep well. We had our new neighbor, Elle, over for dinner. She brought lots of margaritas. I had a few too many. Aunt Fae, too."

I recalled the heartfelt admission by Aunt Fae that I'd been the spark that had brightened her life and I smiled, but I didn't feel like sharing that with Keone right then.

Mr. K smiled in return, adding his trademark dimple to the mix. "And like *I* said, I'm not concerned about how you look. I'm worried about you taking on whatever blame or guilt or whatever it is you're feeling about that guy who blew up his house."

"I don't care much about the guy. He was a mean, probably crazy, dude. I care about whether he killed an innocent girl in the process. I didn't see her, but I saw her pink rubber slippers and I . . ." How could I explain how that image in my mind's eye would haunt me forever?

"Is there anything I could say that would make it better?"

"Probably not. But I appreciate you asking."

We stopped talking and chomped on ham and cheese and chugged down root beer for a while. Having him there eased my grief a point or two, but once his splendiferously uniformed presence left the building, I'd probably be back to square one. I was first to break the silence. "I need to go out there."

"Where? To the scene?"

"Yeah. I need to see the extent of the damage."

"Why would you even consider that?"

"According to Lei, I was probably the last person to see the place intact. I need to see what it looks like now."

Keone pushed back from the table and wiped his hands on a paper napkin. "That's a very bad idea. But it probably doesn't matter what I think, because I doubt the investigators will let you within a half-mile of the place."

"Maybe so, but I've got to try. I owe her that much."

He came around behind me and set his hands on my shoulders, giving them a massaging squeeze. I tolerated it, and after a minute, closed my eyes and relaxed as he rubbed the stiff muscles. "Just so you know, I'm completely against this," he said eventually. "But if you insist on going, I want you to swear you'll wait until I can go with you."

"As you know, Mr. K, I'm not much for swearing." It was true. Growing up in my Aunt Fae's house, she'd insisted on a certain level of what she called "decorum." Cursing was not tolerated. In fact, two decades later, I could still recall the taste of a bar of Ivory soap I'd been subjected to after dropping an F bomb.

"Fine. Let's call it an ask. Please don't go out there without me."

"I won't be going anywhere other than the post office for the next four hours," I said, glancing at the time on my phone. "And you need to get going right now or you'll be late for your preflight check."

"Okay, but how about a hug for your favorite pilot?"

I got up and turned around. Though I wanted a hug in the worst way, shivers shook me; I was afraid to be close, to need him any more than I already did.

I hung my head. "Not in the mood right now."

"You sure?" Mr. K cocked his head and bit his lip. He couldn't have been more appealing; the problem was all me.

"I do love you, Keone. I promise that much." We'd been test driving the "L" word since Christmas, but it was still tough for me to say.

"And I love you. We'll get through this, Kat. I wish I could convince you to take this easier and let me help."

He left and took all the brightness out of the day with him, just as I'd feared he would.

～

LIKE AN ADEPT BORDER COLLIE, I managed to herd the last of our postal patrons out the door at four p.m. sharp.

Pua widened her eyes, seemingly impressed. "Maybe if I was a foot taller, like you, I wouldn't have to threaten bodily harm to clear this place out at closing. I can't remember the last time I was able to pull that shade down on time."

Ask anyone: Pua Chang was way more formidable than most people twice her size. And she knew it. But I'd hustled everyone out and locked up promptly for a reason, so I wasn't going to waste time playing "who's scarier" with Pua.

Keone had asked me to wait until he could accompany me to the scene, but I'd managed to sidestep agreeing to that request. I didn't want him there. Not that I didn't appreciate his love and support, because I did. But this wasn't about that. My need to see the site was about facing the enemy head-on. I had to check whether the pink slippers, or any other evidence of the girl's presence, was out there. I had to see what I could do to either convince the authorities that the girl had been there or convince myself that she hadn't.

THE POLICE HAD STRUNG yellow warning tape across the turnoff to Halepuaʻa Road. A white Maui Fire Department sedan was parked to the side. I pulled up beside it and sucked in a deep "here we go" breath before lowering my window.

A grizzled fire department veteran lumbered out of the sedan and came over to me. "Sorry, Ma'am. This road is closed," he said.

He had the appearance of a guy who was working off his last year or two before retirement and resented being charged with manning the outpost rather than getting his turnout gear dirty in the thick of the action.

"I appreciate you safeguarding the scene," I said. "And this will only take a few minutes."

He leaned in as if trying to establish if I'd been drinking. "Ma'am, I'm serious. No one in or out. No exceptions."

I fetched a business card and presented it to him. "Katherine Smith, Postmaster," I said in my Secret Service protection detail voice.

"Okay. You run the post office in Ohia."

"Correct. And, as the senior federal employee representing the interests of postal service in this area, I need to be allowed to pass."

He took a step back as if he was concerned about catching whatever craziness I was suffering from.

I opened my car door and got out. I'd learned from previous encounters with bureaucratic roadblocks that my size and demeanor went a long way in establishing my authority. I closed the driver door and turned to face him, pleased to note he was at least four inches shorter than I was. "I'm here to ascertain the condition of certain United States Postal Service property that may have been damaged or even destroyed as a result of this incident."

"What in heaven's name are you talking about, young lady?"

"As you may know, rural mailboxes are the property of the U.S. Postal Service, not the homeowner. And I've been tasked with determining if any such property was damaged or destroyed."

He balked, opening and shutting his mouth. I took that opportunity to reopen my door and grab a clipboard I'd brought along for the occasion. I studied it ostentatiously. "I need to document the site and report back to the central office in Kahului within now and close of business tomorrow. Today I will surveil the damage, and tomorrow I'll file my findings."

The firefighter shook his head. "I don't believe they have mailboxes out this way. Last I heard, this was all General Delivery."

"This property may or may not be within the rural route delivery zone," I bluffed. "As postmaster, I can verify that I have never observed the homeowner pick up mail at the post office. That being so, this property may be within the delivery zone."

The man gazed out into the dense vegetation lining the road as if hoping someone above his pay grade would crash through the foliage and give him the go-ahead. Or, better yet, tell me to get my lying behind out of there.

"This is a federal order, sir." I tapped on the clipboard. "You don't mess with the feds." I squinted to read his name badge. "Fire Investigator Moore, is it? I don't know when your shift is up, but I can assure you I'll get what I need to file my report in less than half an hour. Counting travel time. I won't even leave my vehicle."

The man ran a hand through his steel gray crew cut, then backed up, showing me his palms in a display of surrender. I popped back into the driver's seat and took off like a shot down the rough dirt road—the clipboard, loaded with post office box applications, bouncing on the empty seat beside me.

15

THE NARROW, potholed track out to the hermit's place seemed even more impassable than it'd been a few days earlier. Between my last trip out there and now, numerous vehicles had gouged deep ruts in the soft mud and torn through the bushes, leaving branches and rocks strewn across the pitted roadway.

I slowed as I approached the area where the hermit's shack had once stood, leaning forward to peer through Sharkey's windshield.

The entire zone was unrecognizable from what it had looked like only a few days ago. At the end of the road, vegetation was virtually nonexistent, and the few blackened tree trunks left standing seemed like eerie witch fingers pointing to the blue sky above. I marveled that the intense green I'd observed when I'd been there before had been replaced by shades of gray; it was as if I'd seen a movie in color, and now I was watching it again in black and white. The sounds of birds and the swish of palms were gone, too. Eerie silence reigned.

I parked and got out, immediately assaulted by the reek of charred, wet wood and a chemical smell that stung my nostrils.

But that wasn't the worst of it.

Where the dwelling had once stood, there was a hole torn into the earth larger than the footprint of the house and over a foot deep.

I gazed at the swimming-pool-sized crater before me, unable to fathom the magnitude of what it would've taken to cause such destruction.

"You can't be here." I could swear I heard a low-pitched voice behind me, and I jerked around to see the speaker, shivering at the unnerving recollection that those were the same words the hermit had greeted me with a few days earlier.

A young firefighter in full gear covered in soot raised a pike pole and pointed it toward the crater. He resembled a medieval knight getting ready to joust. "No civilians on the premises," he said.

I drew myself up; sure enough I was taller. I tapped the ID badge I wore on a lanyard around my neck. "I'm Kat Smith, Ohia Postmaster."

"This is a secure area. No one's allowed to be out here except the fire and federal investigators."

"Federal agents have been called in?"

"Yeah." The young guy had fresh pink cheeks; he was just a kid. He glanced around as if checking to see if he'd be written up for disclosing unauthorized information, but we were the only people there. "The whole nine yards are on this thing. FBI, ATF, Homeland Security. And those are just the ones I remember."

"Alcohol, Tobacco and Firearms has been called in, too?"

"Yeah. From what I've gathered this wasn't a normal propane tank explosion. Whoever did this knew what they were doing when they set up the explosion. I heard they found evidence of magnesium ribbon."

"I'm not following."

Again, the guy swiveled his head to ensure he wasn't being overheard, then stepped closer. He couldn't resist being the one in the know. "I'm new at Maui Fire," he said. "That's why I got this lousy detail securing the scene. But I just passed the Firefighter One test and I had to know the ignition and burn temps of extremely flammable materials. Magnesium's a big one. Ignites at about eight hundred and fifty degrees Fahrenheit and burns at over three thousand. It's almost impossible to extinguish, and very unlikely to be in the house by accident."

I still wasn't sure what he was getting at, but I nodded to encourage him to keep talking.

"See that white powder over there?" He pointed with the metal pole. "That's what's left of a roll of mag ribbon that was laid throughout this place. You get a fire going after you've laced it with stuff like that and, once it's out, you've got nothing left."

"Three thousand degrees, huh?" My stomach pitched. They'd never know if human remains were mixed in here.

"That's what I'm saying. Twice the temp of a cremation furnace."

My spine tingled with shock as he confirmed what I'd suspected. I thanked him for his time and stumbled back to my SUV. I somehow managed to turn around without landing in the crater, but I had no recollection of the drive back to Ohia.

BACK AT THE K & K office, I was too upset to do the follow-up I'd promised Sophie with the small job she wanted us to complete; instead I donned my swimsuit and did laps in the Bay until I felt calmer.

I was getting dressed after a shower when Keone arrived with takeout from a Hana food truck. I texted Aunt Fae that I wouldn't be home for dinner, then gave Keone a hug.

"I went out to the explosion site right after work," I told him immediately; I had to get it over with.

His jaw tightened and his eyes flashed, but he said nothing, just dropped the bag of food on the table.

"There's absolutely nothing left," I went on. "I've seen photos of the aftermath of IEDs in Iraq, but this was ten times worse.

Complete devastation. Just a hole in the ground, and everything around the area burned."

"Kat, I asked you to wait until we could go together." Keone gestured to his T-shirt and jeans. "I was hoping we could go now."

"I don't want to ever see that place again," I said fervently.

"Banana," he said.

I dropped into my chair at the table. 'Banana' was our safe word, something we invoked when we had an awkward topic to navigate. "Okay. Lay it on me."

Keone sat down across from me. He moved the bag of Bruddah Hutt's barbecue aside so he could make eye contact and paused as if to choose his words carefully. "I'm guessing this situation is reminding you of what happened to you as a kid. A child was in danger and you want to help. That's why you're so driven to find answers. Would you be willing to talk to someone about this situation?"

"You mean Lei?"

"No, I mean a psychologist. A therapist. Someone like that."

"Why is everyone trying to push me toward counseling? First Aunt Fae and now you. Are you telling me I'm crazy?" My voice rose.

"Not at all. I'm saying you shouldn't have to deal with this on your own."

"I'm not. I'm talking to you."

"Are you, though?" Mr. K reached out to take my hand, but I yanked it back as if he'd threatened me with a hot branding iron. "See? This is really messing with you. All the progress you've made up 'til now has been stolen from us by what happened out there."

For years, I'd managed to pass the Secret Service psych exam without anyone picking up on my touchphobia. Now it was hard to admit I'd regressed—that it wasn't just me being hurt.

"I appreciate your concern," I said. "But I prefer DIY when it comes to processing the ugly stuff that comes with the job."

Keone seemed to lose his patience at last. "I sure hope your appendix doesn't burst," he said.

"What?"

"I'd hate to see what kind of a job you'd do on yourself with DIY surgery." He stood up and strode out, closing the front door extra quietly as if to keep from slamming it.

I stayed seated. "That wasn't nice," I whispered.

Once I heard the rumble of his truck's engine disappear, I glanced up at the ceiling of the tiny kitchen in the shack to see Tweedledee and Tweedledum, the resident geckos, peering down at me with pitying expressions.

"What do you know?" I said. "You hang out up there catching bugs and doing your little push-ups. It's way harder down here."

I opened the bag and took out the Styrofoam container holding one of the kalua pig, rice, and steamed cabbage "plate lunches" the food truck was known for. I ate quickly. Hopefully Aunt Fae would want the other one; if not, it would make a nice lunch the next day.

As I stepped out onto the flat beach rock that served as the shack's front porch and turned to lock the door, I felt a presence behind me.

I whirled to check out what it was, stepping out to the edge of the tiny porch onto the beach rock front step, and felt something throw me off. My knee buckled as my bare foot slid off the rock's uneven surface. I windmilled my arms and dropped the bag of takeout. It felt like it took minutes, rather than seconds, to go down, but when I did it was with a bone-crunching *thwomp*. I lay there, splayed out, attempting to pull air into my lungs. The pain in my side, and my head, made it impossible.

Flashes of light. Then darkness.

16

When I awoke, I was awash in blinding white light.

Had I died?

It took me a couple of seconds to recognize Keone squatting beside me, peering into my face. His truck engine rumbled, only a few feet from where I lay; the headlights had me in their blaze. A searing pain in my side made it hard to take in a full breath.

"What happened, Kat?" he said. "I came back to get my dinner and maybe work things out, and found you lying here!"

I tried to respond, but with so little oxygen to work with, I could only hiss out, "Hey."

"Don't try to talk," he said. "You must have fallen. I've got an ambulance on the way. They're coming from Hana, so it's going to be a few minutes."

I tried to sit up, but the fireworks flashing knocked me back down. "I must have hit my head as well as my ribs. I slipped on the rock."

"Kat, please lie still. You must've done some damage because you were out cold when I arrived."

I blinked; it was the only movement I could handle without

causing more pain. "This is so embarrassing. I thought I saw someone by the door, and I turned too fast."

"Rubber slippers aren't great when the footing is uneven," he agreed. He took my hand. "You're so cold. Just try to relax and breathe."

"Breathing doesn't feel good," I wheezed.

The ambulance arrived. When the EMT gently palpated my left side, it took all the grit I could gather to keep from vomiting up my dinner.

"Tender?" he said.

I nodded, light-headed from having to take tiny sips of air rather than filling my lungs.

"I think you may have cracked your ribs. You're gonna need X-rays. First, let's get you to the clinic."

Next thing I knew I was being carefully rolled over and slid onto a backboard. Then they hoisted me onto a gurney. Mental sparklers continued to flicker and flash. Beyond the light display my brain was putting on, I saw a profusion of stars in the black velvet of the Ohia night sky.

Keone watched them hook me up to an IV and check vitals. "Call Aunt Fae," I wheezed.

"Already done," he said. "I'll follow and meet you there," he called, as they closed the door.

"Let us examine you," said a nurse wearing a blue mask over the lower part of her face when we arrived at the Hana Urgent Care Clinic. A female doctor, also wearing a mask, and with dark curly hair similar to Lei Texeira's, arrived soon after and, after checking me over, ordered X-rays. "We don't have the capability here at the clinic, but tomorrow I'll need you to get down to the hospital in Wailuku and get that taken care of. Are you going to need transportation?"

I was too muddled to answer but I heard Keone say in the background, "We're good. I'll make sure she gets there."

The doctor left and the nurse came over and wrapped a wide

elastic bandage around my torso. I winced as each layer of binding cinched my injured torso tighter, but after it was secured, the tape did make me feel a bit more comfortable.

The doc came back in and handed Keone some paperwork and a small white paper bag.

"Make sure she only takes *one* every four hours after this first dose," she said. "These are great for acute pain, but they can become a slippery slope."

I took a couple of the pain pills under supervision, drinking down a full paper cup of water from a dispenser, and then Keone helped me limp back to his truck.

He opened the back of the extended cab and tried to settle me flat on the back seat, but I had to bend my knees up to fit. The pain meds eventually kicked in and I was breathing better, but the trip back from Hana to New Ohia seemed never-ending. I felt every rut, every pothole, and every dip in the road.

Aunt Fae met Keone's vehicle out in our driveway. "I've been worried sick," she said.

"Kat's got to go to Wailuku for X-rays tomorrow," said Keone. "Like I told you when I called, she fell outside the K & K shack. The doctor's pretty sure she's cracked some ribs."

He rattled on about finding me, the trip to the clinic, and the doctor ruling out organ damage and a concussion, but I'd tuned out.

I was focused on his assessment that I'd simply fallen. Now that I was more comfortable and out of immediate danger, I revisited the moments after I'd grabbed the takeout bag and stepped outside.

I hadn't fallen. *I'd been pushed.*

17

THE NEXT MORNING, Aunt Fae drove me to Maui Memorial Medical Center. She was a bit apprehensive about tackling Sharkey's tech-heavy cockpit, but she did just fine as I rested beside her with my seat fully reclined. I'd improved enough not to have to lie in back, but I still grimaced with every jolt along the way.

The verdict was two small rib fractures and extensive bruising on my left side, and a contusion on my head but no concussion.

I wasn't blessed with the grace of a ballerina, but I wasn't a complete klutz, either. The rock stoop outside the shack was flat and, more importantly, its surface was well-known to me. It didn't make any sense that I'd just toppled over.

But I kept my thoughts on this to myself. As ridiculous as it sounded that I'd simply taken a tumble, it sounded even more absurd to accuse someone of pushing me. I had no basis for the allegation, and no idea of a possible perpetrator or motive.

The good news, if you could call it that, was that doctor's orders banned me from serving as postmaster for the next week or so. Extra help was sent to Pua from the main office in Kahului as I was under orders to do "no bending or lifting."

That meant I could spend a bit more time and effort checking into what happened out at the hermit's place.

I started by calling Doug Beachum. "Hey, Doug. How's your route treating you?"

"I don't want to talk about that girl," he said, ignoring my attempt at breaking the ice.

"I do. And I'd like to meet you in person."

"Why? I told everything I know to the cops. And they made me feel like some kind of criminal. Now I'm not sure what I saw."

"Don't feel bad, Doug. I'm much more at fault than you are. I actually went out there and confronted the guy. While I was there, I saw a pair of little girl's sandals. I believe your original story, Doug."

He was silent, so I went on. "I don't think anything you did or didn't do would've made a difference. But I'm trying to figure out what happened. And talking to you would be a big help."

In the end, Doug Beachum agreed to let me buy him lunch at Bruddah Hutt's in Hana. When he showed up, Doug got out of his truck wearing the infamous muddy brown UPS uniform, complete with knee-length shorts that stretched across his thighs. Although he was a big guy, he seemed fit and moved well, reminding me of a sumo wrestler.

I'd alerted Doug to my height and black pants, white polo shirt ensemble, so it didn't take him long to pick me out of the line waiting to order.

"Hey, Kat," he said, shooting me the local pinky-thumb *shaka* greeting.

I tried one in return; he smiled for the first time. "What can I get you?" I asked.

"I'll just have a bowl of saimin. And ice water." He patted his rotund middle and explained he'd made a New Year's Resolution to drop a few pounds and, so far, he'd pretty much kept to it.

I ordered our food. I got myself a katsu chicken salad and a canned lilikoi drink. I didn't need the calories either, but I figured a little sugar in my veins might make the conversation we were about to have feel a bit more tolerable. And besides, I was on the "injured reserve" list.

When I brought the food to the table, we made small talk for a couple of minutes.

"You wanted to talk to me about that girl out in the jungle, right?" he said, getting back on task as he slurped his saimin.

"Just more of a confirmation talk." I filled him in on my brief encounter with the hermit and then my shock at what he'd done early the following morning. Then I gave him a very brief description of the destruction I'd witnessed at the explosion site after my trip out there.

Doug pushed aside his Styrofoam container of saimin and pair of wooden chopsticks; he appeared as shocked and remorseful as I felt.

"I didn't want to get involved," he said. "The cops made it sound like I'd done something wrong, not reporting it. So, I told them I wasn't sure what I saw. I didn't want to get caught in the middle."

I waited. My training in interrogation techniques kicked in. Don't ask another question until you've allowed enough time for the interviewee to finish their thought.

Doug went on, "I mean, I *am* sure. I'm, like, a thousand percent sure. But what good does that do now?"

"Can you describe the girl you saw?" I took out a pad and pencil. "I'd like to try to sketch her face, with your help."

He closed his eyes. "Okay. Um, she had dark hair, I guess. I couldn't see how long it was, but it was straight, not curly. She appeared to be school age. You know, like maybe third or fourth grade. I don't know kids' ages exactly, but I have a *keiki* niece who's nine and she seemed to be about the same size as her."

"Anything else?" I sketched quickly. "Was her hair in bangs, or hanging down?"

He shut his eyes again. "Down. Beside her face. No bangs. Past her shoulders."

"Were her eyes round, or more Asian in shape?"

"Round."

I scribbled more. I wasn't a good artist, but I'd taken a class on interviewing witnesses this way and hopefully, his memory could be jogged further. "And her skin tone? Was she white, or mixed, or . . ."

"Mixed, I think. It was shaded in there but she wasn't super pale."

"See, you know more than you thought." I held up the drawing. "What do you think?"

He shook his head. "I don't know. Her eyes were smaller than that. Closer together."

I erased and redid them. "What about her mouth?"

"Not smiling. Lips were . . . medium?"

I tried an interpretation of that.

"She's dead, right?" he said suddenly.

"We don't know," I said. "Right now, no one's searching for her because you changed your story and my story of the slippers wasn't enough . . . and that bomb blew up any evidence."

He grimaced. "Then why does any of this matter?"

"Everyone deserves to be accounted for. Regardless of the circumstances, it's important to get justice for victims. Even if this girl is dead, we need to find out who she was."

"Okay," he said. "I get it. I do. I feel really bad. I'll tell the cops the truth if they ask me again."

"That's good, Doug. That might make a big difference." I forced myself to pat his hand, comforting him. "I'll let them know. This is important; it could make a difference in whether they keep trying to find her or not."

"If you discover anything, would you let me know?"

"Of course I will, Doug. We'll both feel better if I do."

18

WHEN I GOT BACK to Ohia, I went into the K & K office. I fixed myself a cup of tea, took a pain pill (my ribs were calling for a nap, STAT) and phoned Lei. "I got a sketch of the hermit girl's face from Doug Beachum," I said baldly.

A pause—I heard that whoosh of breath that meant Lei was blowing that curl up off her forehead. "How did that come about?"

"Well, I have a little time off due to falling and getting some cracked ribs, so I thought I'd use it to dig into the investigation," I said. "I called Beachum and took him to lunch at Bruddah Hutt's. He admitted he felt pressured and under the gun with you guys, so he changed his story. He's willing to go on record with it now."

"Okaaaaayyyy," Lei said. "Tell me about this sketch."

"I had a class in sketching once when interviewing a witness. Part of my Secret Service training. I'm no artist or expert, but it turns out he remembered more about the girl than he thought he did. Do you want the sketch?"

"No. But I'll get it from you later to compare after I contact our department ID artist and have her reach out to Beachum," Lei said. I heard the keys of her keyboard rattling; she was probably emailing as we spoke. "There are other powers that be that I'll have to contact, too. I'm actually no longer on the case."

"But I had an additional thought about the girl in the hermit's window," I said. "Who she might be." Lei's silence told me all I needed to know about how interested she was in hearing my thoughts on the matter. I pressed on. "Can you give me a list of reported runaway girls? Especially young ones, like twelve and under?"

"Kat, the MPD has given me direct orders to stand down on this case. The feds are involved now since the bombing, and anything I do alone regarding this matter would be considered insubordination."

"I'm only asking for a list of runaway girls." I squared my jaw. "You don't have to tell them you gave it to me."

"I'm afraid the answer is 'no.' Is there anything else?"

"I guess not." Lei wasn't the only one who could sound frosty.

We ended the call. She hadn't even thanked me for the lead on Beachum. Our friendship was heading toward a breakup like a ship toward a reef.

Of course, that wasn't going to stop me and there was more than one way to skin a mango. I wasn't done mixing my metaphors, either.

AT DINNER THAT EVENING, I filled Aunt Fae in on my meeting with Doug Beachum and my subsequent strikeout with Lei Texeira.

"More than one way to skin a cat," said Aunt Fae.

"I prefer 'skin a mango,'" I said, glancing under the table to where Tiki sat alertly at my feet, waiting for whatever tiny scrap might fall. Good thing she wasn't proficient in English. "Be careful what you say," I said. "You didn't know her when she was feral, but trust me, Tiki can slice and dice."

Aunt Fae shook her head. "All I'm saying is, can't you get what you need from someone else?"

"You're right. Now that I think of it, didn't Rita Farnsworth work for the Maui School District before she retired?"

Rita was one of the newest members of the Ohia Red Hat Society. She'd built a cat sanctuary on her property for strays and had been helpful in a case I'd worked, recovering a valuable lost cat. She and I had gotten along well. Even if she couldn't help me get the information I needed, she might know someone who could.

"Yes, I remember her saying she'd been in education," said Aunt Fae. "I'm playing Bunco with her and a few of the other Red Hat gals tonight. How do you think she could help?"

"I'll bet the schools keep records of kids who are truant. You know, poor attenders. Who could also turn out to be runaways."

I was too pain-riddled to attend the downstairs Bunco tournament and went to bed early, but Aunt Fae talked to Rita on my behalf.

It turned out, Rita hadn't just worked at the school district, she'd been the head of curriculum and instruction for the county. That was like being the offensive line coach of a football team. Next to the school district superintendent, hers had been one of the most influential positions in the whole bureaucracy. She was bound to have access to the information I needed.

I CALLED RITA FARNSWORTH, cat whisperer, early the next morning after getting the deets on her position from Auntie over coffee.

"It's been a while since I worked with the school system. I've been retired for some time," Rita said, when I phoned her with my request for a list of truant elementary school girls.

"I understand, but I'd appreciate any help you can offer with my case."

"We're having a Red Hat soiree tonight at Edith's place. Why don't you join us, and we can talk about what you want to know, and why, in person? That is confidential information. I have to know why you need it."

"Of course," I said, though I inwardly sighed. I'd been made an honorary Red Hat member some months ago when I'd managed to keep Edith Pepperwhite from meeting her Maker before her time. I enjoyed partying with the older ladies now and then. "But I'm off work for medical reasons this week. It might not be good for me to be seen out socializing."

"From what I've heard, you're not working because you're under doctor's orders not to do any heavy lifting after your fall," Rita said. The scope of personal details available on the coconut wireless never failed to amaze me. "And you're in luck," she went on. "Because the only lifting you'll be doing this evening is a wineglass."

"Okay, then. See you tonight."

I ended the call and checked my phone's calendar. I'd almost forgotten that Keone and I were scheduled to be out at Sophie Smithson's client's house in Hana at ten a.m. that morning. I groaned and got up to get dressed; I needed a pain pill as well as food before I hit the road.

Keone and I had agreed to meet three contractors who were coming out to prepare bids for a bathroom remodel at the client's house. I stuffed down my annoyance at the task; the client seemed to be implying that the bonded and licensed professionals who'd be showing up at his mansion were not only untrustworthy, but potential thieves. Not only that, the place already had a full-time caretaker on the premises.

But I didn't have a choice on whether to take the assignment. I'd agreed to assist Security Solutions whenever possible when they had something out this way, and it'd been weeks since I'd been asked to do anything.

Keone didn't have to be there, but he'd been extra solicitous since I'd taken my tumble, texting me several times in the last day and night. He didn't let on that he'd traded a few flights to be with me that day, but I'd heard about it from Auntie, who heard from Opal, who'd heard from Keone's aunt, who'd heard from Pono, and that's how news got around out here.

Keone met me at the K & K office and we took Sharkey out to the estate. The guy's place was a palace inside a paradise inside a bubble of money that mere mortals like me could only imagine living in.

The grounds were impeccable—wide, impossibly green lawns bordered by a profusion of tropical trees and flowers. There was a greenhouse out behind the house, probably full of orchids and costly exotic species, but we didn't take time to check it out.

The mansion itself was built of what appeared to be mahogany or teak or some other precious rainforest wood. Seems the dude could care less that the Amazon Basin and the jungles of Southeast Asia were being deforested at an alarming rate as long as he had a nice setting in which to store his priceless art. A peaked roof soared thirty feet above the floor, with windows that had a one-eighty view of Hana Bay.

The ocean was ten shades of azure, from midnight to the palest baby blue, with a few whitecaps near the horizon. An immense white yacht motored by while I was taking in the scenery. I couldn't help wondering if the homeowner, or one of his celebrity neighbors, might be on it.

The home's art collection rivaled something you'd find in a modern art exhibit in a city the size of Honolulu, Seattle, or Dallas. My art education had only included a survey course my freshman year and then an "Art of 20th Century America" course I took to nab the last few credits needed for graduation, but even I could recognize many of the names scrawled in the bottom corners of the paintings.

Keone checked in each contractor and verified their licenses and IDs, then kept watch at the main entrance as I trailed the professionals through the house and across the grounds while they took measurements and worked their phones and calculators.

The whole enterprise took two hours. Keone seemed preoccupied as we walked back to the car for the drive back to Ohia. We'd taken Sharkey, since I stuck the magnetic Security Solutions logo on the side and we were on official business, but Keone was driving because by then I was exhausted and my ribs were throbbing. I couldn't wait to recline the seat and rest. Besides, if I'd had to brake hard or swerve out of the way of an oncoming tourist who'd crossed the center line, I wasn't sure my mummified torso could manage it.

We pulled away from the client's circular driveway and exited the automatic gate with Keone wearing a scowl reminiscent of Tiki when I run out of kibble.

I glanced at Keone's dark expression as he drove. "That was so boring. Two hours of our lives we'll never get back," I said. "Everything okay?"

"It's not that. I've been putting off telling you this because I don't like to kick you while you're down," he said. *Uh-oh.* Just the thought of being kicked anywhere on my achingly bruised body made me wince. "Sorry, bad cliché." He reached over and squeezed my hand.

"Ok. What is it?" I said. "Lay it on me."

"I'm on a short list for a promotion at work."

"What's wrong with that? Sounds great."

"It could be. But the timing isn't the best."

"What do you mean?"

"If I get it, they want me to get certified on the bigger commuter jets. I'll need to go to Honolulu for training. And then . . ." he glanced at me. "They might want me to move away."

"Ohhh." The air leaked out as if I were a deflating balloon.

"Yeah. I hate to leave, even short-term, while you're injured and you're worried over . . . well, you know."

"You can't let my problems hold you back, Keone. I'll heal, whether you're here with me or in Honolulu doing flight training,"

I said, wiggling in my seat to try to get more comfortable. "And if you have to move, well . . . we'll figure it out."

He smiled; relief softened his expressive eyes. He'd really been worried about what I thought of his opportunity. "It may not come to anything. I'm flying to Honolulu for an interview on Monday, so we'll see how it goes."

We rode the rest of the way back to the K & K office in silence. I said I'd write up the report for Sophie and call it a day. My damaged ribs were screaming for rest and a pain pill, but I didn't want to take one until I was home in bed.

"Want me to stick around and drive you home?" Keone said.

"Thanks, but I can handle it. I appreciate you coming out here today, though. We looked spiffy as a team." We'd both worn the white polos and black pants we put on for our K & K cases, too. "After all, I'm the one who's benefiting by having Sharkey at my disposal. Enjoy the rest of your weekend." I assumed we wouldn't get together again in the next couple of days; I wasn't up to much at the moment.

"How about a kiss?" Keone asked, as I unlocked the office door.

I turned and he took me by the shoulders, staying away from my injured ribs. I let myself get a little lost in the moment; it was all we'd be able to enjoy with this injury, and the threat of his departure had cast a pall over both of us. Our kiss had a touch of desperation to it; we ended with a *honi*, the Hawaiian exchange of breath, our foreheads resting against each other, our eyes closed as we shared the moment.

Dang it. I was really getting attached to this guy. Was it wrong to hope he didn't get the promotion? Yep, it was.

"I'll be in touch," Keone said. He squeezed my shoulders in farewell and left to get into his truck.

He drove off and I typed up the one-page report indicating all had gone smoothly at the art estate. I texted Sophie to alert her to a successful mission and let her know the report had been sent by encrypted email; she called when she received my notification.

"How are you feeling, Kat?" she asked in her crisp as a new five pound note British accent. "I heard you've had a bit of trouble over there."

Unaware of just how much Sophie knew, I played it safe. "Doing much better, thanks."

"Why do I get the feeling you're not as chipper as you claim to be?" Not much got by Ms. Sophie Smithson.

I hesitated to fill her in with my distress over the thought of Keone leaving, and the ongoing flashbacks every time I remembered what'd happened to the girl in the window. "Just tired. My cracked ribs are making it hard to get a good night's sleep."

"I can imagine," she said. "Thanks ever so much for handling this today. I know it was a bit onerous, but I appreciate you stepping in."

"It was nothing. And I want you to know, I'm taking good care of Sharkey."

Sophie started to say goodbye, but I interrupted as I remembered something. "I'm sorry to cut you off, but I have a favor to ask."

"Anything I can do."

"Thanks. I'm thinking of seeing someone about my . . ." I hesitated to finish the sentence. Sophie knew all about my touchphobia and how it had affected my life during my time with the Secret Service, but it was still difficult to say "mental health" or any of its alternatives.

"Yes. Go on. It sounds like you're seeking a referral of some sort."

"I am. I'm struggling with . . . insomnia. And it's not just because of my injury. I think I might benefit from talking to someone about it."

"Insomnia. Yes. We have an excellent psychologist that we work with here at the firm named Dr. Kinoshita. She's brilliant when it comes to getting to the root of a situation. And extremely discreet. Would you like her number?"

Did I really want her number? No. But did I need it? A definite maybe. "I'd appreciate that, Sophie."

"Excellent. I'll put the referral through as part of your employment package. You'll hear from her office within the week."

"Thanks," I said.

I gulped down my apprehension. *It was only therapy.* I'd survived that before—along with politics in Washington, an IED attack, and a few attempts on my life. I could get through therapy, too.

19

THE OHIA RED HAT SOCIETY held their weekly meetup that night and after some rest, I was ready to take them on. Aunt Fae and I rode together to Edith's cozy cottage in Hana, with Auntie at the wheel so I could get a bit more rest. The cottage and I had some history, not all of it good, but I put that behind me and focused on the task at hand, admiring Edith's glorious potted orchid collection as we crossed her porch.

Rita Farnsworth was a woman with a look about her that Aunt Fae would probably describe as "no foo-foo." Her über-natural style (she was a big fan of beige flax, linen, and burlap) aside, the retired administrator and current cat rescue advocate was pleasant as usual.

I drew her away from the rowdy card game underway in Edith's living room, and explained my dilemma about identifying the girl in the window.

At first, Rita focused on grilling me about every aspect of the situation, which I was loath to go over—but go over it I did. I started with the scant details of the UPS driver's description, then my interaction with the hermit, and finally his dramatic last act.

"Oh my," she said. "Of course I heard about the explosion, but I had no idea about any of this. What can I do to help?"

"I was hoping you could help me get information from the school district. A list of truant girls of elementary school age."

She twisted her mouth into an anxious frown. "But why?"

"The Child Welfare Services people say they have no record of a missing girl who fits the UPS guy's description. Maybe she isn't in their system. Maybe she's missing from her school, but so far, no formal missing child report has been filed."

"I see."

"Could you make inquiries and see if there are reports of kids who aren't in school who should be?"

"You'd like a truancy report."

"Yes."

Rita clasped her hands and lowered her head in what appeared to be a prayerful pose. Then, she glanced up and said, "I'll give this some thought and get back to you on Monday."

I thanked her and we joined the other Red Hats in a spirited game of gin rummy. As empty wineglasses were being taken to the kitchen and goodbye hugs were getting ready to ramp up, Edith and Josie traded a glance. Tiny, round Edith was perky in her favorite peaked red witch-style hat, and Josie's long, rippling gray hair was decorated with a scarlet hibiscus; both of them wore secret smiles.

Edith picked up a spoon and clinked her wineglass three times. "Ladies," she said. "We have an announcement to make."

Silence fell. Everyone froze in place like in a child's game of freeze tag.

Edith and Josie reached out and held hands. If anyone there didn't know they were a couple, they did now; and the room was so quiet I heard the ticking of Edith's old-fashioned wall clock.

"We're not getting any younger, and we want to be there for each other going forward— health directives and hospital admissions being what they are and all that. You all know the health scares we've been through." Nods around the room. "So we've decided we should make our relationship legal."

"Do you mean what I think you do?" asked Clara, grinning as she adjusted the deep purple fabric of her flowing dress.

"We're getting married. We're working with Elle Beane at Hotel Hana about having the ceremony next weekend," Josie said.

Spontaneous applause burst out. Pearl made a startled noise and said, "Next weekend? You two need a shotgun wedding?"

Everyone chuckled.

Edith and Josie took turns explaining the reasoning behind their decision. They wanted to be able to assist each other with medical, financial, and family decisions as their end of life came into view. Edith, an attorney, explained that being legally recognized as a married couple would make everything easier.

Clara said, "Are you going to live together?"

"No," said Josie. "We both love our homes and aren't ready to give them up. But one day, we might."

Everyone agreed it sounded as if they'd given this a lot of thought. Pearl, who must have been in on it, produced a bottle of champagne and rolled forward on her standing wheelchair to line up and fill a stack of plastic glasses she'd had hiding in her chair's saddlebag. Once they were filled, everyone toasted the happy couple with a dollop of bubbly. "Congratulations!"

As the group dispersed, everyone agreed that the wedding would serve as next week's get-together.

When Aunt Fae and I drove back home, she said, "That was fun. It's nice to get out, isn't it?"

We pulled into the garage and Aunt Fae cut the engine. As I opened my door, we swiveled our heads to glance at each other in alarm. From inside the house, Tiki's yowl could've awakened the legendary Hawaiian Night Marchers.

20

AUNT FAE BEAT me to the interior door from the garage. It wasn't a fair race, since I was still in pain and fading fast after hours of Security Solutions surveillance and a couple of hours of social activity with the lively members of the Ohia Red Hat Society.

The moment Aunt Fae opened the door into the house, Tiki flew at us in a fury of indignation, hissing and spitting. Her tail was twice its normal size, and her ear was pinned back. I instinctively wrapped my arms around my bandaged rib cage.

"What is it, girlfriend?" I cooed, hoping my solicitous demeanor would calm her.

Tiki turned and streaked through the kitchen. It was all I could do to keep up. She bolted to the living room and skidded to a stop under an open window.

Aunt Fae pointed to the window. "What's that doing open?"

"Your guess is as good as mine. I didn't open it."

"Well, I certainly didn't either."

"I think we had an intruder."

Aunt Fae's eyes widened, and she said in a whisper, "Do you think they're still here?"

I thought about my weapon in my upstairs nightstand. What I wouldn't give to have had it in my pocket at that moment.

From under the window, we heard a tiny hoarse squeak, like a dog toy that had gone eight rounds with a bullmastiff.

"Misty!" we exclaimed at the same time.

"Tell you what, Auntie," I said. "Why don't I check the house and make sure it's clear, while you rescue Misty?"

"On it," Auntie said, but she swung through the kitchen and armed herself with her favorite iron skillet before she hurried to exit the house.

I retrieved the thumb-sized can of Mace from my keyring and began a thorough search of the house. I held the Mace as I would a pistol as I sidled around, using corners of the room as cover in classic defensive mode. My ears were tuned for anything out of the ordinary; there were no unusual sounds now that Tiki had followed Auntie to supervise the rescue of her kitten.

When I reached my room, the first thing I did was check the Glock 19 former service pistol I kept in the top drawer of my night-stand. Its position had been changed—not taken but *moved*.

I always left it in the handle down position so I could easily grab it out of the drawer. Now it was turned so the barrel was facing my bed.

I racked the slide to check it. The one round I always left chambered was still there, so it hadn't been fired. I kept the bullets and spare magazines in a secure box on a top shelf in my closet. When I brought it down and unlocked it, the box was exactly as I'd left it.

I ducked into Aunt Fae's room and the two upstairs bathrooms. I checked the closets, under the bed, the bathrooms. Everything seemed in order.

By the time I got back downstairs, Aunt Fae had brought the kitten inside and wrapped her in a dishtowel. The poor thing was a wet, pitiful ball of gray fur. Tiki wound around Auntie's legs, purring loudly in an attempt to comfort her baby.

"Seems the sprinklers went off while we were gone," said Aunt Fae.

"Maybe that's what scared off the would-be intruder."

Auntie set Misty down on the floor. Tiki, who only days earlier had batted her baby away when she tried to nurse, got right to work licking her offspring back to warmth. The two of them twined together on the dishtowel in the middle of the kitchen floor were a heartwarming sight.

"Did you find anything missing?" said Aunt Fae.

I wrestled with whether to alert her that someone had been upstairs and had touched my weapon, or fib so she wouldn't worry about it. "Seems okay."

"This makes no sense," she said. "Why would someone break in and then not take anything?"

"We live in a state park," I said. "Maybe a curious visitor just wanted to look around the house. I don't think we locked the window."

"The park closes at six. It's nearly ten."

"Since when does anyone around here follow the rules?"

Neither of us remembered the last time we'd checked the locks on the windows. We often kept them open during the day to allow the breeze to cool the house, but the windows had screens. Aunt Fae had found the screen from the open window in the bushes below.

"Maybe Tiki jumped onto the window ledge and the screen fell out," Aunt Fae offered.

"That doesn't explain how the window got opened in the first place."

Troubled, I replaced my stretched-out elastic bandage with a new one before getting into bed.

The out of place firearm and open window continued to trouble me. If park visitors were going around snooping in the houses, I owed it to our new neighbor, Elle Beane, to advise her about securely locking her windows and doors. I made a mental note to talk to her about it in the morning. It'd also be a great excuse to get her take on Edith and Josie's upcoming wedding plans.

I woke late the next morning groggy and sore. The bed felt unexpectedly lonely. I glanced over to see Tiki twined around her kitten in their bed, making a multicolored cinnamon roll.

Sunday was my day to kick back. If Keone's schedule allowed, we usually hung out together. Surfing was our favorite activity, but depending on the weather and our moods, sometimes we'd take a hike or do something else outdoors, then watch a movie or cook a homemade meal together at his place or with Auntie. (When I say "we cooked" I mean, "he cooked" because I'd proven to be deficient in kitchen skills.)

Staring up at the ceiling, I considered calling Mr. K.

No, I wasn't ready to deal with how I felt about him possibly leaving Maui for an extended period if he got the promotion. His interview in Honolulu was tomorrow morning. I didn't want to sway him one way or another, even though I was clear in my own mind which way I hoped it would go.

Auntie was still in bed. Good. I probably wasn't the only one who'd had trouble falling asleep after last night's disturbance.

I slipped into shorts and a T-shirt baggy enough to not chafe my healing bruises by catching on the elastic bandage around my chest. I then put on my Nikes, snagged a coffee in my favorite *Do Not Speak to Me Until this Mug is Empty* cup, and carefully made my way down to Pikake Court.

Elle greeted me as if we were old friends. "Hey, Kat. Great to see you. What brings you down this way?"

After the pleasantries I said, "I wanted to alert you to something that happened at our place last night. Seems we have prying eyes here in New Ohia." I explained about the open window and Misty's tumble into the bushes. I assured her nothing had been taken from our home, but the circumstances were still troubling.

"Hmm. That is concerning," she said. "I haven't seen anything suspicious, but I'll keep an eye out. And yeah, I haven't been locking the place. I'll start now. " She was wearing athletic shorts, a T-shirt and new, blinged-out trainers.

"You a sneaker person?" I said, pointing to the expensive-looking gold and black athletic shoes.

Elle smiled. "I'm a runner. I'm getting in shape for the Honolulu Marathon."

"Isn't that almost a year from now?"

"It is. But the training is year-round. I try to get in five to ten miles every day during the off-season. You want to join me sometime?"

I pointed to my wrapped chest. "I'm pretty much on the bench for a while."

"Ah, yes, I heard you fell." She scrunched up her nose; her dark brown eyes were sympathetic.

I'm not comfortable with sympathy, empathy, or any other display of pity; it's fine for other people, but not for me. Pity equals weakness, and weakness is the root cause of failure.

"I'm healing fast," I said. "When I do, I'd love to join you. The other thing I wanted to talk to you about was Edith and Josie's wedding. They announced it last night at the Red Hat gathering. What's the scoop?"

Elle turned and walked to a padded workout area she'd set up in one corner of the garage. She picked up a weight and began arm curls. "Oh, no big deal. It's going to be an intimate little wedding. They want to have it outside, weather permitting, and we have a lovely, secluded grotto right behind the hotel where we can hold it in relative privacy." Her gaze sharpened. "Hey, I have a number of fun little responsibilities I need to recruit for. You up for doing something?"

"Uh. What did you have in mind?" I didn't want to get tied up in anything too fussy.

"Minding the guest book. Someone needs to monitor and make sure everyone signs it. You'd also need to keep an eye on the gift table."

"Sure," I said with relief. As long as I didn't have to precede the brides down the aisle wearing some ill-fitting flowery getup, I was down with it.

Elle grabbed a bag-style water bottle and slung it on her back, draping the flexible straw over her shoulder for easy sipping. "I'd better get on the road if I want to get my miles in today. I have an event this evening to prep for."

"Sounds good. See you." I shuffled off as she closed up her house with the new level of security I'd suggested. I was sad we all had to worry about that now.

21

ON MONDAY MORNING, I woke feeling more rested and better able to move than I had felt since my fall after relaxing and taking it easy for most of Sunday. I was sipping the Elixir of Life from my mug while doing some gentle stretches and watching the cats play in a sunbeam, when Rita Farnsworth called. "You still want to check into those truancy reports?"

"Yes, please."

"Are you still off from work today or do we need to schedule this for after the post office closes?" The woman was all business.

"I've got a couple more days off before I can get cleared to return."

"Good. What do you say to me picking you up in an hour and we'll head down to the district office in Wailuku and see if we can shake some trees?"

"Sounds perfect. Thanks."

I dressed in my usual black jeans and polo shirt and then thought better of it. We were going to the offices of the educational command center on Maui. I probably should wear something that was a bit more friendly and casual.

I kept the jeans but traded the polo for a pale-yellow button-down shirt. I even folded up a yellow bandana and tied it around my ponytail for a tidy but summery look.

Rita showed up wearing Birkenstocks and a homespun tunic with what Aunt Fae would call "palazzo pants." With her beige hair, light tan face, taupe-colored clothing, and mud brown sandals, she'd be invisible in a sandstorm.

"There you go," she said as she insisted on helping me into the passenger seat of her little electric car. Getting in took some maneuvering to accommodate my six-foot something frame, with or without a battered torso.

We chatted for most of the ride into town. I inquired about her stray cat sanctuary. She assured me she'd left the kitties in good hands for the day. "I'm up to nearly two dozen felines in the cat house now. It was wrong of Chad to use the postal truck to help me get the sanctuary going, but he's such a dear. He comes over now and then and helps me with cleanup and nail trimming, and he's my sitter on weekends. It's so lovely to have a young person around."

We discussed the weather, the upcoming wedding, the price of bread and coffee in rural Hawaii, and about a half-dozen other things that kept us safely away from addressing the distressing case of the missing girl.

About the time we turned onto High Street in Wailuku, where the school district office was located, Rita turned to me and said, "I need you to let me handle this. I'm going to be calling in a few favors, and maybe even doing a bit of fibbing. I hope you're okay with that."

I assured her I was on board.

Rita was greeted like that Greek guy in "The Odyssey" arriving home after years at sea as she swept into the Maui School District office. People left cubicles to come over and hug her as word spread that the much-loved former head of curriculum and instruction was "in the house."

Rita introduced me as the Ohia postmaster, as if somehow that gave me standing, and no one questioned her.

We went from office to office and cubicle to cubicle, greeting those who would've taken offense if she'd failed to seek them out. Then, we made our way over to the area that held what we'd come for—the school attendance department.

"Hi Sheila," Rita said upon entering the office. The plump, curly-haired clerk's name plaque was clearly visible on her desk, so I wasn't sure if Rita knew the woman or not, but Sheila lit up as if she'd spotted a long-lost relative that'd been given up for dead.

"Dr. Farnsworth! How wonderful to see you. May I offer you a chair? How about a cup of coffee or a bottle of water?"

Rita leaned over the desk and gave the woman a perfunctory hug. "It's lovely to be back. But we can only stay a few minutes. I'm hoping you can help me with a personal matter."

"Of course. Anything." Glancing at me, Sheila explained, "Dr. Farnsworth was such a help to me when I first got here. I consider her my mentor."

"Well, it was my pleasure, Sheila."

I had the feeling that if Rita Farnsworth had asked this woman for her left kidney, we'd be leaving for the hospital immediately.

Rita explained what we were searching for. We waited while Sheila pulled up a list of four names of elementary-age kids on the east side of the island who'd been "excessively truant," which meant for more than ten days, in the past month.

"I'll be writing up the February report this week," Sheila said.

Rita stared at the printout Sheila had given her. "Can I ask just one more small favor?"

Sheila's bright eyes resembled a trick dog waiting for its trainer to give the 'go' sign. "Of course."

"It appears one of these children is a boy and the other three are girls."

"Yes, I'm pretty sure 'Timo' is a boy's name. The other names are usually given to girls, but you can never be sure."

"Would you check that? While you're in their files, would you be so kind as to include their ages and addresses?"

"Sure. Give me a minute. Are you sure I can't get you a coffee or some water while you wait?"

"*Mahalo*, but no. We're in a bit of a hurry."

"Okay. I'll get right on it."

Rita kept peeking out into the hall as Sheila pecked and moused her way through the data screens on her computer. After only a couple of minutes Sheila triumphantly handed over a new printout.

"There you go. I hope that helps."

"Again, *mahalo*, Sheila. You're a dear."

Sheila flashed a smile. "It was nothing. My boss is out this week with the flu so I'm not that busy. But I do need to get going on that quarterly truancy report."

"Oh, and about that," Rita said. "Please don't mention I asked you for this? It's not a big deal, but I wouldn't want to get you in any trouble. You're doing a favor for someone who doesn't even work here anymore."

Sheila did a little "cross my heart" gesture and they hugged again. We didn't speak until we got to the car.

"I wanted to move on this fast because I heard Sheila's boss was out. The administrator who runs that department suffers from excessive bureaucratic zeal, so I was counting on him being gone."

We read over the list of three girls' names and ages. One was only five years old, too young to match Doug's description of the girl he saw in the window. The others were aged ten and twelve. Either of those could be the missing girl.

"Thanks again for getting me these names," I said. "I want to visit the addresses and see what I can find out about them, but I don't want to waste any more of your time."

"My dear Kat," she said. "Finding one of Maui's children is anything but a waste of my time. Let's see if either of these kids might be who you're searching for."

We drove out to a remote area north of Wailuku in a back-of-beyond area that rivaled Ohia for being "off-the-grid." As we made our way to the tiny settlement, I had a flashback to driving down the rutted road to the hermit's place. Every few hundred feet was a sign warning that this was "private property" and "no trespassing."

The road narrowed, and we came to a metal barrier which required Rita to stomp on the brake. On either side of the barrier were eight-foot flagpoles bearing flags I'd never seen before. The left-hand pole held a light blue flag with a red and gold emblem in the center. I couldn't make out the emblem in its entirety, but I could see on one side it was a Hawaiian warrior holding a tall stanchion. The other flagpole bore a red, green, and gold striped flag with a center section of green and gold. Again, the center was partially hidden in the folds, but it seemed to be a simple icon depicting a paddle and maybe a shield or feather.

"What do those flags mean?" I said.

Rita bit her lip. "This is a Hawaiian Sovereignty outpost. The people who live out here are advocating for the return of the Kingdom of Hawaii."

"How is that possible?"

"You know the history, right?" Rita said. "The sugar barons and missionary families plotted to overthrow the legitimate Kingdom of Hawaii. They pulled off a coup and got the islands annexed to the United States. These people want to reverse that and reinstate the kingdom. They're very passionate about it."

"Seems if we want to go any further down this road, we're going to have to walk."

Rita clenched her hands on the steering wheel but said nothing.

I went on. "Could our girl have been snatched from here and they didn't report it? Maybe these folks wouldn't want to deal with the local police."

"I agree. I'm afraid if we—" Rita was interrupted by a loud

knock on her driver's side window. We were both startled. I hadn't seen anyone coming, and apparently neither had Rita.

The large, dark-skinned guy standing at the window wore a swath of red and yellow cloth tied around his waist to make a long skirt. That was it. Nothing covering his chest. I couldn't see from where I was sitting, but I bet he was barefoot, as well.

"This is sovereign land," he said, after Rita rolled down her window. Geometric facial tattoos covered his face, making him appear menacing—though his eyes seemed sad rather than threatening. "You don't belong here. You gotta leave."

"I apologize for the intrusion," Rita said. "We're here to make sure one of your *keiki* is safe. I'm from the school district and we haven't seen . . ." She checked the printout and continued . . . "Eliana Ka'aohoe in school for the past few weeks."

"She's safer here than she'd ever be in your occupier school."

"Again, we're sorry to intrude, but do you know the girl I'm speaking of?"

"Yeah, she's *'ohana*. My brother's granddaughter."

"And do you know why she's not been in school?"

"She's being educated here, in our ways. She's not happy at that school of yours."

"You know you can file a form for her to be homeschooled? Then, you wouldn't have people like me bothering you."

He narrowed his eyes and leaned his arms on the roof of the car. "I don't need to apply for nuthin'. This is our home, our land. You have no right to tell us what we can and can't do."

"May I make one final request and then I'll leave?" The man was silent. He straightened up and folded his arms over his chest, inclining his head. "If you tell me that you know that Eliana is safe and being educated at home, I'll do the paperwork. I'll come back for a signature later. We're only out here to make sure she's safe and being educated."

His eyes flashed in anger and he roared, "You took everything from us, and now you dare to accuse us of harming our own *keiki*!

Go back and tell the people you work for that the night marchers are coming. And when they do, this land will be returned to the righteous *kanaka* it belongs to."

Once again, Rita apologized for the intrusion and thanked him for his time. She buzzed her window up and put her car into Reverse. She twisted in the seat, navigating the little yellow vehicle to a wide spot so she could turn around.

After we'd gotten back to the main road, I said, "I'd love to hear more about the Sovereignty Movement. And what does it have to do with the ghost story Night Marchers?"

"A story for another day," she said. "Let's put the next address into the GPS."

I was impressed with how cool she was through the entire encounter, and now we were on our way to the next one.

22

THE ADDRESS for the remaining girl on the truancy list was in the outskirts of Haiku, a town of about nine thousand residents *mauka*, or inland "toward the mountains" in Hawaiian, from the Hana Highway.

After getting lost and asking directions at the Hanzawa Store and gas station, which reminded me of Artie and Opal's store in Ohia, we navigated to a small plantation style home painted dark green with white trim.

The house wasn't derelict, but it couldn't be described as tidy, either: the lawn in front was pocked with weeds, and enormous hibiscus bushes surrounding the house obviously hadn't been trimmed in years. The place consisted of the small main house, a freestanding garage, and either a garden shed or a small storage building in back. All the structures could've used a new coat of paint and the windows a bottle of Windex and a squeegee.

We went up onto the porch. The front door was open, but a rusting screen door stood between us and the living room inside. A TV blared with the raucous laugh track and *whoop whoop* sounds I associate with a daytime game show.

I tapped on the doorframe, then peered through the screen into the gloom and spoke in my loud "official" voice. "Hello, is anyone home?"

A woman who appeared to be at least sixty got up from a recliner and slowly shuffled her bedroom slippers to the door. She squinted through the screen as if pondering whether to slam the door in our faces. Her skin was fair and wrinkled and she wore a faded dress that'd seen better days. Her most distinguishing feature was a long braid of salt-and-pepper hair. She flipped it over her shoulder, and even then it reached nearly to her waist. She'd twisted an elastic band with a yellow plastic plumeria onto the end of the braid. That one bit of effort to "dress up" her everyday attire made me hope she might be more approachable than she first appeared.

"What do you want?" she said. Her voice was muffled as if she was trying to hold a loose upper denture in place with her tongue while she talked.

"We're here about Maile Ortiz," I said. "The school district has reported her absent for more than ten days this quarter."

The woman wound the end of her braid around a finger. "So, they have, have they? What're you wanting from me?"

"Are you Mrs. Ortiz?"

"Not likely. Mrs. Ortiz, as you call her, is up there in the county jail. Drugs, prostitution, you name it."

Rita and I exchanged a glance. She took over. "We're here to make sure Maile is safe. May we come in?"

"I gotta say 'no' to that. I don't know you two from Adam."

Neither Rita nor I had any kind of ID giving us the authority to get past that screen door, so we hesitated. I had clipped the truancy report onto the clipboard I used to bluff my way out to the hermit's bombed-out home. I tapped the paper. "It says here that Maile goes to Haiku Elementary School. Is that correct?"

"You're the one with all the information. You tell me."

"She does. And she hasn't been in school for some weeks. We're here to check on her."

"Who are you? Show me some ID."

"We are concerned citizens," Rita said. "We're volunteers who help the school by doing home visits for students we're concerned about. My name is Rita, and this is Kat."

"I don't have to say diddly to a 'concerned citizen.'" The woman made air quotes with her gnarled fingers. "But since you came all the way out here, I'll tell you that she's gone on a trip to visit family in California."

I absorbed that. I was crushed. This was our last lead.

We apologized for the disturbance and walked back to Rita's car. The electric engine made no sound as Rita backed out of the driveway but a little beep-beep-beep of warning.

My window was down, and I heard a thumping noise, as if someone were pounding on the woman's back door.

"Do you hear that?" I asked.

"What?"

"I thought I heard something."

"It's probably that ridiculous TV," said Rita. "She's got the volume turned all the way up."

"Something's off with that woman," I said.

"*Everything's* off about her," Rita agreed. "The report lists her as Maile's temporary foster parent. Why wouldn't she have called the school to tell them that the girl was off-island?"

I shifted in my seat. My healing ribs itched under the tight bandage. "Do you have time to stop at Haiku School and see if they know anything more?"

"After meeting that woman," Rita said, "I have all the time in the world."

Haiku Elementary School was a low-slung gray building surrounded by green lawns and chain-link fence. It appeared to be like every small-town elementary school from Oʻahu to Omaha. A couple of "portables" were off to the side, likely there to serve as class-rooms when they had a temporary increase in student enrollment, but the main buildings looked like they'd been there for a decade or more.

We went into the front office and, once again, Rita asked me to let her take the lead.

"*Aloha*. I'm Dr. Rita Farnsworth, from the District Office," she said. The words "district office" seemed to instill urgency in the school secretary, who had been sitting at her desk watching something on her phone.

She popped up and ran around to the front counter. "Are you here to see Principal Tanaka? She's not here at the moment, but I can reach her on her cell phone."

It was close to lunchtime. Maybe the principal had stepped out to pick up a bite.

"This is merely an administrative request," said Rita. "We'd like to speak to the teacher who has Maile Ortiz in their class. Is he or she available?"

The secretary hesitated for only a moment, but it was enough to alert me that something was amiss.

"Um, Miss Lokemani is still with her class for another ten minutes. Would you mind waiting until the lunch bell rings? Then she'll be able to talk with you." She offered us a seat where a row of heavy blond wooden chairs lined the wall. I remembered those seats from when I was in elementary school. Did every school in America get issued a set of those intimidating straight-backed chairs?

We were about to sit when a woman of about fifty with short blonde hair came out of an adjoining office.

"Hey there," she said. "I'm Mrs. Miller, the school nurse. I over-heard you inquiring about Maile Ortiz. Dr. Farnsworth, can I speak to you in my office for a moment?"

Rita gave me a glance that said, "stay put" and went into the small room, closing the door behind her.

I found myself fighting to control my emotions as I settled on the hard chair. I heard the ordinary sounds of a school in session: the murmur of voices, the squeak of shoes on linoleum, the drone of an adult reading aloud.

My mind went back to the mental picture I had of the girl in the window of the shack that was now a hole in the ground.

I'd been that little girl. Alone in a demolished car on a snowy night, I'd waited for help to arrive as my parents died. Fortunately for me, paramedics showed up and freed me, then took me to Aunt Fae. But no one had showed up for this little girl. She was just gone . . .

I was deep in dark thoughts when the nurse's office door opened and I heard Mrs. Miller say ". . . no trouble at all. So, we're concerned."

Rita nodded and thanked her for the information. She returned to where I was sitting. I waited to ask until she'd settled back on her chair. "What was that about?"

Rita said in a soft voice, "I think we've found our girl. Maile was having emotional problems and often went to the nurse with tummy aches."

"But what about the California thing?" I hissed.

Rita shook her head and pinched her lips together.

The bell rang. The halls filled with young voices and rushing feet. Maile's teacher appeared a few minutes later. "I'm on cafeteria duty today, so I'm afraid I only have a minute," she said. "But if you're concerned about Maile, let me weigh in that I'm extremely worried about her. She's had a horrible year. First her mom gets arrested, and now there's an issue with the foster mom." Miss Loke-mani touched her fingertips to her lips and her eyes widened. "This *is* about the foster parent, correct? I hope I haven't said something I shouldn't have. Are you from Child Welfare Services?"

"No, we're not," said Rita. "We're from the school district following up on an attendance issue. You say Maile's in foster care?"

"Yes, since before winter break. She was struggling with being taken from her home. Really sad and upset—she wasn't making a good adjustment. Now the temporary foster parent appears to be completely negligent in getting her to school. We haven't seen her in almost two weeks."

"The foster parent—at least that's who we think we spoke to—told us Maile went to California to stay with family," Rita said.

The teacher shook her head. "No. There are no family members there, or she would have been sent to them. I was with the CWS people when they met with our team about her placement here at Haiku. We're not her home school. Even that was new for her this year. I'm sorry, I have to go." She hurried off.

Rita turned to the secretary, who was watching open-mouthed. "Please leave a message for the principal that a truant officer should be sent out to Maile's foster parent's address to find out why she isn't in school. CWS should also be notified."

"Of course," the woman stuttered, taking notes.

ON THE LONG drive from Haiku to Ohia, Rita and I said little. Each of us seemed lost in our personal struggle with the dilemma at hand. As Rita drove to my house to drop me off, she sighed. "I'm feeling guilty," she said.

"Why?"

"Working at the school district, you feel as if these little ones are your responsibility. Discovering something like this has gone unreported is a complete failure of the system."

I thanked her for her help and promised her, as I had Doug Beachum, that I'd let her know what I discovered about how Maile Ortiz might have ended up at the hermit's place.

I called Lei as soon as I got into the house. "Hey Kat," Lei said when she answered. "I heard you've been down for the count. How're you doing?"

"I'm much better, thanks. I'm calling with new information on that explosion we had out here."

"I thought I told you we're not working that anymore. It's gone to the feds."

"Right. But this isn't about the explosion, per se. It's about the little girl that may have been out there."

"Kat, I—"

I cut her off. "Please, just hear me out. I tracked down the name and address of a local girl who fits the description and who's gone suspiciously missing. I visited the address and it's a foster parent's house. The woman wouldn't let us in and lied about the girl's whereabouts. I went to her school, and they confirmed she's been absent for almost two weeks." I deliberately kept Rita Farnsworth's involvement out of it in case the whole thing blew up in my face.

"Do I want to ask how you obtained this girl's name and place of residence?"

"You don't, and it doesn't matter. The fact is, we now know there's a missing girl who matches the description offered by Beachum. Do you want me to send you what I have on the girl?"

"Yes, please do. I'll follow up within the hour. And Kat?"

"Yes?"

"Thanks. I'm still hoping you're wrong on this, but it's important we check it out."

I ended the call with a warm fuzzy feeling that counteracted the pain in my chest; though Maile was gone, at least we knew the girl in the window was real and had a name.

AN HOUR and a half later Lei called. "I found Maile Ortiz in the system. Do you want to go with me to Child Welfare Services tomorrow? You've been working this so if you'd like to join me, you're welcome."

"I definitely want to go. I have a doctor's appointment at two, so could we make it a morning meeting?"

"No problem. We'll get there early, before they've had a chance to get their CYA straight." CYA, or Cover Your A**, was a well-known acronym to anyone who'd worked in a government bureaucracy.

I gripped my hands into fists to keep them from shaking. As the little girl in the window became more of a real person and less of an imagined apparition, it was becoming harder to not want to fly into action, guns blazing, to avenge her death—but there was nowhere to go with that energy. The hermit was dead, too.

That night as I was donning my Jessica Rabbit sleep tee and getting into bed, Keone called from Honolulu. I had been so caught up in the missing girl situation I'd forgotten to worry about how his test and interview were going.

Keone sounded hopeful over his performance on the tests and getting the possible promotion. "But I'm still worried about the training time. It sounds like they'll want me here for at least a month."

"Do you want to fly those bigger planes?"

"Of course. Who wouldn't? The pay's better, and I'd have a better schedule—a few days on, several off. It's all good except for having to be away from you. How are you feeling?"

I told him I was doing better.

"You sure? You were pretty upset last time we talked."

"I meant my ribs." I crossed my fingers so the lie wouldn't count as I went on, "I'm accepting the bomb situation. It wasn't my fault, after all."

"There's nothing you could've done."

I still didn't really believe that. "Part of what's making me feel better is that, with Rita's help, I found out who the girl in the window was." I brought him up to speed on recent events. "So even though she's still gone, at least there's a name to go with the face Doug Beachum saw."

Keone was silent a moment, absorbing this. "You didn't let it go, did you?"

"I couldn't. Not until I knew who she was."

"I love that about you, even when it gets you into . . . pardon the use of your nickname—*Trouble*."

"Good one. I love you, too." I said goodbye, then leaned back into my pillow and patted the bed. Tiki jumped up and came alongside me, purring like a chainsaw in need of an oiling, and that was all I needed to send me right to sleep.

23

I DROVE out to Kahului to meet Lei first thing in the morning, grateful my ribs were steadily improving and no longer bothering me every time Sharkey hit a bump. Lei joined me in the parking lot of the big central police station and led me over to her silver Tacoma.

"Is it me or does it seem like at least half the people on this island drive a Toyota truck?" I said.

She laughed. "Seems like it. How're you doing?"

"I'm better physically, but this thing with the girl in the window hits pretty close to home."

"Goes with the job," Lei said as we got into the truck.

I lobbed a fuzzy stuffed toy into the back seat of the extended cab, where it landed in a child seat that had to be her daughter's. "I have to constantly remind myself that I'm in the 'justice' business and not the 'saving' business. I guess that's why I'm pretty fired up about what we're about to check out."

"Do you think Child Welfare Services dropped the ball?"

"I think I appreciate you letting me come along to find out," I said.

We soon arrived at the CWS headquarters, which, along with

the Maui School District office, was located in an office building in Wailuku.

"They work out of a number of places here in town," Lei said. "But I checked, and this is where they keep the files on the temporary foster kids."

At the front desk, Lei flashed her gold MPD badge.

"What can I help you with?" said the blue-haired coordinator. "Do you have an appointment with anyone in particular?"

"I'm investigating a possible child endangerment situation," Lei said. "May I see the social worker assigned to Maile Ortiz?" She spelled the name.

The manager typed it into her computer.

"It's Candace's case. She's out on a home visit. I can call her for you."

The social worker answered the call, and the receptionist told her that two police officers were there to see her. I glanced at Lei to see if she was going to correct the woman that I wasn't actually an officer with the department, but she just lifted a brow to indicate she was going to let it slide.

The coordinator listened to the other side of the call and then hung up. "She's on her way back now. Do you want to wait or leave your card for her to call you?"

"It's urgent that we speak. We'll wait."

We sat on metal tubing chairs in the waiting area and worked our phones to pass the time; I sent Keone a text message with some 'kiss' emojis on it, asking to get together. I was missing him and ready to prove it.

Ten minutes later, a trim young woman with dark-blonde hair wearing an aloha shirt in a muted taupe and black print and khakis came in through the door. She lugged an eight-inch stack of manila files in one arm, and a tote bag bursting with additional files in the other. Her sunglasses were perched on her head and she had a sheen of perspiration on her nose.

"I hope you haven't been waiting long," she said. She set the heavy tote on the floor and shifted the bundle of files from her right side over to her left. She then stuck out her hand, and Lei shook it. "I'm Candace Casey, and these are this week's case files."

Lei introduced herself and introduced me as simply, "Kat Smith from Ohia."

We followed Candace back to her tiny cubicle. Her desk seemed like a city with stacks of files standing in for skyscrapers.

"I knew when I took this job that we'd be understaffed," she said. "But ever since the pandemic it's been like being caught in a riptide."

"You surf?" said Lei.

"Not anymore." She grimaced. "No time."

My indignation over CWS being negligent was quickly being replaced with the realization that the demands of the job were impossible to keep up with.

Candace flopped into her office chair and gestured for us to squeeze in along the cubicle's wall. "I got a call from Haiku School yesterday about Maile's attendance but haven't had a chance to follow up. Barbara Long, Maile's temporary Family Resource Parent (FRP for short) isn't one of our gold star guardians, but she's never had a real complaint we could nail down. There have been rumors about her care, though. What's going on?"

I told Candace about my visit to Haiku Elementary to check on Maile's attendance, which had triggered the call to her office. I was relieved when she didn't press to see my credentials.

"Tell you what," Candace said. "I'm not scheduled to do another home check out there for a couple of weeks, but I have a bad feeling. What say we pay our FRP an unannounced visit right now?"

"We were hoping you'd say that," Lei said.

Candace rummaged through the piles on her desk and pulled out a slim manila folder.

"May I see Maile's file?" Lei asked.

Candace handed it over. Lei flipped it open. A three-inch school photo was stapled to the inside of the cover. I only got a quick peek at Maile's hopeful smile, but it made me gasp with recognition: I could tell that the girl's sweet face nearly matched the sketch I'd developed with Doug Beachum. Lei slanted me a glance, and I nodded. "That's the girl the UPS guy saw."

We hunched over the slim file and skimmed through information that matched what I'd gathered at Haiku School. Lei filled Candace in on how we'd reached this point in identifying Maile as a possible homicide victim.

"We'll need a copy of all of this," Lei told Candace. "Digital is fine. Send it to my email at MPD." The two put their heads together and got that going.

I stared at Maile's large brown eyes in the file's headshot. I sneaked my phone out and took a picture of it to keep for myself. I wanted her image close to me.

"Ready to find this girl?" said Candace, standing up. She crackled with energy in that moment, and I revised my opinion further: this social worker DID care—the system had just buried her under too many manila folders to keep up with.

We nodded and followed the blonde woman out to head for Haiku.

FORTY-FIVE MINUTES LATER, we pulled up outside the plantation cottage that Rita and I had visited yesterday. We went up the cement walkway to the front door in single file: first Lei, then Candace, and finally me, bringing up the rear. The two women who had the authority to get through that screen door were poised to do so.

Up on the porch, Lei rapped briskly on the doorframe. When Barbara Long appeared, a silhouette behind the screen, she flashed her detective ID and Candace followed with her CWS ID.

"I know who you are," Ms. Long said. "What can I do for you

today?" My, how the foster mom's attitude had changed as soon as she glimpsed the gleam of the ornate badge on Lei's belt.

"We're here to do a check on one of your temporary foster kids," Candace said. "May we come in?"

"Of course," she said, stepping back and holding the door open. "Don't mind the mess. With these darn kids coming and going, it's hard for me to keep up."

The inside of the house was shabby and cluttered, but not especially dirty. Once again, the TV was blaring in a corner of the room.

"Please turn off the television," said Candace. "We need to talk."

The woman hesitated, then went over and flipped off the TV.

"I'll get right to the point," said Lei. "Is Maile Ortiz currently at this residence?"

The woman's eyes darted to the door. I half expected her to make a dash for it, her long braid flying out behind her, so I stepped in front of the screen to block it.

"Yes or no, ma'am, it's a simple question," Lei rapped out.

I'd never heard Lei call an older woman "ma'am;" she usually used "auntie." She clearly wasn't in the mood to be messed with.

"Maile's not here right now. Why should she be? It's a school day." Barbara Long fiddled with her long braid.

"But she's not at school, either," Candace said. "We're here about her lack of attendance. We are here to physically see her. *NOW*."

The foster mom gripped her hands into clawlike fists. She stared down at the threadbare rug on the floor.

"I'm going to check the house for her," Lei said. No one spoke as Lei moved out of the room. We heard her in the hall opening and closing doors.

Lei returned. "No one else is on the premises. Where is Maile Ortiz?"

We waited for Ms. Long's response, but she stayed silent. My chest squeezed; it must've been so frightening for Maile to have been left here with someone so unfriendly.

Candace broke the silence. "Was Maile still in your custody when I came out here almost two weeks ago? At that time, you told me she wasn't on the premises because she was attending an after-school activity."

"No. She ran away." Ms. Long said in a low voice.

"What do you mean, 'ran away'?" said Candace. "She's ten years old. Where would she go? And—why didn't you report that to me? CWS is responsible for her."

"Well, I thought she'd come back. I mean, she's a feisty one, that girl. She was mad about her mom being busted and she tried to take it out on me. One day, I took her and some of the other kids to the Goodwill Store down in Kahului to do a little shopping. The next thing I knew, she'd up and taken off."

"When was this?" Candace continued.

Lei took out a little notebook and began taking notes.

"Weeks ago. I can't recall the exact date."

"And you never once considered calling and letting us know?" Candace's voice had risen. "There will be consequences for this. Severe consequences!"

Lei stepped in. "When you noticed Maile had gone missing in Kahului, how did you imagine she'd make her way back here to Haiku?"

"Well, that girl's tough. I figured once she'd had enough of living on the street, she'd hitchhike or take the bus or something back to my place. She'd want to return to where she got three meals a day and her own bed. Frankly, I'd had enough of her lip. She wasn't much for following rules, let me tell you."

The room went quiet. I picked up a faint thumping noise, much like what I'd heard when Rita and I had been out there the day before.

"Do you hear that?" I said, frowning. The sound seemed to be coming from behind the house, as if something padded was hitting the back door.

"I don't hear nothin'," said Barbara Long.

"I do," said Lei. "It sounds like someone thumping or knocking. Is there anyone else on the premises?"

Long shook her head. "I still don't hear nothin'."

Candace seemed spooked; her cheeks had gone pale. "You have two other children to care for besides Maile. Where are they?"

"The other children are at school," Long said.

Lei headed for the door. "The noise is coming from outside, behind the house."

The three of us hurried out the front door. We went around the building in single file, until Lei drew her weapon and gestured. "You two stay back. The sound is coming from that shed."

We plastered ourselves against the wall as Lei approached a stout wooden shed in the backyard, her gun held in the ready position. Now that we were closer, we could hear that the thumping was punctuated by a keening sound.

"Come out with your hands up," Lei ordered.

The banging stopped. Then, a small voice said, "I can't. I'm in time-out."

Lei holstered her weapon and grabbed the padlock on the door's hasp. "Candace, get the key."

Candace spun on her heel and marched back into the house through the back door. A few moments later, Barbara Long exited with Candace shoving her to keep her moving forward.

"Unlock this shed," Candace said. "Right now."

Long took a handful of keys out of her pocket and unlocked the shed's padlock. She stood blocking the door as she undid the hasp and slowly opened it. From the darkness inside, a child's high-pitched voice said, "I'll be good. I won't do it again. Please let me out."

Lei shoved Long out of the way and entered the pitch-black shed. Candace followed her. I stood beside Long to prevent her escape.

Candace found an overhead light and pulled a short chain. A bulb turned on, illuminating a little boy wearing dirty shorts and a well-worn T-shirt. He was huddled in a corner, barefoot. The shed held no light, furniture, blankets or any evidence of food or water, though a camp bucket emitted toilet smells. The wood floor was completely bare.

"What in the name of heaven is going on here?" said Candace.

"He's in time-out," said Barbara. She fiddled with her braid nervously.

"This isn't 'time-out,'" said Lei. "This is imprisonment, and it qualifies as child abuse."

Candace took a deep breath. "I'm going to need to write this up and you will be permanently removed from our rolls as a Family Resource Parent."

"I was told I could use appropriate discipline when necessary. Nothing physical, and I haven't laid a hand on him. Check that boy. There's not a mark on him," blustered Long.

Candace squatted down. "What did you do to get 'time-out'?" she asked the child.

He hung his head. "Nothin'." Then he seemed to think it might be better to come clean rather than risk being locked up again and added, "I took some bread and ate it in the bathroom. I was hungry after dinner. I'm sorry."

"See?" said Barbara Long. "He admitted to stealing. I think I have a right to put a stop to that kind of behavior."

Candace stood up to her full height, all but vibrating with rage. "And I have a right to make sure your version of discipline never happens again. Like I said, you're no longer employed by Child Welfare Services. And I can't speak for the Maui Police Department, but this detective will no doubt be checking into charging you with child neglect and abuse." Candace took the little boy by the hand. "How about we go get something to eat?"

"Yes please," he said meekly. She led the child out into the sunlight and toward her car. As they were getting in I heard him say, "Am I in trouble?"

"You are definitely not in trouble. You and I are going to go get some lunch. What would you like to eat?" I couldn't hear his response, but the gratitude on his face made me want to break down and cry.

As they pulled away, Barbara Long squinted at me. "And just who are you, missy? You haven't said much."

I locked eyes with her. "I'm the one who just got you fired. And you know what? I wish I could've done it years ago."

24

LATER THAT AFTERNOON, Aunt Fae drove me to the Hana Clinic for my follow-up exam. I was too exhausted from the morning's activities to argue with her insistence that she not only come with me, but drive.

After an examination, the doctor cleared me to return to work, but for clerical work only. "No heavy lifting for another two weeks or so," she said, providing a note to back that up.

I grimaced; Pua was NOT going to like helping Chad with all the packages. Maybe Mr. Hanoi, my boss, would leave the clerk he'd sent to help out until I was able to move stuff again.

Afterward, Aunt Fae reluctantly dropped me at the K & K office on the way home; Keone had called and told me he was back from Honolulu, and he'd be hanging out at the office hoping to see me.

"I'd rather you came home and rested," said Aunt Fae. "But I know you're raring to get back in the saddle and for life to return to normal."

I wasn't "raring" for anything, but I *was* eager to see Keone and try to get our relationship back on track. I waved goodbye to Auntie and went up onto the tiny porch.

I winced as I took a deep breath, and then opened the door.

"Kat!" Keone got up from the table and came to me, looking delicious as hot chocolate in a snug brown tee and jeans. "Hug?"

"How about a *honi*, instead? I'm feeling a bit banged up after all the prodding and poking at the clinic."

We leaned in and touched foreheads. I wanted more, and I could tell he did too, but I pulled back after only a few seconds. We sat down in our usual chairs. "Can I get you anything?" Keone asked. "Some water? A pain pill?"

"No, thanks." Even while the doctor had been checking my ribs, I'd been seriously close to hyperventilating over the physical contact. She'd asked if I'd had any issues with the pain meds and I assured her I hadn't used them all. "Keep the rest of the prescription just in case," she'd said. "But make sure they're locked up. We see too many cases of kids getting into their parents' medicine cabinets."

Thinking about kids brought to mind the picture of Maile Ortiz now on my phone. She'd gone from a 'maybe' to a 'for sure' as the girl in the window, and I could easily imagine what she'd looked like with her hands pressed against the glass.

Rita Farnsworth had said she felt "guilty." For me, it was "regret." I'd probably been within fifty feet of Maile when I'd gone out to the hermit's place. Why had I allowed him to intimidate me with that machete? Would he have used it on me? Or was it just an act? Didn't matter. I could have tried to disarm him, and now I'd never know.

Maile paid the ultimate price because I'd lacked the courage to call Dragoon's bluff.

Keone gazed at me, worried, as I shook my head and came back to the here and now. "I'm sorry. It's been an intense day."

"Tell me about it?"

"We know who Maile is, and where she came from. We don't know how she ended up with the hermit." I told him about the home visit. "We might not have helped Maile, but two kids are going to be better off because we shut down that foster home." I rallied with an effort. "Do you think you'll be offered the new job?"

"I don't know. They said they have their eyes on three people." He smiled. "You'll be glad to hear that one of them is a woman."

"Hey, I'm all for affirmative action, but in this case, I hope the best *man* wins." I forced a smile.

"Do you mean that? I mean, I'd be away for at least a month during training. I could probably come back for weekends, but that's not for sure. If I got the job, I'd likely be stationed in Honolulu."

I considered what I was about to say, and decided to focus on my personal process. "I need to let you in on something, Keone. While you were on O'ahu, I didn't want to bother you—but the truth is, I'm not doing that great. Now that we know who the girl is, I'm having a tough time with it."

"But you said you were okay." He cocked his head. He wasn't annoyed, exactly—more like sad and frustrated.

I blew out a breath and winced as it twinged my ribs. "That's the problem. I wasn't being completely honest with you. I can't stop feeling that it was my fault. I set that whole tragedy in motion."

Keone shook his head. "I don't know how to help."

"You can't."

Mr. K swaggered over to the Murphy bed, currently strapped to the wall, and patted it suggestively. "Let me distract you."

"Oh, you know how to play dirty."

"As a mud wrestler. Let me show you exactly how far I'll go to make you feel better."

"Gah. I'm sorry, I can't!" I threw my hands up. "I'm the worst girlfriend ever. You might as well dump me and get it over with!"

Keone left the bed and came over to me. He set his hands slowly and deliberately on my shoulders, then squeezed gently. He leaned in and kissed me on the lips; I let him, and gradually the gentle contact melted my resistance—but he didn't push it further and try to grab for more. The man was a saint. "I'm here when you need me," he said. "And for all our sakes, please consider getting some professional help."

Okay, nope. Not a saint.

Mr. K kissed me lightly on the cheek, grabbed his backpack, and left without another word.

I turned and addressed the geckos, ever-present on the wall over the stove. Miss Prissy was off hunting somewhere else, thankfully. "I deserved that, didn't I?"

The two bobbed and chirped in the affirmative.

"Sophie said she'd set up a referral for this Dr. Kinoshita, but I haven't heard anything. I guess I can follow up on that," I said.

Tweedledum got distracted and ran after a moth. Tweedledee chirped loudly that I should make the call.

But I didn't. Instead, I turned off the lights, locked up, and walked slowly back to our house in New Ohia. Maybe Aunt Fae would have dinner ready and I could get to bed early; after all, tomorrow was another day and things just had to get better.

Aunt Fae glanced at my pale face as I limped in and commanded me into one of the recliners in front of the living room TV. "I'll nuke us some frozen dinners," she said, turning on the news. "You just rest here."

As Auntie busied herself in the kitchen, I watched the screen with glazed eyes—but turned up the volume when the top story came on: *the report from the investigation at the Halepua'a Road explosion site had been completed!*

Neighbor island news is rarely featured on the Honolulu television news stations due to a lack of time after they reported all the murders, burglaries and general mayhem that takes place on O'ahu, but tonight, East Maui was front and center.

"Federal and local agencies have concluded the explosion that obliterated a house on Maui was arson. They agree that the perpetrator used high-grade explosives and accelerants, resulting in total destruction of the dwelling and the surrounding area to the point that human remains in the ashes would be undetectable," said the coiffed anchorman, his tanned face suitably grave.

The scene switched to a traditional briefing, this one on the steps of the Honolulu courthouse. "The occupant of the house on Halepua'a Road on Maui hasn't been seen since the explosion, but unlike most arson scenes, this one left nothing behind," said an agent standing at the podium wearing the customary navy-blue FBI windbreaker. "We can't confirm or deny loss of life, as we found no physical evidence on site, nor would any have remained after a fire that hot."

The agent concluded by expressing condolences for anyone who might have perished in the blast but concluded that the FBI and the other agencies working the case agreed they'd examined all the available evidence and were suspending the investigation as "inconclusive" for now.

He then opened up the press conference for questions.

I sat frozen. There was much more to know about what happened out on Halepua'a Road than the authorities were going to uncover now.

Aunt Fae set my TV dinner in front of me on a folding tray. "You have to eat," she said.

"Thanks." I finished the food quickly, without tasting it, so she wouldn't worry further. "I've got work tomorrow, Auntie. I need to get to bed."

I used the banister to pull myself upstairs. I needed a shower, and the doctor had replaced the uncomfortable elastic bandages with a lightweight Velcro brace. She'd apologized that the only color they had available at the clinic was black.

"Women usually prefer the white or beige, because they don't show as much under clothing," she'd said. "But the black brace is better than the wrapping was, right?"

I agreed it was. The eight-inch Velcro strip made a loud noise when I peeled it open. *Skrittttch.*

Tiki, who'd come to the bathroom door to greet me, hissed at the sound and ran to nestle into her kitty bed with her baby. Misty mewed a "Welcome back, Mommy."

The hot water relaxed me, and we were all tucked away for what I hoped would be a much-needed eight hours of blissful slumber, when my phone rang.

I checked the caller ID before answering. The screen showed *Edith Pepperwhite.* "Kat, I'm sorry to call so late," said Edith. "But it's Lola."

I straightened up. "Is there a problem?"

"She's here. At my house. And I'm pretty sure she's been drinking."

25

LOLA REEVES, the fifty-something daughter Edith had given up at birth due to being single and in college, had been in recovery for months. Lola and I had had our differences when we met, culminating in her shooting at me not once but twice. Her lawyer had gotten the charges reduced to illegal discharge of a firearm, a misdemeanor, and she'd been released with time served and was now on probation. She and Edith had been mending fences, and since she'd joined a recovery meeting program, Lola had been a model citizen—until now.

"What can I do to help?" I asked Edith. I was exhausted and hoped she'd say she simply wanted to alert someone to the situation but was convincing Lola to go home and sober up.

"I know it's a lot to ask, but I was hoping you could come over. Josie's had some problems with her CPAP machine, so I don't want to wake her. Would you mind?"

I heard a loud *boom* from Edith's side of the connection.

"What's going on?"

"I think she's trying to break down the door. Help me, please!"

"I'll be there as soon as I can." I pulled my weapon from my nightstand and grabbed a full magazine from the storage box and snapped it in place. I hoped I wouldn't have to use it, but I did the math: with Lola, I had two shots in my favor to make things even between us. They'd have to be inaccurate, because hers had been— but "forewarned is forearmed," I said aloud.

Rain pattered on Sharkey's windshield as I drove to Edith's tidy cottage in Hana. Driving the highway at night felt like spelunking an unexplored cave; the darkness was as thick as gravy.

I pulled into Edith's hibiscus lined driveway and slowly advanced with my lights on high beams, hoping the blast of brightness would cool Lola's aggression. Once at the house, I got out of the SUV and tucked my gun into the waistband of my jeans.

Lola stood on the front porch rhythmically pounding the door with something. As I got closer, I recognized it was a small cement-colored tiki, one of many from Edith's collection of yard art.

Bam, bam.

"Lola," I shouted over the commotion. "What's this all about?"

She turned and, with a move I didn't see coming, pitched the tiki in my direction. I dodged the heavy concrete missile and it sailed past me into the yard.

"Get out of here," Lola hollered. "This is between my mom and me." Her speech was slurred, and came out more like, *"Gee owd o here. 'Tween mum an me."*

"Lola, have you've been drinking?" That was one of those "duh" questions I'd been trained to avoid in hostage negotiations, but I wanted to establish a baseline. If Lola admitted she'd fallen off the wagon and seemed remorseful, I'd move forward with suggesting we call her sponsor.

"My mom's gotta listen to me. She's making a huge mistake."

No, not remorseful.

Edith peeked through a crack in the curtains. Illuminated in the harsh headlights, her eyes resembled one of those Felix the Cat clocks with the eyeballs that click back and forth marking off the seconds.

"You're scaring your mom," I said. "Can we go inside and talk things over?"

Edith shook her head in a forceful "no" from her side of the window, but that was too bad. She'd got me out of bed and over here to deal with her loose cannon of a daughter. It was going to take a pot of strong coffee and an hour of artful negotiation to get Lola sober enough to communicate enough for conflict resolution.

I advanced toward the porch, keeping my hand down by my side in case I needed to quickly pull the Glock. Since Lola had been using both hands to ram the door, I doubted she had a weapon at the ready.

Smash! The sound of a broken front window reverberated through the night air like a thunderclap. Edith squealed from inside the cottage.

I pulled my pistol. "Lola, I'm armed. I'm ordering you off the porch. Come down the steps, slowly."

"You're not the boss of me." Lola giggled drunkenly. "Make me."

Clearly Lola wasn't intimidated by my gun; she hadn't been the other times, either. Edith must've retreated to a back area of the house because I heard nothing from her after the initial crash.

"Lola, I will use force if I have to," I said. "In Hawaii we have what they call 'castle laws' which means people are allowed to defend their homes. You need to back off, now!"

"This isn't your castle," Lola said. "It's my mom's. And when she marries that woman, it will be Josie's. What about me? What do I get? Nothing, that's what!"

"Showing up drunk and belligerent isn't going to help your cause," I said.

"S'not right," Lola mumbled. "It's jus' not right." She stumbled off the porch, coming down the steps toward me. I kept my gun on her in case whatever she'd been using to break the window should come flying toward me, but she weaved past me without incident. I watched intently as she staggered down the driveway and out onto the road.

And then the heavens opened. Rain came pelting down in one of the sudden, heavy showers this side of the island was known for.

I hadn't seen a car parked anywhere nearby when I navigated the driveway, but at no time did I get a prick of conscience to offer Lola a ride to wherever she was staying.

Instead, I went up on the porch and, through the hole in the window, called out. "Edith! Lola walked off. She's gone."

My friend, wrapped in a leopard print plush bathrobe that made her look like a designer fire hydrant, came out from where she'd been hiding. She flicked on the porch light.

I picked up the metal orchid planter Lola had used to break the window glass and set it upright. The area beneath the shattered window was strewn with potting soil, glittering glass shards, and the smashed flower. Fortunately the deep roof overhang sheltered the area from the heavy rain that roared on the corrugated tin over the porch.

Edith unlocked and opened the door. With the inside lights shining on the door, I could see the damage the cement tiki figure had wrought. A couple more blows and the wooden door would've caved in, for sure. Glass littered the living room.

Edith's cat, Butter, peered from behind the rattan sofa, her eyes wide with fear. Edith didn't appear to be much better; her skin was pale and her blue eyes round. Her white hair stood up like a porcupine's quills as she tightened the robe reflexively. "Are you sure she's gone?"

"Yes. She's gone. The rain will sober her up fast."

"I'm so sorry to drag you into this," she said. "Again."

Edith and I had gone a few rounds with Lola and Lola's daughter, Ana, in skirmishes around the same topic: the two of them felt entitled to Edith's money. Things had been quiet since Ana had fled the country. Until now.

"Well, Lola fell off the wagon in a big way," I said. "And all bets are off when that happens with an alcoholic. Seems like Lola is angry about you marrying Josie?"

"Let me make us some tea," Edith said. "I'm too upset right now."

I considered leaving for home instead. My ribs were screaming for rest and the rain had really started to pound in earnest on the roof of the cottage. But one glance at Edith's trembling hands told me I wouldn't be able to sleep unless I stayed long enough to be certain Lola wouldn't change her mind and come back. "Where's an umbrella? I'll go turn Sharkey off and join you."

Edith pointed to a stand behind the door that held walking sticks and a couple of umbrellas. I grabbed one, dashed through the wet to the car, and shut the vehicle off.

Back inside the house while Edith rattled about in the kitchen, I scanned for something to use to block the wind coming in through the broken window. I spied a large metal tray on the coffee table. I picked it up and brought it to the doorway of the kitchen.

"Do you mind if I put this tray over the hole in the window? It's better than having the weather come in."

"I never liked that tray," Edith said. "It was a gift from a friend, so I had to display it. But it's kind of ugly, don't you think?"

I gazed more closely at the tray. The dark green metal featured a red and gold center design depicting a chicken surrounded by various other animals in a wheel resembling a clock.

"I don't get it," I said.

"It's from a friend. That's my Chinese New Year animal. I was born in the Year of the Rooster. She said rooster year people are witty and tidy."

I glanced around Edith's fastidious kitchen. "Well, it may be an ugly tray, but the sentiment is right on. Find me some duct tape, and I'll get this in place."

After I taped the tray into the window, Edith closed the curtains while I swept up the glass. We went back to the kitchen to wait while the tea brewed. The chamomile smelled comforting in the cozy confines of the bungalow. Edith rustled through the cupboard and set out a plate of macadamia nut cookies.

"These are store-bought," Edith said. "But they're not bad. Try one."

I'm not usually a middle-of-the-night snacker, but the sugar went down well after the burst of adrenaline that'd shot through me when Lola lobbed the tiki in my direction.

"Do you always carry that gun around?" Edith's frown signaled she wasn't a big fan of unfettered Second Amendment rights.

"I do when a friend is in danger," I said. "I have a permit. And I regularly recertify to keep my skills up."

"Would you have shot my daughter?" she asked.

I let Edith's question hang in the air, so she repeated it. "Would you have shot my daughter?"

She continued to stare at me until I squirmed.

"I wouldn't have shot Lola unless she was armed too," I eventually said. "Please remember. Your daughter has fired a gun at me twice already. Third time might be the charm."

"I guess that's fair." Edith picked up her mug and took a sip of the tea. The china rattled against her teeth.

Would I have shot Lola if she'd broken down the door?

No.

But I'd been fretting over my lack of action with the girl in the window. I had to keep in mind that taking action could wreak just as much havoc as doing nothing. Sometimes more.

"Do you want to call the police? File a report?"

"No. That's why I called you. Lola's on probation. A police call will send her back to jail."

I was not opposed to that idea. "I'm sorry, but I won't cover for Lola again. If she comes back, you can reach out to me, but know that I'll be calling the police. It's 'enabling' when an alcoholic is shielded from the consequences of their actions."

Edith covered her face with her hands; I heard crying behind them. She was so small and fragile that I pushed past touch aversion to wrap an arm over her. "I understand how hard this is. You're her mother, and she plays on your guilt."

Edith lowered her hands, grabbed a dishtowel, and mopped her face with it. "I have to disinherit her now," Edith said. "She has to know it's got nothing to do with Josie but is a result of her own behavior. Can you imagine what she might do to Josie if I died first?"

"I can, and I'm sorry," I said. "And I hate to bring this up, but what if Ana comes back? Those two haven't changed. You're not safe until you change your will."

"Ana's out regardless, but I reinstated Lola as part of our reconciliation," Edith said sadly. "I'm going to leave income for life to Josie, but now the bulk of my estate will be left to an alcoholism recovery charity with just a little something for Lola. I'll have her served with a copy of my will as soon as I can get it redone."

"And you better be somewhere safe and far away when she gets that notice," I said. "In fact, it's time you put a fence and a gate around this place."

"Ugh," Edith said. "You're right. I don't think I'll sleep well here again until I do."

"May be a good time to go stay with Josie," I suggested.

We finished our tea and cookies. I walked my friend back to her bedroom and tucked her in.

After making sure Edith's place was as secure as it could be with a badly damaged door and broken front window, I dragged myself home.

Aunt Fae met me as I came inside.

"It's nearly two o'clock in the morning," I said to her. "What are you doing up?"

"I couldn't sleep when you were out late when you were young, and tonight I heard you leave. I was worried. What's going on?"

I briefed Aunt Fae on Lola's attack on Edith's cottage.

"What's wrong with that girl?" she said.

"Girl" was charitable considering Lola was a middle-aged woman, but I understood the underlying message: parent-child relations could be fraught under the best of circumstances.

Lola had been raised by adoptive parents who abandoned her to the system. It was impossible to know whether she thought of her biological mother as family or simply as someone who owed her recompense for her troubles.

Either way, Edith and Josie needed to protect themselves.

"I'm going to call Lola's probation officer and let her know Lola's had a slip in her recovery." I had to use the banister to drag myself upstairs to bed as Aunt Fae trailed worriedly behind. I was not looking forward to work tomorrow.

26

THE NEXT MORNING, the doorbell rang as I was finishing my first cup of coffee. Good thing it wasn't a half-minute earlier, as I concur with the message on my favorite coffee cup: *"DON'T TALK TO ME UNTIL THIS MUG IS EMPTY."* I set the mug in the sink and headed to the front door.

Elle stood on the porch, jogging in place. Her constant motion reminded me of a little girl who had to use the bathroom.

"How goes the running?" I said.

"You up for a lap or two this morning? Get the blood pumping?"

"I've got to be at work by nine and I was out past two last night." I yawned so widely my jaw creaked.

"A short jog might be good for you. I've got to be at the hotel by eight thirty, but that doesn't mean we can't put in a mile or so."

I considered my options. With my healing ribs I'd neglected even the most rudimentary exercise for the past week. "I'm still under doctor's orders to take it easy," I said. "So go easy on me."

"Fine. We'll take it slow. Any time you want to turn back, just let me know."

I had dressed to stretch in a jog bra and yoga pants, so I slipped on my white Nikes. They appeared sadly worn next to Elle's high-tech gold and black sneakers.

For the first ten minutes we said little as we trotted along the smooth curving asphalt streets of New Ohia. I focused on getting in rhythm with Elle's quicker pace, trying to keep my breathing shallow and even. If this is what she considered taking it easy, I was in for some pain.

Elle glanced back at me, and my expression must've given me away. "Tell you what," she said. "I'll bring it down a notch and provide some entertainment."

Unsure as to what that meant, I nodded. A few beats later, Elle spoke. "You want to hear how I really ended up out here in New Ohia? An eight-year Army medical professional now advising couples on flower arrangements and cake options?"

"Tell me." She'd slowed down just a bit but the fog of weariness was ebbing away. My side was beginning to ache.

"I'd been at Schofield for nearly two years. We were doing some cool research on blood replacements: you know—artificial blood to keep soldiers alive while they're being transported. I worked on a dengue fever project out here in Hana during my first year there, but the artificial replacement stuff was more of a priority. Dengue is pretty much limited to tropical environments, and right now the Army doesn't have much going on in those parts of the world.

"Anyway, my team was cleared to publish a breakthrough paper in a prestigious hematology journal when it all came to a halt. And nobody knows the word *halt* better than a smarmy lieutenant colonel with an agenda."

The stitch in my side now screamed for mercy. "Speaking of halt," I said. "I've got to take a breather."

"Of course." Elle slowed and we stopped.

I bent over and rested my hands on my knees. Elle wasn't even winded though my breathing was ragged. "Sorry, but according to the doctor, my rib cage is still pretty messed up."

"Got it. You want me to go on?" she said.

"With your story, yes. With the running, no. Give me a minute more."

"Well, my immediate superior at Schofield got transferred and in comes this colonel who should never have been there in the first place. I was a good soldier. I'd been all 'yes, sir,' and 'no, sir,'—whatever it took to get the job done, for my entire career."

I motioned that we could start moving again.

Elle pointed back to the way we'd come, and I nodded in gratitude. We moved out at a brisk walk.

"We both need to get to work, and this story is too long," she said. "What do you say we put it on pause until another time?"

"Sure. Your tale might have something in common with mine. There's a reason I ended up as postmaster of Ohia from the Secret Service." I prayed I had enough gas left in my tank to make it through the day at work.

"You did great," Elle said as we approached the turnoff to my cul-de-sac.

I snorted. "No I didn't. Swimming might be better for me until I recover more. Do you surf?"

"Nope."

"Want to learn?"

"I'm afraid that's another 'no.' I appreciate the offer, but I'm strictly an earthbound organism. No water sports for me." She waved as she picked up speed past our turnoff.

Under a cold shower designed to wake me up further, I replayed our conversation.

Earthbound organism? What was that about?

LATER, I unlocked the front door of the post office just as a red Ford Mustang tore into the parking lot, flinging gravel around like party confetti. It screeched to a stop four feet from the front door.

I stood back as Lola charged up the steps. Lola was a short

woman, about five feet if she stood on tippy toes, but her blue eyes blazed with the ferocity of a warrior doing a *haka* war chant before going into battle. Her bleached blonde hair stuck out like a fright wig and her barrel-shaped body was packed into a lavender velour outfit with pants that puddled around her ankles.

"Good morning, Lola," I said keeping my voice level. "I see you've got your favorite rental car again. Are you here to pick up mail?"

"Don't 'good morning' me, you traitor. I thought you and me were good. And now, you're all cozied up with my mom and that, that . . ." She thrust a finger at me, ostensibly to intimidate. That wasn't frightening since it barely reached midriff level, but her glittery nails were long enough to make me step back. I could smell the remnants of her bender the night before wafting off of her, strong enough to make my eyes water.

A customer had followed Lola, and she stopped and stared. I didn't know the woman's name, but it didn't matter: the gossip mill would be firing up big-time after this.

"What's going on?" I said, keeping my voice low. "Are you still upset over your mother's wedding? Or is it something else?"

"Don't act like you don't know what's going on here, Kat," Lola bellowed in response. "My so-called mother and that crazy Hawaiian woman are doing this to mess with *me*. This isn't just a wedding, it's a slap in the face. First, Edith dumps me off as a baby. We go through years of estrangement and now, when all I want is for her to act like a mom and make things right, she's dumping me again. And you're egging her on. Last night she called you to run me off when all I wanted was to talk to her." Lola punctuated her speech with her pointy-nailed finger jabbing away at my middle like she was putting in a passcode at an ATM.

"Lola, you were drunk and you scared your mom. She called me because you were about to break down her door." I tried to defuse Lola by raising my hands in a surrender gesture. "Okay, tell me your side."

"I asked nicely for her to let me in. She wouldn't. So, I had to find a way to get her to listen to me."

"Lola, will you admit that you had been drinking?"

"I may have had a nip or three, but that doesn't give my own *mother* the right to lock me out and refuse to talk to me."

"It gives her every right." Two more customers had come through the door; they goggled at the confrontation going on.

"Edith owes me," Lola shrieked. "And I'm not losing out on anything more on account of her marriage."

"I think you're jumping to conclusions. You need to calm down." The customers were making faces as if they'd come upon a pile of dog poop that hadn't been scooped by the pet parent. After months on Maui I'd learned that "living aloha" doesn't condone airing your 'ohana private matters in public. "Lola, you're making a scene in a federal government facility. If you have no postal business to conduct, you need to leave."

"Oh, I've totally got 'postal business,' as you call it. Mark my word. Mom ran my sweet daughter into the arms of a narco criminal and now I may never see my darling Ana again. I don't care what happens to me—whatever it takes, Edith Pepperwhite will *not* be getting married next weekend."

She reached out and with one swipe sent everything on the counter flying. A pen holder with half a dozen pens, a stack of green change of address forms, a tent sign promoting the newest commemorative stamps, and a pile of flat rate cardboard envelopes all went flying to the floor.

"Back off or get caught in the crossfire," Lola threatened, with one last finger shake. And then she slammed out the door. A minute later the Mustang roared off—but not before I'd memorized the license plate.

I was definitely calling Lola's sponsor and her parole officer. She'd just made a serious threat as well as a scene in public.

The clock on the wall ticked off a few seconds as we all stood frozen. I turned to the customers with a forced smile. "Sorry we all had to start the day that way, folks. Anything I can get for you this morning? Stamps? A general delivery package? A new set of eardrums?"

Nervous smiles and a titter from one of the ladies got us all moving again. Pua, pristine in a cream-colored linen sheath, lifted the counter flap for me to step behind. One of the customers who'd come in, clearly trying to break the ice, spoke. "Wasn't that shower last night intense? The weather report says we're due to get more rain in the next day or two."

"I heard that too," Pua said, with a glance to me that said she would handle the front so I could go back to my office. "Sounds like we all need to batten down the hatches."

"In more ways than one," I muttered, as I unlocked my office door and headed for the phone.

I MADE MY CALLS, leaving messages for Lola's probation officer and her sponsor. I also called Edith and ended up waking her; I told her to order the fence and gate today, and then to go to Josie's, which already had one. Lola was on the warpath, and I wanted everyone safe and alert.

Edith regretfully agreed. She told me she had a lot to do today already, and that included prep for the upcoming wedding. "Thanks for keeping me informed."

"And so you know, I called Lola's parole officer and her sponsor," I told Edith. "Sorry, but after the way she acted in the post office this morning, I had to."

"I understand," Edith said, her voice heavy and sad. We ended the call.

After that, the rest of the day was uneventful, but by four o'clock I was ready to crash. After dealing with Lola trying to break down Edith's door the night before, the early morning run with

Elle, followed by the altercation in the lobby and a full day's work, I was drained.

I ate an early dinner with Aunt Fae. We cleaned up, she turned on her favorite TV program, and I headed toward bed with a romance novel that had arrived from the "Lust of the Month Book Club" subscription Auntie had given me for my birthday. I called Tiki out of the kitchen to keep me company. "Hey, sweet girl. Come snuggle with me."

Tiki seemed more than pleased to accompany me to my room. She and Misty scampered up the stairs and gazed back down as I took each step one at a time, leaning on the banister for support. Tiki's expression seemed almost empathetic, and she rubbed against my leg with a purr when I reached the top. "Thanks for the encouragement, Tiki. Only a catastrophe of epic proportions will get me out of bed for the next nine or ten hours."

I took a shower and climbed in bed. Tiki hopped up beside me, and this time Misty clawed her way up onto the bed, too. The two were a comforting presence beside me as I started Chapter 1 of *The Scotsman's Sexy Kilt*—and immediately dozed off.

Unfortunately, the next sound I heard was the phone ringing.

27

ALTHOUGH I'D PUT my cell phone on vibrate, the thing still woke me up when it started buzzing and inching its way across my night-stand like an angry rattlesnake.

The clock next to my bed said it was eleven thirty-eight, close to the middle of the night. I grabbed the phone, ready to tap "Decline" and let the call go to voicemail, when I saw who was calling: *Opal Pahinui.*

Opal wasn't usually awake at this time of night, let alone calling. Something must be wrong. "Hey, Opal. What's up?"

"I'm sorry to call so late, Kat. Were you sleeping?"

What is it about admitting you've been asleep that makes us uncomfortable? I don't know, but I said, "No, it's fine. I'm awake now."

"I hate to bother you, but I've got a problem and need your help. Artie's fallen. I can't seem to wake him."

Now I was wide awake. "Did you call nine-one-one?"

"I did, but the ambulance in Hana is already on a call so they said it might take a while."

"I'll be right there."

I threw on the same jeans and polo shirt I'd worn to work that day and made it to the general store in record time. Opal had left the door that led to their apartment open. I hurried inside without knocking; Opal met me, tying her robe on over an old-fashioned nightgown. The overhead lights cast deep shadows under her round, terrified eyes. "Artie got up to use the bathroom and fell just inside the doorway. Follow me."

She directed me to where he lay, and I had to hold back from crying out when I saw how he was splayed across the floor, his arms and legs at angles to his body. His slack face was the color of putty, and his eyes were partially open.

Opal's face was nearly as pale as Artie's. She sucked in her lips and gazed at me as if hoping I'd be able to perform a miracle.

I dropped to my knees beside Artie and felt for a pulse in his slack neck; it was there. His chest rose and fell. "I think it looks worse than it is," I said—like I had any clue; I only knew basic first aid and CPR.

I fumbled my phone out of my pocket and called Elle Beane; she was the closest thing to a nearby medical professional I could think of. I was relieved when she picked up, and I gave her the basic facts.

"Is he breathing?"

I checked again. "Yes. Slow, but it's there. He has a pulse too. Already checked that."

"Any bleeding?"

"Not that I can see. Do you want me to roll him over?"

"No. Don't move him. If there's no obvious blood loss, it's better to keep him still."

"Opal called for an ambulance, but who knows when they'll get here. The dispatch told her they were already out on a call."

"I'm on my way," Elle said. "Until then, cover him to keep him warm and check his pulse. Get a count for me."

Opal had sunk to the floor beside me; she took Artie's limp hand. "Come on, sweetheart. I bet your insulin is off," she murmured.

I thumbed my phone to the timer in the Clock app and picked up Artie's other hand to check his wrist pulse. "Opal, can you get something to cover him with to keep him warm?"

"Of course." She stood up with a creaking of knees and pulled a thin quilt off their bed. She draped it over him, tucking it under his chin.

The lights from Elle's car flashed through the bathroom window and then swung across the walls as she pulled in and parked. Opal hurried out to meet her. Elle would need assistance finding us.

Soon, Elle bustled over to where I was still holding Artie's wrist. "What's his pulse?"

"I'm getting 55 beats per minute."

"Okay. He's in mild bradycardia, but that's not unusual with someone who's unconscious."

Opal said to Elle, "I've seen you in the store these past few weeks, but I didn't realize you were a nurse."

"I'm not," said Elle. "I used to be a U.S. Army medical specialist."

"Maybe his insulin is off," Opal said. "I'll check his blood." She fetched a little lancet and pricked his finger.

The ambulance wailed into range suddenly. After they came in, we stayed back as the EMTs bustled around and questioned Opal and took Artie's vitals. They got him on a gurney and shuttled the couple out onto the Hana Highway for the long drive to Maui Medical Center. "Any idea what it was?" I asked Elle as they pulled away.

"No telling at this point. You say he's had diabetes for some time?"

"Yes. Opal didn't have time to tell us if it might have been a diabetic coma. As you probably realized when you've shopped here, the disease already blinded him. He's had trouble with his feet and who knows what else, too."

"He's a very talented musician though," she said. "He's always singing and playing an instrument when I come up this way. I hope he'll be okay."

"Well, thanks for coming down. I was glad not to be the only one with them."

"My pleasure. I like helping people."

"Me too. I know exactly what you mean."

"How's your ribcage doing?" she asked.

"Much better. I'm tender right now because I'm not wearing my sexy black Velcro 'corset,' but the bruising is down."

"Great. Let me know when you're ready to pound the pavement again. I've been running at dawn since we've been so busy at the hotel. Who would've thought so many people would be booking events out this way in February."

"Why do you say that?"

Elle smiled. "Everybody on the continent thinks Hawaii is this paradise with perfect weather, welcoming people, and nonstop fun and games, especially in the winter. And, for the most part, it is. But when things go bad out here, they really go bad. I hear there's a big storm on its way this weekend, and the locals tell me that if we stay here long enough, we'll have stories to tell about all kinds of things that don't jive with living in paradise."

Elle hadn't been brought up to speed on the many stories I could *already* tell about my non-paradise life in Ohia. "A storm might be the least of it," I said. "I have to get back to bed, but someday I'll tell you about how the state got New Ohia Park back from gangsters. Now that's a story."

"And in the meantime, fingers crossed your friend is okay."

28

WHILE I WAS GETTING ready for work in the morning, I got a call from Opal at the hospital. She'd stayed the night in Artie's room while they ran tests.

"His insulin was off. Part of why he passed out," she said. "But there's more going on with him, and we don't have answers yet." Her voice cracked. "Kat, I'm sorry to bother you once again, but is there any way you could come fetch me after work today? I love my husband with all my heart, but if I have to spend another night in that visitor's chair, I may need to be admitted right alongside him."

"Of course," I told her. "I'll head out as soon as the post office closes."

Aunt Fae had offered to mind the store for them for the day and was already down at their place getting coffee going and the doors open. I stopped in on my way to my postal duties to check on her progress. "How's it going?" I asked, walking through the dimly lit aisles to where my aunt kept watch over the tablet they used to tally up goods at the back counter.

"Good thing your co-worker Pua showed up early at Opal's request. I usually help out here in the afternoon, so I had no idea how to run the newfangled coffee machine Artie and Opal put in last week."

I glanced toward the postal building. Sure enough, Pua had already turned on the lights in the post office. Knowing her, though, she hadn't unlocked the doors to customers yet. She was prompt and tidy, but not a complete glutton for punishment. When she'd gotten her job back after a hiatus due to her crime family's activities, she'd encouraged me to keep to the scheduled hours even if we had to fall behind sometimes.

"We're running a post office, not a twenty-four-hour diner," she'd said. "People need to plan accordingly."

I chatted briefly with Aunt Fae and told her about my upcoming trip to Wailuku later that day.

"I can go get Opal this morning," she said. "I bet if I called in the Red Hat posse, they'd be more than willing to watch the store for a while."

"Thanks, but I have something I want to check into while I'm there. And I think although Opal is complaining about spending the night in a chair, she's not going to be ready to leave Artie until they've figured out what's going on with him."

The hours at the post office that day seemed to drag. I kept checking the clock, hoping maybe it would magically say four o'clock when I knew it was probably closer to noon.

"You're worried about Artie, aren't you?" Pua said.

I nodded. "And I also feel bad because, since I can't lift anything, I'm not much help to you with these heavy boxes and bags of mail."

"You saw Chad stay and help get the packages sorted and the bags dumped," she said. "No need to feel guilty." She flexed hands covered in purple gloves and patted the crisp white apron she wore over her stylish clothing. "I'm fine with this. But tell you what. Why don't you go ahead and head out for the hospital now? I can close up."

"You sure?"

"I like closing up," she said. "It's my one chance to throw my weight around."

That was a joke; Pua's "weight" was all in her attitude. Her petite frame was half the size of mine.

I fired up Sharkey, and drove the infamous "backside" from Hana toward the central part of the island. Traffic was light with the incoming rainy weather, so I made good time.

I was antsy to get to town because I wanted to drop by a government agency that, by sheer luck, was only a block away from the hospital. I had to get there before they closed.

I needed to find out more about the property where Maile had vanished. It would help me move on if I knew the hermit might have had another reason for blowing up the house other than freaking out after my quick visit.

I MADE it to the Department of Land and Natural Resources office less than an hour before closing time. The male clerk at the front desk glanced at the stark black and white clock on the wall as I made my way towards him.

"We close promptly at four," he said by way of greeting.

"Yes. I'll remember that. I'm here to request a public records search."

"For what exactly?"

"I want to learn who owns some property out in Ohia."

"Ohia? That's out east, right? Near Hana?"

"It is."

"We're totally online now for property records information. All you have to do is search for the property in question and all the public records pertaining to that property will pop right up."

I checked out his name plate—*Jason Ka'aohoe.* I was pretty sure that was the same surname as the first truant girl that Rita and I had checked into, the one who lived out at the sovereignty camp;

but, with Hawaiian names having so many vowels and few consonants and as a newcomer, it was hard for me to be sure. Besides, it was getting near closing time and this guy didn't want to extend the deadline. "Sounds good. I'll check it out online."

I went back outside and got into Sharkey for the two-minute trip to the hospital. I parked in the Visitor area and picked up the paper bag of items Opal had asked that I bring. I entered the building and asked at the Information Desk for Arthur Pahinui's room. A woman with thick glasses, bright blue hair and penciled-on eyebrows directed me to the third floor.

Opal was standing by the window when I reached Artie's room. Her face was pale with purplish half-moon pouches under her eyes. The bright teal tentlike gown she'd thrown on for the ambulance ride had various crumbs and food spots dotting her ample bosom. Her short white hair stuck up on top but was completely flat in back after a night in the hospital chair. "Hey, Opal."

"Oh, thank goodness you're here, Kat." She opened her arms for a hug, then closed them, clearly remembering my touch aversion.

"I was able to get out here a little early. You have Pua to thank for that." I went over to the bed and sat on a plastic chair beside it. I picked up Artie's large hand; it felt dry and cold. "How are you doing, Artie?"

"Is that my Kitty Kat?" Artie's voice was weak. His robust complexion was ashy and his milky eyes were sunken. "I hope you've come to spring me from this jail. Did you bring a hacksaw hidden in some *haupia* pudding?"

"Well, someone's sounding a lot better than the last time I saw him," I said. "Seems the hospital food agrees with you."

"Ha. I'd rather eat *poi* and *laulau* any day."

Opal scowled from the other side of the room. "He's supposed to be resting."

I set down Artie's hand and crossed to where Opal was standing by the window. "I'm sure you must be exhausted after a long night in that chair." I pointed to the bile green fake leather recliner in the corner. It had a permanent depression in the seat that seemed like it'd supported many anxious family members over the years.

"I am. Do you have all the stuff I asked for?"

That afternoon, Opal had called and given me a list of things to bring for Artie. I pointed to the bag I'd set beside the chair and rattled off the items . "Razor, toothbrush, toothpaste, deodorant, pajamas, a bathrobe, and warm socks. It's all there."

"*Mahalo*. He's so cold in this room. They keep it like a refrigerator in here. You're sweet to help us out like this."

"Speaking of helping out, Pua helped Auntie get the coffeemaker going and also offered to close the post office today so I could get down here before dark." Pua had been, and maybe still was, one of Opal's dearest friends so I thought I should give credit where credit was due. "So, how's the patient? Any word on the test results?"

Opal glanced over at Artie, then back to me. "Like I said, he needs his rest. Let's take this discussion out into the hall."

"I'm not seven," Artie called out as we left the room. "I'm seventy. I can handle bad news."

"Ignore him," said Opal under her breath. "He's been acting like a child all day."

I'd never heard Artie and Opal pick at each other like this, but a medical scare can do that to even the most loving couples. Once we got out into the hallway, Opal told me the doctor had said the tests showed Artie had experienced a mild heart "event."

"Does that mean heart attack?"

She shrugged. "You know how they are here. They call everything either something you can't understand, or they make it sound like it was nothing. But you saw him last night, right? Did that seem like a 'mild event' to you?"

"No. It seemed serious." Seeing Artie unconscious on the floor had been downright frightening.

"They're making him stay here one more night just to be sure his vitals are stable. But they've told me it's best if I go home. I guess they think people in the room make it harder for the patient to rest." She'd used finger quotes around the words, "people," as if it certainly didn't apply to her, but she could see how they may have had problems in the past with troublesome family members.

Back in the room, we put the robe and socks on Artie and stowed his toiletries. We said our goodbyes and I promised Artie I'd send in the cavalry to scoop him up as soon as he'd been cleared to go home. Opal lovingly kissed her husband goodnight after tucking in his blanket, and we made our way out to the car.

She gazed up at his third-floor window before getting in Sharkey on the passenger side. "I've hardly been away from him overnight for more than twenty years," she said. "I can't imagine my life without him."

"And you don't have to," I said stoutly. "Artie's going to be fine."

I wished I was as certain as I sounded.

29

FRIDAY MORNING BEFORE WORK, I went online to see what I could find out about who owned the property on Halepuaʻa Road. The guy at the DLNR office had said that all public documents regarding land ownership in Hawaii were available online via the Bureau of Conveyances.

I navigated my way to the website, created a user account and accessed the Document Search & Ordering system. When I found the form that would provide me with a name, I hit a wall. I had the road name, but no address and no parcel number. The name of the route, "Halepuaʻa" was kicked back as "Insufficient Information."

How had the feds been able to locate the landowner? At the press conference they'd said the presumed occupant hadn't been the owner, but they'd left it at that. Clearly they had a lot more resources than I did for tracking down that kind of information.

It had been steadily raining since the afternoon before. At noon, I dashed between water-filled potholes to visit Opal at the store before my break was over; my evening had been taken up with helping Auntie and Opal get through the store's bookkeeping, then making sure Opal ate something and got into bed early.

Now, she was at the cash register wearing a bright yellow dress with a gold velvet shawl secured with a sparkly pin depicting a parrot. Her face was pale and her freckles stood out like paint, but she was trying to hide her worry behind an overly bright smile to match her lurid outfit. "*Aloha*, Kat," she said. "Cold out there, isn't it?"

As a New Englander, my notion of "cold" and the local residents' perception of it were miles apart. Today was simply wet. Cold didn't kick in until the temperature dropped to single digits.

"You're looking much better today," I fibbed. "How's business?"

"It's been pretty busy, which is good, since it keeps my mind off missing Artie. I heard on the weather radio that this rain might keep up for a few more days. If it does, the electricity will probably go out. That's always a concern out here when the rains come hard like this."

"Have you heard anything about when Artie will be released?"

"The doctor said he might be able to come home later today."

"Do you need a ride down there? Or did you find someone else to take you?"

Opal bobbed her head. "I'm fine bringing him home myself. Our truck has four-wheel drive if one of the streams gets flooded."

"Okay, but let me know if something changes." I gave her a quick, comforting hug, and ran back to the post office. The afternoon went quickly with everyone coming in to retrieve their mail and share predictions about how long the rain would continue. Older folks took the opportunity to reminisce about former storms.

"Last time it rained like this, we didn't see the sun for a week."

"I was here back in the 90s when the whole side of the cliff out by Black Sand Beach gave way."

"We've had rains so bad out here we couldn't get to Wailuku for weeks."

At two, Elle came in and asked if we had anything for her in General Delivery; we didn't.

"I've been working at home today, but I've got to go to Wailuku to pick up some monogrammed party items for Edith and Josie's event this weekend. In this weather I'd rather not go alone. Care to come along, Kat?"

My mind wandered when she mentioned "monogrammed." It hadn't occurred to me that the two ladies might combine their names into one hyphenated name. "Josephine Manahuli-Pepperwhite" would be a mouthful, for sure.

When I didn't answer, she pressed. "How about it? Can I talk you into riding shotgun with me to town, or do you need to stay here until after four? I have to pick up the napkins before five, so I'll need to leave soon."

Pua had her back turned to the counter, but she waved a hand. "Go on ahead. I can close up here. Again."

"Are you sure you don't mind closing the post office without me —again?" I put my hands on my hips. "Your lips say one thing, but your tone says another."

Pua shook her head "I'm in no hurry to leave—in fact, I may not be able to. My neighbor called and said the road to my place is washed out. I have no idea how I'll get home. Maybe I'll be sleeping here in the office tonight."

I assured her she wouldn't be spending the night with her head on her desk. "We've got an extra bedroom at our house and you're more than welcome. I'll call Aunt Fae and make sure the guest room is ready."

"I appreciate the offer, but I'm worried about Sassy," Pua said, referring to her strident little white dog.

"Do you have anyone on that side who can go to your place and feed her?"

"That's not the issue. She has a self-watering dog bowl and an automatic food dispenser. I just feel bad leaving her alone, especially in this bad weather. She hates getting wet and thunder makes her anxious. I'm going to have to ask my neighbor to put down some puppy pads for her inside."

Sassy wasn't a pooch that had taken to me, unless you consider wanting to take a bite out of my leg as developing a special bond.

But I remembered how much I missed Tiki when she'd been lost at Christmas; I knew what "pet parent guilt" felt like.

"Well, we'll have you stay at our house tonight. That's a done deal." I turned to Elle. "Any chance you could drop me off to handle an errand while we're in Wailuku? It's right by the hospital."

"Are you seeing a doctor about your injury?"

"No, I'm not going to the doctor or hospital this time. Opal is bringing Artie home on her own. I just need to check out something at an office near there."

"Sounds good. We can both get errands done, and I'd appreciate the company on the drive."

Rain poured down hard as we hurried out to Elle's white Jeep Grand Cherokee.

"Whew," Elle said as we climbed in. "Somebody better call Noah. We're gonna need an ark."

She drove the Hana Highway carefully around the "backside" as I had done yesterday. Her midsize SUV took the puddles in stride, but there were areas where the water was flowing across the highway with the force of a rushing stream. Late in the day most of the tourists would be gone regardless of the weather, but the torrential rain had probably kept them on drier parts of the island to begin with.

Elle eventually dropped me off at the building that housed the Department of Land and Natural Resources. I hopped out and promised to be outside waiting for her within twenty minutes.

"It might take me a bit longer than that to get back here," Elle said. "Stay dry until you see my car."

I sprinted across the parking lot to the DLNR office, where once again, Jason Ka'aohoe was sitting at the reception desk.

"Hi, Jason. Remember me? I was here yesterday inquiring about some property out in Ohia. I still need your help."

Although I saw a flicker of recognition in his eyes, I didn't see delight. "Not sure what I can do to help."

I told him I needed to find the name of a property owner of a parcel of land. He started with his spiel. "As I told you yesterday, all of that's online now. All you have to do is—"

I cut him off. "I searched online, but it doesn't work if you don't have a street address or a parcel number."

Jason leaned back in his chair. "You're talking a blind search, then."

"I guess I am."

"Well, that's different. Do you have map coordinates? Maybe an old deed? Or a satellite image?"

"Uh, I'm afraid I've got to check the 'none of the above' box on that. All I know is the property is on Halepua'a Road near the town of Ohia."

"Could you find it on a map?"

"Probably. I could get close."

"Okay, here's what we'll do. I'll pull up the map on the computer and you mouse around until you think you've got it. Then I'll overlay the parcel grid and we'll see what we get from that."

"Sounds good."

He tapped his keyboard for a few seconds. "Take a look at this." He motioned for me to come around to his side of the desk.

I was amazed at the detail of the satellite image. I could make out the roof of the Ohia post office and the Pahinuis' store, even the clubhouse roof at New Ohia and our place.

"It's more *mauka* than that," I said, proud of myself for using the local word.

He moved the mouse a bit further down the Hana Highway and inland. "More like that?"

"Getting warmer."

"Why don't you play around with it for a minute? I'm going to get my stuff from the break room. I need to lock up right at four." He offered me his chair.

"Thanks, Jason. I'll see if I can find it by the time you get back."

I cautiously shifted the mouse until I got to a spot I recognized, the clearing right before the turnoff to Halepuaʻa Road.

Bingo.

The image had been taken before the explosion. The jungle canopy was an unbroken swath of bumpy greens and browns. No burned-out crater, no blackened foliage, no ash gray soot covering everything for a half-acre.

I closed my eyes and sat back in Jason's ergonomic office chair. If only we could freeze time like a satellite image. Before the destruction, loss, and pain.

I heard Jason's footsteps in the hallway; hopefully I was closer to an answer that would give me peace.

30

When Jason returned, I gave him back his chair, and with a few flicks of the mouse he overlaid the parcel grid on the geographic area I'd selected. "Huh. This parcel number was recently requested in a different search. Are you with the federal government?"

"Yes." As postmaster, I was indeed a federal employee. Hopefully he wouldn't ask what branch.

"In that case, I'll give you a printout of the information for this property. Do you want the full report or just the owner's name?"

"The full report, please."

Jason tapped a few keys. A printer started up with a *whirr* in a room behind us. He left, and retrieved the report. He handed it to me and we both glanced at the wall clock. It clicked from three fifty-nine to four. "How about that," he said. "Right on time."

"Thanks, Jason. You've been a big help."

I made my way back down the hall to the lobby as he followed, carrying a ring of keys. I had the information I'd come for, so it was worth it if I got a little damp.

I waited under the building's roof overhang, and Elle's white Jeep pulled up a few minutes later. I folded the report to keep it from getting wet as I dashed to the car. "All set?" Elle asked.

"Yes." At the red light, we waited to turn onto the highway. I glanced down at the rolled-up report in my lap and was tempted to peek. The light changed and Elle accelerated through the intersection, splashing water like a speedboat cutting through waves.

"I've got about a dozen details to clear up for Edith and Josie's wedding this Sunday," Elle said. "But I was able to pick up the dresses Edith and Josie ordered for you and the other bridesmaids."

I frowned. "I thought I was minding the guest book."

"Oh, sorry." Elle slanted me a mischievous glance. "That was the gateway commitment. Once you said yes to that, Edith upgraded you to bridesmaid."

"What!" I'd been in a wedding or two through my twenties and it was something I'd enjoyed. "Do you know how hard I am to fit? Let's not forget how tall I am."

"It's a pretty dress. Maybe you'll even be able to wear it again sometime."

"That's what they always say. Is the wedding even still on? This weather's horrible and I thought you were holding it outside."

"I called Josie yesterday to confirm. She claims since everyone who's coming is local, it shouldn't be a problem, and the hotel has an indoor celebration center we can use if it's raining. Don't forget the rehearsal's on Saturday."

"Okay. But what about shoes? Those are even harder to find in my size."

"Any kind of black heels you already have should work with the gown." Elle dodged around a puddle the size of a small pond. "I'm sorry if this was an ambush. Edith said she wants her most special people close on the big day."

I softened at that. "I guess it's fine if you already got the dress and it fits. Hey," I said. "You never got to finish your story about what happened to you at Schofield. You want to talk now, or do you need to focus on driving?"

"I can walk and chew gum. Let's see how far I get driving and flapping my jaws." She grinned, a mischievous expression on her pretty face. "Where was I? Oh yeah. This clueless lieutenant colonel was assigned to take over the lab. He was fine at first, pretty much letting us do our jobs. But one night when I stayed late working on a project, he came in and asked if we could have a drink. I told him I didn't socialize with senior officers, especially married ones."

"Let me guess, he claimed he wasn't happily married."

She nodded. "Seems you've seen this movie."

"I'll bet most women over twenty, and some younger than that, have seen some version of it."

"Well, it didn't stop there. The guy alternately badgered and flattered me nonstop. One day at lunchtime when I was the only one who hadn't gone out to eat, he came in, cornered me, and put a hand on my boob. In the middle of the day!"

I had to blink several times to regain my vision as black spots circled in my peripherals. Elle's story was getting under my skin as I flashed back to the congressman's moves on me. I'd had to fight him off, and that's what had led to my "exile" and sideways career change to Ohia.

Elle glanced over at me. "Are you okay? You seem spooked."

"Remember I told you I had a story about why I ended up post-master of Ohia after being in the Secret Service?"

"Oh no! Not a similar thing!"

"Sadly, it was. Powerful men don't like to hear 'no.' But finish your story, please."

"I went to my commanding officer and told him I was being harassed. He begged me not to file a complaint. He said he'd had five complaints on his watch, and a sixth could mean the end of his career."

"What'd you do?"

"I let it ride for another couple of weeks. But then 'BLC,' that's what we all called him, for 'Bootlicker Lieutenant Colonel,' gave me a lousy performance review for my work in the lab. Totally unfair and inaccurate." She breathed out a gusty sigh as the wipers labored to keep up with the waterfall on the windshield. "I told my CO that it was him or me. If he didn't do something I was going to break chain of command and go over his head with my harassment complaint. But by then, it seemed as if I was just trying to get even for the bad review."

"Same movie, different actors."

"I was three months from the end of my posting at Schofield, but in the end I agreed to leave quietly with an honorable discharge and severance package. My CO knew a guy who knew someone at the Hawaii State Parks office who owed him a favor, and I was offered the house in New Ohia until I could find more permanent digs. They put in a good word for me at the hotel, too, and I got the job."

I forced my clenched hands to open and turned to give Elle a smile. "In my case, things ended well. I wouldn't have seen myself being happy in a place like Ohia, doing a job like the post office, but I am. Maybe you'll land on your feet, too."

Elle had the kind of smile that lit up dark places. "I already have. Turns out I'm darn good at event planning, and it's such a relief to have low stakes worries like whether someone's party napkins ought to be peach or ecru." She squeezed the steering wheel tighter. "And I'm going to use those feet I landed on to win a marathon next."

"I believe you," I said. "Want to know how the New Ohia development came to be a state park? I had a role in it from the first day I arrived in Ohia."

"Seriously?" Elle's big brown eyes flashed with interest. "We've got time. Tell me everything."

So I did, and that took most of the drive home.

31

ELLE PULLED into New Ohia at nearly seven o'clock, having taken almost an hour longer than usual to drive the twisting highway due to the heavy rain, but thankfully, we made it without incident.

Once I was inside our house carrying the zipped plastic bag that held the bridesmaid dress, Auntie told me that Pua had taken me up on the offer to sleep over with us in New Ohia. She'd already gone up to rest in the guest room, but Aunt Fae told me she'd made dinner for us first.

Aunt Fae lifted the lid on a pot simmering on the stove with a flourish. A delicious aroma hit my nose and activated my taste buds; I closed my eyes to breathe it in. "That smells amazing."

"Pua asked me if we had flour, butter, eggs, chicken, celery, onions, garlic and carrots. I told her we did. Then she made her own noodles and whipped up some fantastic chicken soup. All I did was watch." Aunt Fae had the bedazzled eyes of a groupie.

"And Pua makes another fan for life. I sure am hungry."

Aunt Fae dished me up a hearty serving, heavy on the home-made noodles. "I haven't had noodles this good since I was knee-high to a grasshopper."

"I can't remember eating homemade noodles, ever, at all. Was I ever that small, Auntie?" I slurped the hot, tasty soup. "Knee-high to a grasshopper."

"No. You didn't stop growing until you were in your twenties."

I rolled my eyes. "I know. I was there. But was I always tall for my age?" My childhood memories prior to going to live with Aunt Fae at nine were fuzzy. A psychologist had told us that was a side effect of the trauma from the way my parents had died. The accident had not only stolen them from me, but most of my memories of our life together.

"My brother told me when they brought you home from the hospital you were the size of a two-month-old. I was living too far away to see you right away. I didn't meet you until Christmas of the year you were born, and you were quite an armful by then."

"So I was knee-high to a horse."

"Yeah." Auntie patted my shoulder. "A big, beautiful horse."

My phone pinged, and when I checked the message, it was a weather alert. "Wow, Auntie. The highway department closed the Hana Highway at mile marker 32, near Waiʻānapanapa State Park. Elle and I were probably one of the last cars to get through to this side."

Auntie frowned. "I better go check the news and see what's up."

It'd been a long day. I was still recovering from a week with too many sleepless nights, and my head pounded from the strain of peering through the pouring rain for two hours on the Hana Highway. I was eager to call it a night, but I couldn't sleep until I'd found out whether Opal and Artie made it home before the road closed. I also wanted to review the report I'd gotten from the Bureau of Conveyances.

A quick call to Opal verified that yes, they'd made it home okay. Artie was resting comfortably, and Pearl and Clara from the Red Hat Society had brought them a meal and were keeping her company. "Oh good. Will you need any help tomorrow at the store?"

"Clara has volunteered to take the morning, and your auntie is covering the afternoon," Opal said. She yawned loudly in my ear. "That's if the power stays on. It often goes out when we have flooding."

"Noted," I said, and ended the call.

I bid Auntie goodnight and trailed the cats upstairs. The guest room door was already firmly shut; smart Pua was already in bed.

The cats preceded me to my bedroom and hopped up on my bed. "I see how it is. You girls should be in your own bed." Tiki turned her back and began grooming, ignoring this suggestion.

I took a shower and did my nighttime routine, got into my sleep tee, and retrieved the rolled up report from my bag. Settling against the headboard and switching on the bedside lamp, I began reading the report on the hermit's place.

The land Hugh Dragoon had built on was deeded to "Wabash River Associates, LLC." I wasn't sure where the Wabash River was —Wisconsin? Indiana? Ohio?—but it certainly wasn't in Hawaii.

Apparently the owners had applied for a change of zoning, from agricultural to hotel and multifamily housing in the year 2010, but that had been denied. "No kidding," I muttered. "Like that was going to fly way out in the middle of nowhere." The property taxes, which were minimal, had been paid promptly each year. The address for the LLC was a post office box in Chicago.

So the property was owned by a mainland outfit whose big plans for development had been nipped in the bud. "So Hugh Dragoon was free to squat and build on it without interference."

From my time in the Secret Service, I'd learned that even the most innocuous detail, something that didn't seem to matter all, could be the spark that lit the fuse of what became an aggressive act.

What had set off Hugh Dragoon?

Even with how tired I was, sleep was slow in coming as my brain refused to let go of the image of Maile's sweet, haunting face.

THE NEXT MORNING I lay in bed listening to the patter of rain on the roof. I patted around on the quilt beside me and discovered the cats had gone back to their cozy bed. It was Saturday, which meant I had two more days until I had to be back at work: two more days for my ribs to recuperate, but two days that were already heavily scheduled. First up was Edith and Josie's wedding rehearsal and dinner, and then Sunday would be taken up by the ceremony and reception.

I got up and went downstairs in search of coffee. As I passed through the living room on my way to the kitchen, I could see through the window that the soil around our house was so saturated that pools of water surrounded the base of every bush.

Out the kitchen window, I spied a steady stream of water sluicing down the asphalt driveway and, although it wasn't visible from that vantage point, I could imagine the stream joining up with a wider one rushing down the entrance road to New Ohia.

Our model home had nearly every conceivable upgrade, from instant hot water to a top-of-the-line air conditioning system, but it didn't have gutters. Rain poured from the roof as if we were living under a waterfall.

I reached over and flicked the switch for the overhead light.

Nothing.

I flicked it again. Same result.

I gazed at the shiny appliances in the dim confines of the kitchen. The blue clock readings on the microwave and oven weren't illuminated. Cocking an ear, I couldn't hear the refrigerator running.

As Opal had predicted, we'd lost power during the night.

"Ugh." No coffee maker. No cell phone chargers. No TV to watch the weather report to see when the storm would pass.

Aunt Fae joined me in the kitchen a few minutes later. "Power's out?"

I nodded.

"I was afraid of that. The clock by my bed is as dead as a dodo."

"Well, we need coffee. Unfortunately, the stove is electric."

"Oh, poo," said Auntie. "We won't have anything to offer Pua when she gets up."

"I'm more worried about my total caffeine withdrawals. Opal won't be opening the store without power, so we can't get any there, either."

Just then, someone knocked on our front door. We both hurried to answer it as if the arrival might be the only small bit of entertainment we'd get that morning.

Elle stood on the stoop wearing a bright yellow slicker. Her bright smile made her appear unfazed by the weather and lack of electricity. She stepped inside, holding a cardboard box which she lifted like a trophy. "Elle L Beane to the rescue!"

"What've you got there?" said Aunt Fae.

"A French press, ground coffee, and a chafing dish heater with canned heat," she said. "I was concerned we might lose power, so I brought this stuff home from the hotel earlier in the week. I thought we all might need hot coffee on a morning like this."

I could've kissed her.

Pua, dressed and coiffed, arrived from the guest room as Elle was making her way to the kitchen with her rescue kit. I introduced them.

"You work with Kat at the post office," Elle said. "You helped me fill out my mailbox request."

"Of course. Lovely of you to bring us what Kat calls the Elixir of Life," Pua said. "Unfortunately, a request is only a spot in line at the Ohia Post Office. We've got customers who've been waiting for years to get a box."

"No worries," said Elle. "I rarely get mail. Besides, I like to check out the local 'talk story' while I wait in the general delivery line."

Elle measured water into our pot and lit the chafing dish heater. She placed the metal teapot over the heater and measured preground coffee into the French press. Within fifteen minutes, each of us had fresh brewed coffee. The French press could only hold four cups, so we carefully divvied it up among us.

"It's so sweet of you to think of us," said Aunt Fae.

"I can handle most types of deprivation, but lack of coffee on a rainy day constitutes a violation of the Geneva Convention," Elle said.

"We have that in common, too," I said.

My phone vibrated—thankfully, it was still working, and I picked up for Keone. "Are you okay out there? I'm in Kahului, hoping to get a flight out that way later today. Right now, the airport in Hana is closed since there's no power for the runway lights and visibility is next to nothing."

"We're okay here," I told him. We kept the conversation short, though, because my phone was down to twenty percent and I had no idea when I'd be able to charge it up again. We agreed to catch up later at the rehearsal dinner if he made it out this way.

"Let's hope they get the power back on," Keone said. "Until then, stay safe, Kat."

I hung up, realizing belatedly that Keone's tone and words had been strictly business. No "I love you" or even "Miss you." A little hole opened up in my heart as I considered the rocky content of our last encounter. Were we in trouble as a couple?

Elle said she had a few things she needed to do at work and asked if someone would mind taking her to Hana. "My fuel gauge is down to 'E' after my trip to Wailuku yesterday, and since gas pumps require electricity to operate, I'm out of luck until the power comes back on."

Pua offered to drive Elle to the hotel. Soon it was just Aunt Fae and me at the kitchen table, with Tiki and Misty at our feet.

"I think I'll go check on Artie and Opal," I said. I could've just called them, but the dim confines of the kitchen walls were starting to close in. In similar situations in Maine, Aunt Fae was known for coming up with various chores for us to do to pass the time. These included such heart-pumping activities as organizing the spice rack into alphabetical order or wiping imaginary dust from the tops of all the canned goods.

Besides, given the power outage, I wanted to check and make sure everything in the post office was okay. I couldn't think of anything that could be harmed by a lack of electricity, but I'd never experienced this situation before, and as Aunt Fae liked to say, "You don't know what you don't know."

I put on my Nikes and a parka and walked down to Opal and Artie's store. The "Closed" sign was in the window.

I knocked on the back door. A few minutes later, Artie came to open it for me. His color had returned, and he appeared to have regained his usual cheerful demeanor. "Artie! How're you feeling?"

"Hey there, Kitty Kat. Never better. Come in and have a cup of hot tea."

"Don't mind if I do." I hung my parka on a hook on the door. Opal bustled in. She scowled. "He's much better, physically," she said. "But a cooped up man is never a happy man."

"You got that right," Artie said. "I'd rather be on the porch, strumming my guitar."

"No reason why you can't do that, whether the store is open or not."

He smiled. "Something to look forward to later, when the day warms up."

"It's not really cold now, but it's still raining," I said.

Opal had fired up a small gas-powered lantern for light, and a hot water kettle burbled on the one-burner Coleman stove set up nearby. We sat at the little kitchen table in their personal quarters. While we waited for Artie to prep the cups and tea bags, Opal took out a little notebook from her flowing dress.

"You remember when I cast the runes about what happened out there at the hermit's place?" she said.

Although the hermit and his horrendous act had been top-of-mind for me, I'd completely forgotten about Opal's rune reading. "You never interpreted them, right?"

"Not to you. But while I was sitting here in the dark this morning, I revisited my notes. You want to hear what I came up with?"

"Sure."

"The three most important messages I saw were destruction, revelation, and, see this one that looks like an 'X'?" She pointed to her illustration. "It means 'a gift.' Maybe there's some good that will come from what happened out there. Can you imagine what it could be?"

From where I was sitting there was absolutely no good that could come from a crazy man and a little girl being blown to smithereens. I shook my head.

"In any case," Opal said. "I thought you might want to know."

"Thanks, Opal." I couldn't muster anything more; I was too depressed over the whole thing.

We talked about the rain. I asked if she and Artie had lived in Ohia when they'd closed the road before.

"Oh, lots of times. These roads are forever getting closed due to slides and washouts. No tourists can get out this way, so it's just us chickens." Opal cackled as if pleased to be cut off from civilization, and Artie nodded in agreement.

"Snow days in Maine were like that for us when I was growing up," I agreed.

I thanked them for the tea and hopped, skipped, and jumped around puddles until I got to the back door of my own place of business.

The interior of the post office was downright creepy in the dark. I walked from room to room, checking that we had surge protectors for all the electronics and that everything was either Off or unplugged. I had to remind myself that flicking the switches wasn't going to do anything to dispel the gloom. After I locked up, I walked around to the front to check that the door was locked.

I frowned. Someone had left a cardboard box on the steps, tucked under the eave of the roof.

The airport warning: "Do not leave bags unattended. If you notice an unattended item or suspicious activity, immediately report it to the police or airport personnel." flashed into my mind. This box was that kind of item.

32

I SURVEYED THE AREA: no one was anywhere around. The parking lot between the post office and the Ohia General Store was empty but for Opal and Artie's sturdy SUV, parked beside their home.

The road was, for once, empty of traffic due to the flood closures.

The palm trees at Ohia Bay gyrated in the gusty wind; the beach was pretty much empty of anything but a crab or two. By squinting, I could also make out a turtle pulled up on the sand.

Fine misty rain wet my cheeks as I turned back to survey the cardboard box.

Perhaps someone new to the area didn't know we were closed on Saturdays.

Maybe it was an old empty box someone had dropped off for us to recycle. Since we handled so much cardboard material and junk mail through the postal system, many patrons dumped unwanted boxes and junk mail into our garbage cans in the lobby. Maybe this time someone had dropped one of them off outside. Pua and I didn't appreciate this, but couldn't seem to get the habit to stop. A guy from the main district came around about once a month to pick up recyclables which Chad helped us bundle and store.

I couldn't conclude the box was a threat without investigating it further. I gingerly approached the item. The rain had eased to a light drizzle, and the cardboard was out of the direct rain, flush against the door under the roof overhang.

I gently touched a corner of it. The cardboard felt soggy, as if it had been sitting there for a while. I squatted beside it to examine the thing without touching it further.

Where the address should have been, in neat, felt-tip pen block letters, it read: "Kat Smith, Post Office."

The box wasn't sealed with tape; the four flaps had been tucked inside each other.

I processed the scenario: an abandoned box, with no one around, after a nearby dwelling had been blown to smithereens only ten days earlier.

I glanced across the parking lot at Artie and Opal's place. If the box contained a bomb, it might be powerful enough to demolish the post office and their store and home with them in it.

I hesitated and sucked in a breath, wishing there was someone, anyone, I could call to handle this instead of me. But with flood conditions blocking the road and no power, it was up to me to see if the box contained an explosive. "Big girl panties, Kat. You got this," I muttered.

I scanned the box visually for any wires or other booby traps; there was nothing visible. I gently unfolded and lifted one of the flaps and peered inside.

The box wasn't empty, but in the gloom of the cloudy morning it was hard to make out what it contained. I peered in closer. The object at the bottom of the box was coiled around the four corners, leaving an open area in the center.

My first impression was *snake*.

But there were supposedly no snakes on Maui?

Thankfully, the item wasn't moving or making any noise.

I gently lifted the box and tilted it to capture whatever feeble sunlight was available.

I gasped: *it was a long braid of human hair.*

Salt-and-pepper gray human hair, shorn at one end and held together with a decorated elastic band at the other.

I turned the box upside down and dumped the item out. The severed braid tumbled onto the steps, the yellow plastic plumeria ornament that held the braid together making mockery of the macabre souvenir.

I had no doubt who this braid belonged to.

I went inside and used the landline to call Lei. She didn't answer so I had to leave a message. "Lei, please call me. I just opened a package that was left here at the post office and it contains human remains," I said. I thought better of that. "Not remains, more like human waste." I hadn't described the contents of the box correctly but I was too rattled to think straight. "I mean, evidence of a human . . . mutilation? I guess. Just call me. It's an emergency."

I paced around my dim office. How long would I have to wait? There was nothing to do in the gloomy space but take a dustcloth to the furniture and office supplies on the counter.

Thankfully, ten minutes later, Lei called back. "What are you talking about, 'human remains'?"

"Remember that really long braid of Barbara Long's, the foster mom in Haiku? With the yellow plastic plumeria at the end of it? She cut it off and brought it up here to freak me out. She left it outside the post office on the front steps. I don't know how she got it here," I said. "I think the road's still closed."

"It is." I could hear Lei's keyboard rattling in the background. "Did the box have any identifying marks on it? Return address, anything like that?"

"No. It was creepy. Left on the front steps of the P.O. with my name on it. I was worried it was a bomb." I chuckled nervously. "Do you think she did it to get back at me for getting her fired?"

"Pretty weird." Lei sounded distracted.

"So, what do you—"

"I don't know, but I don't like this. Pono and I are heading out to Haiku to check on Long's place right now. See what's up with her."

"Do you think—suicide?" My stomach lurched. "And it's my fault."

"Stop it, Kat. Go home and wait for a call from us at your house. That's an order." She ended the call with a bang of the receiver.

"Okay," I said to the dead air. I locked up the post office and walked briskly back to our house. I was on the front steps, taking off my parka, when Pua pulled into the driveway.

She got out and shut the door of her Honda. "Sorry, Kat, I'm still your houseguest. Can't get to my place." She zeroed in on my face with that keen stare she had. "What's happened? You look like you've seen a ghost."

Turned out, I hadn't seen a ghost, just the dire possibility of one. "Something super weird is going on. It's postal business because . . ." This was getting complicated. I hadn't kept Pua up to speed throughout the case, but now, since the box had been left on the post office steps, she deserved to know everything. "Let's talk out here in your car. I don't want Auntie to get alarmed until we know more. She's had some lightheaded spells and I don't want to frighten her."

We were still in the car, hashing it out, when Auntie came to the door and waved the cordless landline phone at me. "Kat! It's Detective Texeira for you. She says it's official business."

I hopped out and ran to take the phone from her. "Thanks, Auntie. I'll fill you in on everything in a minute." I avoided her reproachful eyes and hurried past her, taking the stairs two at a time to get privacy in the upstairs office. "Lei? Is everything okay at Long's place?"

"No." Lei blew out a breath. "But it could have been worse. It's a good thing Pono and I went out to the house when we did, because Barbara Long was imprisoned in her 'time out' shed behind her Haiku home."

"What? How? Is she okay?" My voice rose.

"From what the EMTs were saying, Long's condition could go either way. She was unconscious, and we think she was put in there shortly after we made our home visit—so several days without food or water," Lei said. "She'd been smacked around a bit too."

"That's horrible." Barbara Long more than deserved a taste of her own medicine, but that was beside the point. My mind was scrambling. "Could she have somehow gotten herself locked in there?"

"No. She was tied up. On a chair. She had knocked it over, but couldn't get loose. You saw the lock on the shed. This was deliberate."

I didn't say anything as I considered the possibilities.

"And yes, Long's hair had been cut off, so the braid you found at the post office was hers, if the decoration matches the one we saw," Lei went on. "When the road opens, I'm going to need to come get the box you found along with its contents. Evidence for our investigation."

"Of course." I recalled carefully replacing the braid in the cardboard box and bringing it into my office, then locking the door of my private work space. I wasn't sure how much help the box would be in identifying the perpetrator, but regardless, I'd be glad to have the creepy hair coil out of my possession. "Why do you think her braid was left on the front steps, addressed to me?"

"The perp wanted you to know he, or she, had done something to Long. That's my guess."

"Right. But how did they know I had any connection to her?"

"If we knew that, we'd be halfway to solving this case. Oh, and one more thing," said Lei. "Evidence from inside the home points to the possibility of someone other than Long staying there for the past few days."

"What? What kind of evidence?"

"From what we can ascertain, the home invader may have stuck around for a while after locking Barbara Long in the shed. There are dirty dishes everywhere, and the refrigerator is empty. Forensics is working on fingerprints and trace collected, but so far, no matches to anyone in the system."

I sat down, hard. Since I'd arrived in Ohia, there'd been a string of bizarre events. With this imprisonment of a woman I'd met only a few days earlier, I was well on my way to having a reputation as a "mayhem magnet." *Kat Smith moves into town and the social order goes haywire.* "Do you think this crime against Long had anything to do with her getting the boot from CWS?"

"The timing speaks to it, but we can't assume anything," Lei said. "As the social worker pointed out, Long wasn't a good care-taker. I'm sure there are plenty of kids, some of them grown now, and maybe even a few bio parents, who had issues with her abusive child-rearing. Maybe the news that she'd been busted got out from the agency. Candace says she kept Long's disciplinary action confi-dential, as she's supposed to, but her superiors knew. The agency could have leaks."

I thanked Lei for filling me in and ended the call, setting the cordless phone on its useless charger. Thankfully, that landline still worked as long as the battery held.

Glancing around the room, I felt like I was returning to my body. "Wow. That's a lot to absorb."

I didn't want Auntie or Pua to know any of this until it was more resolved. Lei hadn't sworn me to secrecy, but it went without saying that what she'd told me was for my ears alone.

33

AT ELEVEN-THIRTY A.M., the power came back on.

"Finally," said Pua, gazing out the kitchen window. "I'm going to drive over and check on Opal and Artie. I'll leave my car at the post office for the weekend. I've found a ride home."

She told us that she'd been contacted by a fearless neighbor who drove a jacked up four-wheel drive vehicle with enormous nubby tires. He'd offered to come pick her up at the post office; he was sure his vehicle could make it across the swift creek that now ran across the back road.

"I have the rest of the weekend to figure out how to return to work on Monday," she said. "I can't leave poor Sassy alone that long if I can possibly help it."

"But you'll miss Edith and Josie's wedding," I said.

"I may, but that's a chance I'll have to take. Sassy's probably going wild thinking I've abandoned her. I've got to get back. If I don't make it, I'm sure the ladies will understand."

She said her goodbyes, and soon Auntie and I were lunching on Pua's leftover soup seated at the breakfast bar. "Tiki was acting strange this morning," Aunt Fae said.

Like that was something out of the ordinary. "She was okay

when I was up in my office taking Lei's phone call. She and Misty were napping in their bed. What was she doing?"

"Growling and pacing and just all-around acting upset. This was before you got home. Earlier."

"Did she want to go outside?" After the incident with the open window, I'd added a slide-in pet door to the patio slider, so Tiki and Misty could come and go easily. Tiki hadn't taken to the idea of muscling her way through the rubber flap. I'd only seen her use it once, and the expression on her face had 'not acceptable' written all over it.

"I don't think so. Maybe I'm reading too much into it." Aunt Fae rolled her narrow shoulders back deliberately. "The wedding rehearsal's in three hours at the Hotel Hana. You think everyone's going to be able to make it?"

"The power's back on and the road workers have been clearing the highway for the past day. Anything's possible."

We ate in silence for a few moments. Finally Aunt Fae said, "Okay. What's going on that you don't want to tell me?"

I set my spoon into my empty bowl and pushed it aside. "Oh, Auntie. There *is* something going on, but I can't tell you about it yet. It's an active police investigation." I swiveled the kitchen counter barstool to face her. "It's another strange crime that I seem to be in the middle of. Since I got to Ohia, it's like I'm attracting crime and disaster."

"Stop it. That's no way to talk. You are a caring, inquisitive, can-do sort of person. It's natural that you want to find answers—but that doesn't mean you caused the issues in the first place."

"Maybe." But it seemed more like I was a fulcrum, a tipping point that had resulted in two violent crimes: first the explosion, now some sort of trigger for what happened to Barbara Long. Not an easy thing to shrug off, especially for a former Secret Service agent who'd valued the agency's motto: *Worthy of trust and confidence.* "I hope you're right, Auntie."

Keone called as I was loading the dishwasher. He said he'd

made it to Hana, but now he'd had to pick up an extra flight. He wouldn't be able to make it to the rehearsal dinner, after all.

The nagging feeling that he was avoiding me persisted. "See you at the wedding tomorrow?" I asked.

"I'll do my best."

"You better not miss it. I'm going to need some encouragement, because the dress that Edith and Josie picked for me to wear is . . . well, let's say it's challenging."

"Give me a hint."

"I guess the operative word is 'skimpy.'" I grimaced. I'd only had time to peek at the gown Elle had picked up for me, but that glimpse was enough to be worrisome.

"Then for sure I won't miss it. See you there." He ended the call.

I went upstairs to take a closer inspection of what I'd been charged to wear in the wedding. The gown was made from a gorgeous silk fabric in an amethyst purple that accented my blue eyes. It was expertly stitched, and the drape of the fabric was excellent. The problem was, there simply wasn't enough of it.

I'm over six feet tall, which both Edith and Josie are well-aware of, but as I held the dress against myself, as I'd suspected, it ended only a couple of inches below what Aunt Fae referred to as my "hoo-ha." No way could I bend down or climb stairs without some "I see London, I see France" underpants action going on.

I tried the dress on next, tugging the back zipper up with a little ribbon attached for that purpose.

The top was fine, a scoop neck with little cap sleeves. The waist was tight enough that it held my ribs in without need of further support. I slid my feet into the faithful black pumps that had seen me through many a state dinner, then walked over to the mirror on the back of the bedroom door. I sucked in a breath. "Dang, this dress is short!"

Keone was definitely going to approve—I was showing about a mile of leg. But was it appropriate for the wedding of a couple of old ladies? "Not hardly. What were they thinking?"

I rifled through my garments and found a cute pair of black satin 'boy shorts' underwear that provided enough coverage and didn't ruin the dress's (tight) rear view. I swiveled to and fro—yep, I needed to be careful with any bending.

Edith had overstepped by not including the bridesmaids in the dress decision, let alone failing to ask me directly to fulfill the role. But was it worth it to call her and complain so close to the event? No. The whole thing would be over by Monday, and hopefully I'd make it through without a wardrobe malfunction.

By AFTERNOON, the skies were gray, but the rain had finally stopped. I trotted down to Opal and Artie's to see if they needed a ride to the rehearsal later.

Artie was in his usual spot on the front porch, picking out a tune on his guitar.

"Kitty Kat," he sang out as I approached.

"You ready for the rehearsal tonight?" I said. Opal wasn't actually in the wedding party, but the brides had asked Artie to play a couple of tunes during the ceremony, so she'd be bringing him to the run-through practice we were doing before the dinner.

"I'm playing both in the wedding ceremony and for a while at the reception," he said. "I had to strong-arm those women into accepting my playlist. Josie wasn't a problem, but Edith wanted some strange tunes."

"Strange, how?"

"You ready for this?" he said. "'Fifty Ways to Leave Your Lover,' by Paul Simon. Or how about, 'You Give Love a Bad Name,' by Bon Jovi? I told Edith, those might be favorites of yours from back in the day, but this is your *wedding*."

"Good of you to stand your ground. I've got my own strange situation." I told him about the silk micromini dress as Opal came outside to join us.

She handed me a frosty root beer from the cold case. "On the house. What's this about a dress?"

I repeated that my bridesmaid dress was too short.

"I'm sure they didn't mean for it to be too skimpy in a bad way," she said. "Those ladies think you're beautiful and they want you to enjoy it. From what I hear, Josie was quite the *wahine* surfer back in her day. Maybe they're encouraging you to 'flaunt it while you got it.' Too bad it goes so quickly."

Artie took Opal by the hand. "You're all the *wahine* this old man will ever want, my *ku'uipo*."

"I love the sound of that word," I said. "What does it mean?"

"Sometimes we shorten it to *ipo*, but it's my darling or sweetheart, just the same."

I wanted to remember that word. I had yet to hear a Hawaiian phrase that didn't sound better to the ear than its translation into English.

I finished my root beer and thanked them, then made my way back to New Ohia. I had less than an hour to get ready for the rehearsal and the fancy dinner that followed.

It'd been a tough couple of weeks. The explosion, my cracked ribs, the break-in at our house, followed by the road closure and power outage, the creepy box on the post office steps, and now the imprisonment and abuse of a negligent foster mom.

I was due for an enjoyable night with nothing to worry about. Even my flashy bridesmaid dress wouldn't be an issue until the actual ceremony on Sunday.

I swiped on mascara and shimmied into the trusty black sheath dress I'd brought from Washington. I anticipated nothing more stressful than a quick dry run of "who stands where" at the wedding, followed by a night of tropical umbrella drinks and chef cuisine with some of my favorite people in the world.

Everything was going to be great. Right?

"Right," I said out loud. Tiki sat up in her kitty bed and glared, flattening her ears. "Yep, I'm going out," I told her. "Keep an eye on the place, will you?"

She yawned as if saying "of course." Even Misty seemed to agree, chiming in by prancing over, her little tail flicking from side to side, to wrap her fuzzy little body around my unfamiliar high heeled feet and ankles. "You kitties know how to make a girl want to stay home."

But of course, duty called—and I was bound to answer.

34

AUNT FAE and I arrived for the rehearsal and walked into the lobby of the Hotel Hana to discover Edith and Josie clinging to each other beside the fountain like a couple of orphaned capuchin monkeys. Edith's face was drained of color. Josie had a glazed look in her large brown eyes and was sucking deep breaths of oxygen through her cannula.

"What's going on, ladies?" I said.

"It's Lola," murmured Edith. "She's here."

I'd forgotten all about Lola's crazed vow to sabotage the wedding. I whipped my head around. "Where is she?"

"In the indoor chapel celebration room we're using. She's raving about locking everyone out." Josie leaned in and whispered, "I think she may have been drinking earlier." Even through the closed doors, Lola's yelling echoed above the peaceful Hawaiian instrumental music playing in the open-air lobby.

Aunt Fae pulled out her cell phone and walked away, punching in a number.

Elle Beane appeared, gorgeous in a fitted orange dress that made the most of her toned figure. In a strained but chipper tone, she asked for everyone to gather in the hotel bar. "We're putting finishing touches on the chapel arrangements, so let's practice the ceremony in there instead," she said.

"I'm so mortified," said Edith, a tear sliding down her cheek. "I can't tell you how sorry I am about this," she said to Josie.

"Don't be. We simply won't let her ruin our day." Josie pulled herself up to her full height and jutted out her chin. She had to tug on her oxygen line to get a bit more length, but it did nothing to diminish her regal countenance. Her eyes fixed on the entrance to the bar. She swept a stunning monstera leaf patterned *pareo* over her shoulder. "This is our time, *ku'uipo*," Josie said, taking Edith's arm. "We will not allow *hewa uhane* to take even one bit of joy from us."

"What does that mean?" Edith said.

Josie clasped both her hands over Edith's and gazed into her partner's face. "Actually, I just made a little Hawaiian to English pun. In Hawaiian, a *hewa uhane* is an evil spirit. And what is happening here is truly the work of alcoholic spirits, which for your daughter are the very embodiment of evil, wouldn't you agree?"

Edith nodded and did her best to smile.

"Now, come on. Let's go." She sallied forth, and short Edith had to trot to keep up with statuesque Josie's longer stride.

I made eye contact with the other bridesmaids, Pearl and Clara from the Red Hat Society. We all trooped into the bar area, where tables had been moved aside for us to stand. The officiant, a Hawaiian priest who was a relative of Josie's, ran us through the short program. The ceremony on Sunday was going to include a procession into the chapel, an exchange of vows, a short musical interlude by Artie, and then a reverse procession out to the reception area.

Fifteen minutes after the rehearsal started in the bar, we all reentered the lobby. I glimpsed Aunt Fae confiding with a tall, elegantly dressed woman with coffee-toned skin and an elaborate hairstyle of expertly coiled tiny braids. *Where had I seen her before?*

I squinted my eyes, as if closing off the scene in front of me would help jog my memory.

Ah, yes. That was Betty, Lola's alcoholism sponsor. Aunt Fae must have been calling her before the rehearsal began.

Elle waved us over to a banquet room where the rehearsal dinner was getting underway. I held up a finger, alerting her that we'd be in as soon as we could, and I approached Aunt Fae and her companion.

"Betty," I said, extending my hand. "Kat Smith. I think we met at a Red Hat gathering some months ago."

"Oh, yes. I remember it well. I believe you've seen Lola at what we in the program refer to as 'rock bottom.' On behalf of my 'sponsee,' may I extend an apology? I feel horrible she has chosen to abandon all the good work she's done, especially at a wonderful event such as this."

Lola's sponsor shouldn't be offering apologies instead of the woman herself. But then, I have a thing about personal responsibility. "It's nice of you to come. Are you going to try to talk to her?"

"Of course." Betty adjusted clinking gold bangles on her arm. "I'll try to get her to a meeting right now."

"Lola's over there, in the chapel. Let's see if you can talk some sense into her," said Aunt Fae.

We left Betty to give Lola her best attempt at an intervention and headed for the banquet room. The large area had been sectioned smaller with a long accordion wall, and Edith and Josie were already seated at the end of a long table. In the few minutes Aunt Fae and I had been conferring with Betty, someone had instructed the waitstaff to remove all the wineglasses from the table. The guests, including family members I didn't know and the other bridesmaids, were quiet. It was as if everyone was holding their breath, waiting for someone in charge to explain what was going on. The waitstaff stood in the doorway but no one moved.

Elle bustled in and hit a switch on the wall. Immediately, Hawaiian slack-key guitar rarified the air. She then whispered something to a guy manning the freestanding bar, where a host of fancy drinks filled a large tray. Then, she turned and addressed the table.

"We have a wonderful treat for you all this evening," she said. "Kai is a 'mocktail' master. He's here to show you all the fabulous ways you can enjoy a healthy, alcohol-free drink that tastes as good as any tropical cocktail on the island. Kai, tell the people here what you're featuring tonight."

Kai, a tall, powerfully built man wearing a black and white aloha shirt that seemed like it had been tailored to show off his wide shoulders, took a quick bow. "I've got three beauties for you this evening. First, the 'Moody Maui.' It's like a Blue Hawaiian, but instead of rum and blue curaçao, I'm using pineapple and guava juices, and a wild blueberry syrup. The second one is the 'Happy Honeycreeper.' It's got hibiscus and cardamom flavors along with bright notes of cherry juice. The final one is the 'Hula Moon,' a creation using ginger ale, a touch of light cream and almond. Each drink comes with a tropical fruit pick and tiny umbrella."

Kai held up a fruit pick with a pineapple chunk, slice of mango and a piece of apple banana in one hand and a pink paper umbrella in the other, as if demonstrating how festive the mocktails would look. The guests went over to choose their drinks. I overheard Edith say to Josie, "Was this your idea? It's wonderful."

"I wish I could take credit," said Josie. "But Elle came up with this all on her own."

I picked up a Hula Moon and took a seat beside Aunt Fae as we waited for the food service to begin. Even surrounded by the other guests, I missed Keone. After the past week of relationship bumps and blunders, I didn't think I could take another romance-related occasion without him.

Half an hour into the dinner, Lola appeared in the doorway. Edith stiffened in her seat.

Lola was a wreck: mascara streaks ran through her thick foundation makeup. Her brassy blonde hair seemed like it hadn't seen a brush. She wore all black: black pants, a black shirt, and even a small black veiled headband. Her funereal appearance said it all. For her, her mother's impending wedding was a tragedy.

"Relax, mother," Lola said. "I'm here to say something and then I'll leave."

Betty, standing just behind Lola, gave her a nudge. The two of them came inside the banquet room. "I need to make amends to those I've harmed with my drinking. I want to say, 'I'm sorry' for what happened earlier. I didn't really want to ruin your wedding, but I thought you—"

Betty nudged her again.

"Right," said Lola. "I'm not here to make excuses. I just came to say, 'I'm sorry.' If you don't want me to come to the wedding tomorrow, I won't."

Another nudge.

"But if I do come, I will not make a scene and will wish you and Josie all the best." Lola turned and raised her eyebrows at Betty as if asking if she'd said enough. Betty nodded.

Edith straightened her gown and went over to her daughter. "I also want to make amends. I made a mistake in not including you in my decision to marry Josie. I should have explained why. I apologize for leaving you out of such an important decision."

The two women reached for each other. Josie got up and joined the hug. One by one the people in the room got up and joined in as if they'd all wordlessly decided to go for the Guinness World Record for largest group hug.

I held back since that wasn't my thing. Elle came over to me and whispered, "I'm aware of your touch 'thing.' Someday I'll tell you about my water 'thing.'"

After a delicious and satisfying dinner, Aunt Fae and I were heading out to the parking lot in the pitch black of a Hana night, when Keone popped out from between two cars.

"Whew! You startled me," I said.

"Sorry. I didn't want to go inside; I was on my way home and decided to stop in, hoping to talk to you."

Aunt Fae waved a hand. "You two take all the time you need. I'll catch a ride with one of the Red Hat gals. I'm about tuckered out."

"No worries, Auntie," he said. "I'll make sure she gets home in plenty of time for her beauty sleep."

Aunt Fae made a *pfft* sound. "Even in the dark I can see she looks even more beautiful now that you're here."

I rolled my eyes; she was definitely in favor of 'K & K' becoming a permanent fixture. We watched as Aunt Fae made her way back to the lobby.

"Want to go get a drink inside?" Keone said. "Or sit in my truck?"

I explained about the alcohol-free rehearsal, and how everyone had made amends. "I'd feel guilty having a drink after all that booze-related drama."

"Then I guess that means we stay here," he said.

We got into his Toyota truck. As I shut the passenger door, I realized I hadn't been inside it for nearly a week. The little feathered warrior helmet hanging from the rearview mirror made me recall our first date so many months ago. Since then, we'd been working and hanging out together almost daily at the K & K office. The fact that we usually went on dates at least a couple of nights a week as well made the long hiatus feel ominous.

"You want to tell me about taking the promotion?" I said. "When are you leaving?"

"Never one to beat around the bush, are you?"

"I like to say what needs to be said. If you're making plans that don't include me, I need to know."

"Kat, that's what I want to get a handle on." His eyes gleamed in the dim light, and so did his white pilot uniform. *Did he have to still be wearing that for this talk?* Unfair! "The thing is, I don't know what you're thinking about 'us.'" He made air quotes for that word. "One minute we're a couple, and then *wham*! Something happens and you're pushing me away. I can't get a read on where this is going."

I rolled my lips inward and pinched down; everything that came to mind to say sounded whiny or defensive. *He was right.*

"And lately I don't even know what's going on with you and the hermit thing. First you tell me you're handling it well, and then you admit—"

"Seriously? Is this what you wanted to talk about? Let me assure you, I'd like to know myself. It's not a simple matter, Keone. It might sound crazy, but it's like that little girl who died out there was *me*. I shouldn't see it that way, because Aunt Fae was the best guardian ever, but for whatever reason, I felt abandoned, just like that girl. Right now, I can't reconcile my part in causing her death. It's hard to give energy to things like 'us' with that going on."

Keone stayed silent.

I took a breath. "I need to get beyond this, I know. Sophie Smithson gave me the name of a psychologist. I should probably call her."

"You said that before, but have you done that?"

I didn't answer; we both knew the answer.

"I want us to have a future, Kat. I love you, you know? But I'm in the dark here about what *you* want for us, and this conversation isn't telling me anything about that. If I hang around waiting to find out what's what with you, I'm going to miss this opportunity, and I'll regret that later."

"So, you're taking the job?"

"It's a good opportunity. A natural progression in my career."

"Fine. I need to get home now."

I got out, slammed the door, and weaved through the lot to where Sharkey was parked. I didn't get inside, though. I stood next to my vehicle, hoping he'd follow. Hoping Mr. K would press past the wall I'd thrown at him. Hoping he'd love me enough to want me in spite of my brokenness.

Instead, I watched as the red taillights on Keone's truck receded into the inky dark of the Hana Highway.

"Oh, dangnabbit. I'm going to lose him." I leaned over and rested my forehead on Sharkey's roof. I banged the metal gently with my head; it was my head that had sabotaged "us."

As I got in and turned the key, I tuned in to myself. Part of me felt empty and alone, but another part was relieved. I didn't have to live up to his expectations and end up letting him down. I already had done that.

But I'd done enough "fake it 'til you make it" to last a lifetime in the Secret Service; I couldn't pretend the explosion and everything about it hadn't brought up my past. I'd told Keone as honestly as I could what was going on with me. He didn't want to live in limbo, and now there wasn't going to be an "us" to worry about.

35

THE MORNING of Josie and Edith's wedding dawned clear and bright, as if someone had flipped a switch and turned off the storm. The doom and gloom of the week's flooding were replaced by a glowing sapphire sky and piercing golden sunlight. Every palm frond gleamed and yellow and red hibiscus blooms burst forth like fireworks against shiny emerald bushes refreshed by days of rain.

I wasn't so sparkly. I got ready for the early afternoon festivities with a heavy feeling in my body; every limb weighed a ton and my chest hurt. I showered and made my way down to the kitchen and sat at the table, where I forced myself to eat a few bites of fresh banana bread Aunt Fae had heated up for us.

"You don't like this recipe?" she said. "I got it from that nice lady down in Ke'anae. She sells dozens of loaves a day to tourists driving out this way."

"The banana bread is great, Auntie, but I might be coming down with something. I'm just not feeling well."

Aunt Fae squinted at me. "I don't think this is physical. Want to talk about it?"

"No thank you."

Tiki seemed to sense my gloom. She wound her furry body

around my legs a couple of times before plopping down on my feet. Her warm body felt like fuzzy slippers. Her ferocious purr added a bit of massage therapy to the mix as she leaned in against my legs. I closed my eyes, enjoying how sweet she was being.

I could really appreciate this moment because I remembered how far we'd come.

"Are you feeling any better about wearing that va-va-voom dress?" Aunt Fae asked.

"Not really. I'm still puzzled why they'd choose something so over-the-top for me to wear." I pushed my fingers through my hair, giving it a tug. "I have to remember not to bend over. *At. All.*"

Aunt Fae patted my shoulder. "It's a small price to pay to make the brides happy, wouldn't you agree?"

"That's the goal, right? To make the brides happy."

I went back to my room and got dressed, putting on the silly little dress. Then I did makeup, which for me was a two-minute operation: a stroke of blush on each cheek, a few swipes of mascara, and a whisk of lip tint. That was as much glamour as I could handle, especially while flashing so much leg.

"What happened to the sparkly eye shadow?" Aunt Fae said as I came downstairs for inspection.

I groaned. "Ugh!"

I'd forgotten the hideous glittery gold eye makeup Edith had handed out right when we left the rehearsal dinner. She'd said, "Josie and I saw a photo in a bridal magazine where all the girls were wearing this. It seemed so festive in the pictures. Since all of you ladies will be in slightly different purple dresses, it's the one thing that pulls you all together."

I told Aunt Fae that if looking like a string of Vegas pole dancers was the thing that "pulled us all together" it didn't bode well for the overall theme of the wedding.

"What the brides want, the brides get. You remember that when it's your turn," said Aunt Fae.

I muttered under my breath. "Like that's ever going to happen."

"What's that?"

"Keone's decided to take a new job if they offer it. He'll be flying bigger planes which means more time away. He mentioned it's a step closer to possibly even getting some mainland flights."

"So? You see how many planes take off and land from Kahului? Let alone Honolulu. A hundred families have loved ones either in the cockpit or crewing in the cabin of those aircraft. They make it work. You and Keone will work it out too."

"That's not the biggest problem."

I told her about my ongoing angst about the little girl in the hermit shack. "I just can't shake it."

"I did my best," Aunt Fae said. "I could never replace your dear mother, not to mention your wonderful father, but every day you were with me, I did my level best to give you a loving childhood."

"I know. And you did." I got up and put my arms around her. My battle with touching others didn't extend to Aunt Fae. "I didn't mean it like that. You were the best guardian ever. I'm not talking about you being like Maile's awful foster mom. This has to do with feeling like no matter how much I work at being strong and self-sufficient, there's something out there that's stronger, that could take everything away at any time."

"There is something stronger," she said. "It's called 'love.' Love will always be stronger than pain and loss."

I nodded and broke away, heading for the stairs. "I'm going up to get that gold eyeshadow on now, Aunt Fae."

But my quick departure was so she wouldn't see me swiping away the tears.

AUNT FAE WAS ALREADY SEATED as I was about to clamber up into Sharkey, no small feat wearing the teensy dress, when my phone rang. I took the call, wrestling the phone out of my clutch purse, when I saw it was Elle Beane. "You need to get down here as soon as possible," she said.

"We're not late, are we? Edith said to be there by noon."

"It's not that. There's someone here you need to see."

"Lola?" I'd about had it with her dramatics.

"Just please hurry," said Elle before hanging up.

I hustled Sharkey to Hotel Hana in record time. It was dicey taking the twists and turns and one-lane bridges ignoring the speed limit. Driving to Hana at eleven o'clock on a Sunday morning meant dodging oncoming traffic and not getting stuck behind slow-moving tourists gawking at waterfalls.

We arrived at Hotel Hana and parked near the front in a loading zone. If Elle wanted me to move my car later, I would. But she sounded like whatever was going on justified time-saving measures. "I've got to go see what's wrong," I told Auntie.

"Of course." She flapped a hand. "I'll take my time and bring in our gifts."

Elle was waiting for me just inside the lobby. Her jaw had the resolve of an Army officer about to send her troops into battle.

"What's going on?" I said, trying to smooth the dress further down my thighs.

"Follow me." She speed walked through the lobby. Once outside the courtyard area, we crossed a manicured lawn ringed by hibiscus bushes sculpted into perfect spheres. At the edge of the area, Elle turned toward a duplex bungalow with stairs leading to a roomy porch. The property made me recall one of Aunt Fae's favorite sayings, "*neat as a pin.*" We hurried across the lawn, my size eleven heels punching holes in the turf as I took strides as long as I dared in the skimpy dress.

I started to kick off my shoes as I reached the stairs, when I saw something that made me gasp.

Resting on the welcome mat of the bungalow was a pair of muddy, child size pink rubber slippers.

36

I WAS STANDING FROZEN when Elle caught up with me. I grabbed her arm, a very uncharacteristic move. "What's going on here?"

"Hard to explain. Better to see."

My heart was pounding as we went up onto the pretty porch and Elle knocked lightly on the door. No one answered, so she unlocked it with her passkey. In a friendly voice she sang out, "*Aloha*, hello. We're here to see what you'd like to eat for lunch."

She pushed the door open. I slid my heels off and followed her inside. There was no one visible in the beautifully furnished room.

"*Aloha*," Elle called again. "Come out and we'll bring you something yummy to eat."

My pulse thundered in my ears. I tried to push down my hope for a miracle, but it was there, nonetheless.

After what seemed like hours but was probably more like minutes, a small face with big brown scared eyes peeked out from under the bed. In the way that a combination lock clicks into place with the last number, I recognized the child scooting out from under the bed.

"There you are," said Elle. "I'll bet you'd like to have lunch. How about a grilled cheese sandwich? Chicken fingers? Or some maca-roni salad?"

I'd seen her photo in the file at Child Welfare Services and kept a copy of it in my phone. I'd mourned her death. Yet here she was, somehow, some way. "Hello," I breathed. "I'm so glad to see you."

The little girl I hoped was Maile Ortiz slowly stood and crossed her arms, as if protecting herself. She wore a grimy T-shirt and ripped shorts that had probably been a sunny color at one time but were now a drab pale yellow hidden by mud and grass stains. Her shoulder-length brown hair looked as if there'd been an effort to comb it, but it desperately needed to be shampooed.

Elle tried again. "Are you hungry?"

She cast her eyes down and nodded.

"Would you like to pick something from the menu, or would you like me to pick for you?"

"You pick." The girl said, her voice hoarse as if it hadn't been used in a while. Hearing her brought the reality home for me: she was real. *She was alive!*

I clapped my hands to my cheeks as tears welled in my eyes and coursed down my cheeks.

"Are you sad?" The child glanced at me sideways, hiding behind her dirty hair.

"No, no, I'm not sad. I'm incredibly happy to see you. That's why I'm crying. I thought something bad happened to you, and I've been searching for you. Lots of people have."

She lifted her head and gave a hesitant smile but said nothing.

"Please tell me if your name is Maile Ortiz," I said.

She stared down at her bare feet, tightening her arms across her chest; then, she spun around and dove back under the bed.

"Tell you what," Elle said after a few beats of silence. "You wait right here, and we'll bring you back some lunch. Would you like that?"

No response.

We went outside. I brushed the tears off my cheeks and cleared my throat in an effort to speak. "How did you find her?"

"I didn't. She was brought here this morning by a guy working on the road crew. He said she just walked out of the jungle out by Wai'ānapanapa Park. He said she didn't seem sure where home was, so he brought her here since the road's still closed to Kahului. When I got to work this morning, I couldn't help but wonder if she was the little hermit girl you've been worried about."

"I'm sure she is. Why won't she confirm her name?"

"Good question."

"Did you call Child Welfare Services?"

"The manager of the hotel did when she was dropped off, but they can't get out here because the road is still closed." Elle said she was going to put in an order for a kid's meal while I pulled out my cell and searched through my contacts to make a call.

As the call went through, I said to Elle, "I've got an idea. Could you make it three kids' meals?"

"No problem ordering three kids' meals. I'll make it four, and have one of everything," Elle said, her fingers flying on the menu tablet. "I've got to get back to the wedding."

She took off as my call went through, and I spoke for a few minutes, then went back inside the room. I turned on the water, got it to a comfortable temperature, and showed the girl the sweet-smelling soaps and shampoo in the hospitality basket in the bathroom, holding it down where she could see the toiletries next to the bed.

"I've got some friends your age coming to visit. You want to look nice for them, right?"

The child nodded, clearly wary of taking her clothes off in my presence.

"I'm going to be sitting right out outside if you need me. You can lock the bathroom door." A girl who'd been abused would be grateful for a locked door. It took a while, but I eventually convinced her to take a bath.

Thirty minutes later, a battered truck pulled up at the hotel and Elle called me to come greet the arrivals.

The Nakasone girls got out of the vehicle, accompanied by their dad, Joe. Sandy, who was almost ten, and Windy, aged nine, wore party dresses that were probably secondhand but had been freshly washed. The girls had long black hair which had been pulled into braids. Windy wore an assortment of barrettes, bows, and a sparkly headband. Sandy had opted for a plain black velvet ribbon tied in a bow at the crown of her head.

I went to the driver's side of the truck and talked with their father, Joe Nakasone. "Thanks for getting here so fast. I really appreciate it. I think the girls will be a big help in solving a mystery we have here."

He smiled. "Huh. Seems these girls are always in the middle of your mysteries."

Joe had gone through a tough year after his wife's death, trying to parent two rambunctious girls with the help of his sister, but things were smoothing out. He'd landed a job closer to home, and his grief, although still very much front and center, had eased to a point where he allowed himself to smile now and then.

"Do you mind if I bring them home after the wedding?" I asked. "I think the girls will have fun at the reception. There will be others here for them to play with."

"A day to myself watching football sounds good to me. You said for me to pack three swimsuits and an extra set of Sandy's clothes, and it's all here. I also put in some sunscreen. It's all in that little duffle Sandy's carrying."

"I really appreciate you doing this, Joe. I will make sure all of the clothes get returned in good condition."

He drove off, a smile on his face at the thought of his girls being invited to the wedding reception and having a fun day at the hotel.

I briefed the girls on the situation in a way I hoped would resonate with pre-teens: I told them there was a girl their age who was alone at the hotel. She had no friends and was all by herself;

she had appeared out of the jungle and was probably lost. "It would be really nice if you two would play with her and make her feel welcome."

I told Sandy that I'd asked her dad to bring clothes for the girl because her own clothes were too dirty to wear. "Is it okay for her to wear your clothes for a little while? I'll make sure they get washed and back to you as soon as possible."

Sandy frowned. "My dad put in my very favorite T-shirt."

"I promise she won't do anything to ruin it. And if there's any problem, I'll buy you a new shirt. Cross my heart." I made a little X on my chest.

Sandy scowled but nodded her agreement.

"We'll have lunch first, and then afterwards, maybe you can all go swimming in the pool."

Windy countered with, "What do we get for lunch?"

"I think it's something you'll like. Grilled cheese sandwich maybe, or chicken fingers."

"I love chicken fingers! They're not really fingers, though. Just little pieces of fried chicken. Most of the time they come with dip. Like ranch dressing," Windy said.

"Yes. So, can you two be nice to a lonely girl?"

"We know all about lonely," said Sandy. "We were lonely when our mom died."

"I'm hoping you can make her feel better. Do you want to try?"

The girls glanced at each other and nodded. "What's her name?"

"That's part of the problem we hope you'll help us with. She won't say."

"We can get her to talk," Sandy said confidently.

"Good. Then let's go meet her."

Elle had arranged for room service to bring the meals to the bungalow, and the timing was perfect as the Nakasone girls and I followed the server up the steps.

I tapped on the door. "Lunch is here. Along with some friends for you to meet."

We went inside. The child came out from the bathroom, where she was engulfed in one of the hotel's adult-size robes. Her hair and skin were clean, but her arms were still wrapped around herself protectively as I introduced the girls. I waited for her to introduce herself, but all she said was, "Hi."

The server set down a large tray covered with dishes. Windy took the metal lid off one and explained about chicken fingers. Soon the three girls got to work making the food disappear.

I left them to it and went out onto the porch. The fewer adults in the middle of this delicate bonding situation, the better.

Seated in a rattan chair outside the room, I called Lei on her cell. She didn't answer, so I left a message. "Sorry to bother you on a Sunday, Lei, but I have some possible new information about Maile Ortiz, the missing foster child. I don't have an ironclad ID at this point, but I'm hoping we've found her. She's clean and appears healthy. Call me."

A few minutes later, the Nakasone sisters' aunt Lani, a waitstaff at the hotel, arrived in her slim fitting uniform dress with a plumeria behind her ear. "The manager has asked me to keep an eye on the girls, since you have wedding duties," she said.

"Great!" I explained that I was giving the girls some private time to bond.

Lani smiled; she was a real knockout when she did so. It gave me a pang to remember that she and Keone had dated before I arrived in Ohia. *Would he go back to her?*

"I totally get it. And I'm happy to put my feet up out here and still be on the clock." She pulled a woven rattan ottoman out from under one of the porch chairs and did so. "Just tell them I'm here if they need anything."

I stuck my head inside the room. The girls were done eating and had turned on the TV. The three of them were watching something from the big king-size bed. "Sandy, Windy. Your aunt Lani is out here on the porch if you need anything. I have to go take care of the guest book for the wedding."

"All good here," Sandy said. Windy nodded. The girl gave a tentative smile that warmed my heart.

I shut the door gently, waved to Lani who was scrolling on her phone, and set off back to the main lobby.

It felt like I was walking on a trampoline; my spirits had been so lifted by the lost child turning up. Yes, things were still sketchy with Keone, but smiling at the guests was going to be so much easier now that I knew the girl in the window was alive.

37

ELLE HANDED me a pretty box containing a red fascinator to wear at a jaunty angle on the side of my head. "From Edith," she said with a smile. The thing resembled a tiny doll's hat, wreathed in folds of shiny red tulle finished with red glitter. In my micro dress and itty-bitty, quirky hat, I imagined Alice in Wonderland after she drank the potion that made her grow to gigantic proportions.

I was first to greet guests for the ceremony, waving a plume-decorated pen toward the guest book. With the constant stream of arrivals, it seemed as if all of Ohia had been invited to the wedding. The Red Hat Society ladies who were my fellow bridesmaids showed up, each gowned in purple topped by a red *chapeau*, ranging from Clara's cloche to Pearl's geisha-like headpiece of red feathers and a fan decorated with tiny white orchids. Edith and Josie had stayed the night at the hotel so I wouldn't be seeing them until the ceremony, but I had no doubt they would be dressed in memorable outfits as well.

The lobby became a hubbub of noise and laughter. I managed to get most of the wedding goers to sign the guest book.

But only fifteen minutes before the ceremony was to begin, Keone had still not shown up.

My concern was amplified when Pono, Keone's cousin and Lei's partner at Maui Police Department, walked in wearing a crisp aloha shirt and freshly pressed chinos. Lei soon followed; she wore her usual black jeans with a polo shirt and her badge on her belt.

"The road must be open! Are you here on official business?" I waggled the plumy pen. "Or wedding business?"

"Both," Pono said. "My cuz can't make it, so I'm taking his place walking you in."

"And I'm here to see about the missing girl," said Lei. "Where is she?"

At that point, my emotions didn't know which way to go. *Keone wasn't attending the wedding and had sent his married cousin to walk me down the aisle!*

AND: *I'd found the girl who'd haunted my dreams for the past two weeks and now I could share that excitement with my favorite detective!*

I decided to lean into the joy and save the tears for later.

I laid the feathered pen in the open guest book and angled it so anyone else entering would be able to sign it. "Come with me," I told the detectives. "The girl's in a bungalow here on the property. I'm pretty sure it's Maile Ortiz, but for whatever reason she won't tell us her name."

We crossed the immaculate lawn toward the bungalow with Lei throwing questions at me with every step.

"How did she come to be here? Have you ascertained her state of mind? How much has she told you about the circumstances surrounding her abduction? And where has she been for the past couple of weeks?"

I didn't have many answers but I shared the little I knew. "I invited some girls her age over to help her feel more comfortable."

"I'll let you ladies handle this, then," Pono said. "Too many cooks in the kitchen with a matter like this." He turned and was soon accompanied by Lani as she hurried back to work.

I tapped on the door. Sandy answered it, her hand on her hip. "We're done with lunch and TV. Can we go to the pool now?"

"We'll see. I want to introduce you to my friend, Detective Lei. She's here to talk to . . ." I faltered over whether to address the girl as "Maile" since we hadn't yet actually established that was her name.

Lei gazed at the girl sitting on the bed in Sandy's clean clothes. She pressed her lips into a restrained smile, but her eyes were wide and bright. If I was reading it right, she was nearly as overcome with emotion at seeing the child alive as I had been; but she managed to maintain her professional demeanor better than I had.

"Her name's 'Maile,'" Windy informed us from where she sat on the bed beside the girl. "She wants us to call her that even though her dad called her something else."

Whoa.

Her dad? Who could that be?

I leaned into Lei and whispered. "Mind if I stay for this part?"

"Wouldn't have it any other way. In fact, I should have another adult present for this interview. How about we 'talk story' with her for a few minutes and see what she will tell us?"

For the next ten minutes Maile Ortiz provided us with a limited, but completely believable, account of her kidnapping. She had been shopping at the Kahului Goodwill store in late December. A bearded man saw her with Barbara Long, and when Maile went over to the toy section by herself, Hugh Dragoon came over and asked her if that was her foster mom.

She didn't answer him because her mom had always told her she shouldn't talk to strangers.

Dragoon told her it was okay for her to talk to him because he wasn't really a stranger—he was a friend of her real mom. He said her real mom had asked him to find her daughter because she needed his help in taking her home.

Maile had asked him, "You know my mom? Is she out of jail now?"

The man said she was, but her car wasn't working so she couldn't come and get Maile. "What he said made sense, because a lot of the time my mom's car didn't work. I was real happy when he said he was there to take me to my mom. Mrs. Long was mean to us a lot of the time. One time I made a mistake and called her 'auntie' and she made me go to the time-out shed."

Once she arrived at the hermit shack in Ohia she realized he'd lied, but according to Maile, he treated her well.

"He made us food and lots of it. We played games like 'Clue' and he taught me how to play poker. He called me 'Jennifer' or 'Jenny.' I told him that wasn't my name, but he said it was my new name because I was his daughter now."

"Were you scared living out there?" I asked.

She shrugged, her eyes down. "He didn't want me to go to school, and I didn't get to play with other kids or anything, but he was nice to me. He finally told me that my mom was still in jail. He said she'd probably be there for a long time."

She seemed oddly accepting of her fate. It sounded like Maile had been at the whim of capricious adults for her entire life. Her birth father abandoned her; her mother was an on-again, off-again druggie who fed her habit by dealing meth and doing sex work; and the temporary foster mother she'd lived with was a selfish, harsh woman who took in children because it paid the bills. For Maile, the shack where the man lived was no better or worse than any other home she'd lived in.

"After a while, my new dad told me he'd been a soldier in 'I-rack' and while he was gone, his daughter died. Her name was Jennifer Ann. He said I was about her same age and I looked like her."

I pressed, "You said your 'new dad.' Do you know what his name is?"

I knew it must've sounded odd to Lei that I'd used present tense when talking about the hermit who'd blown himself up. But I felt the little girl didn't need to deal with any more trauma at this point.

"No. He told me to call him 'Dad.' So I did."

"Okay."

The wedding ceremony was about to begin, and I had to leave. "Do you girls want to come to the wedding with me, or stay here?"

They sang out in unison. "We want to go to the pool!"

Lei agreed to accompany them to the pool. The girls raced into the bathroom to put on the swimsuits that Joe Nakasone had brought with the girls. Lei said she'd let them play for a while and then she'd take Maile down to the Kahului police station to get a recorded statement.

I had an idea. "Why don't you wait until after the ceremony and I'll see if Edith will agree to step in as her legal guardian? You could get the statement done here, instead of subjecting her to a trip to the station. I doubt she's keen on police after watching her mom get arrested and taken away." Edith was a practicing attorney and, even though it was her wedding day, I was certain she'd agree to helping out a little girl.

I hurried back to the lobby and was just in time to be escorted into the chapel on Pono's arm, holding a small bouquet of Edith and Josie's favorite blooms: tiny white dendrobium orchids and pikake flowers.

The ceremony was, as we'd rehearsed, a brief but beautiful event. Edith wore a flattering fitted gown in lavender with a red hat with a veil; glittering shoes peeked out from beneath the hem. Josie wore a flowing *muumuu* printed with violet and red hibiscus and trimmed at the neckline in velvet. Her veil trailed from the edge of a dyed red *lauhala* hat.

It seemed like the whole town was packed into the celebration room to watch them take their vows, which were followed by Artie's ukulele rendition of "Somewhere Over the Rainbow." Then we marched back out.

I walked with Pono since Keone still hadn't shown up.

"What happened to him?" I asked.

"I think it had something to do with work. He said he was at the airport, and he'd get here as fast as he could, but I don't see him." Pono glanced around the grounds as we made our way to the reception area. "Not like Keone to blow off an *'ohana* event like this." Pono raised a thick black brow, glancing pointedly at my dress. "By the way, has he seen you in *that*?"

I smoothed down the skimpy skirt; my black boy shorts were peeking from beneath the abbreviated hemline again. "No, he hasn't."

Pono grinned. "He's gonna be mad that he missed it."

I peeled away from the crowd, hoping to reconnect with Lei and the girls. The trio of girls were in the pool playing Marco Polo. Luckily, there were no other guests in the pool area. Lei was on her phone as I approached. I waited to speak until she ended the call. "How's it going?"

"Fine. Maile's still not saying much about how she got here to the Hotel Hana, but I'm hoping the girls are making her more comfortable about opening up. Great idea bringing them in on this."

"Are you ready to take her statement?"

"Yeah," she said. "I'm going to start by asking where she's been recently. Don't forget, I'm conducting an ongoing home invasion and attempted murder investigation into what happened to Barbara Long."

"True. But you don't think she had anything to do with what happened to her foster mom, do you?"

"That's what I need to find out."

That sounded ominous.

I glanced at the pool. The three girls were laughing and splashing, an idyllic scene. For once, all three kids, who'd been through so much, were acting like the children they were.

Could Maile have been involved with what happened to Barbara Long? My stomach tightened at the unwelcome thought.

38

As I was leaving the pool area, I heard Lei call out to the girls, "Five more minutes, and then we need to go back to the room."

They groaned, but it didn't sound heartfelt. Even Marco Polo had its limits.

The reception was well underway when I returned. The brides were seated at a head table receiving guests as the crowd passed by on their way to the buffet. I took a spot at the rear of the line and was relieved when no one followed after me.

"Edith, I'm so happy for you and Josie," I told my friend. "You both look beautiful."

"And so do you, dear. That dress is a little short, though." She put her glasses on and chuckled. "You're pulling it off just fine!"

I snorted. "I was wondering what got into you, ordering it for me!"

"Speed, my dear. We ripped through the catalog picking items and told Elle to grab them at the store. Anyway, it was our trip to Honolulu last year that started this whole thing. You saved my life, and I started thinking about my future. I had that little heart event, and you saved me again. If there's anything I can ever do for you, please don't hesitate to ask."

"Funny you should say that." I filled her in on the Maile Ortiz situation. "Would it be too pushy to ask for your help on your wedding day?"

Josie had overheard this. She piped up, "Absolutely not. Edith will help. Right, dear?"

"Of course. What a blessing on our special day!"

"That would be the best wedding gift of all," Josie chimed in.

Shortly thereafter, Edith and I made our way to the bungalow. The three girls were sitting on the bed, each wrapped in a huge striped beach towel. Sandy and Windy had taken up a spot on either side of a stricken-faced Maile, who was refusing to answer any of Lei's questions.

Edith removed her veiled hat and bustled forward; she was the white-haired grandma anyone might wish for—twinkly-eyed and kind. "Hello, Maile. My name is Edith Pepperwhite. I'm not a foster parent; I'm an attorney. It's my job to help you answer the questions Lei asks you. So, if you get worried, or confused, or you just don't know what to say, look over at me and we'll work it out together. Does that sound good?"

Maile's knitted eyebrows broadcast her doubts about whether Edith was friend or foe. However, when Lei announced that Sandy and Windy would have to leave, the tiny lawyer piped up, "I think that's something we should ask Maile. Do you want your friends to stay or go?"

Maile reached out and grasped the two girls' hands. "We're staying," said Windy. "And that's final."

Lei brought out her phone and turned on the audio app. She announced the date, time, and people present.

Over the next half hour Maile added to the information she'd offered earlier. She said her "dad" had become agitated after someone had come to their house the day he'd butchered a wild pig. That afternoon he drove her out to Wai'ānapanapa Park.

"He gave me some cooked meat and bread in a backpack. He told me that he loved me and wanted me to be happy, but I couldn't stay with him anymore. Then he drove away. I was real sad when he left."

"What did you do that night?" Lei asked.

"I hid. I thought I might be in trouble from Mrs. Long. It started to get dark. I found a place to sleep inside a cave. There was a pretty beach and it stayed warm in there all night. Dad had given me a sleeping bag so I was okay."

"How about the days after that?"

"Every day tourists came and I'd hide. When they'd leave, I'd go through their garbage. They always threw away lots of good food and stuff. I even found a blow-up beach floatie that I could use for a bed."

I shuddered at the thought of this sweet girl dumpster diving, but she was resourceful and resilient. She'd done what she had to do to survive.

"Your 'dad' never came back?"

"No. I think he knew I wasn't really his daughter and that he'd get in trouble for having me at his house and pretending I was his kid."

"How did you get to where we are now, the Hotel Hana?"

"After some good days at the park, it started raining. A lot. People stopped coming. There was no food and it got really cold and wet at night. When I got really hungry, I went out to the road and asked a man working there if he'd give me a ride home."

"Where is home?" Lei asked in a low voice.

Maile teared up and hung her head. "I don't know. I wanted to go to Dad's house, but I didn't know where it was. And I didn't want to get him in trouble. I couldn't tell the man where to take me."

"So, he brought you here?"

"Yes." By now Maile was crying. Her thin body shook with emotion. The girls scooted closer to their new friend and Sandy put her arm around Maile's shoulders.

Edith said, "I think that's enough for now."

Lei picked up her phone and tapped it, shutting off the

recording and ending the interview. "Thank you, Maile," she said. "You've been very helpful, and I appreciate you answering my questions. I'll be in touch if I need to talk with you more."

"Can I go back to Dad's house now? Please don't make me go back to Mrs. Long's place."

The adults in the room shared a glance. No one wanted to disclose that both of her former guardians were dead or nearly so at this particular moment; the girl had been through so much.

"Tell you what," I said. "Why don't you three go with Ms. Pepperwhite and get some wedding cake? Would you mind taking them with you to the reception, Ms. Pepperwhite?"

"It would be my pleasure. We have cake and *haupia* pudding and all kinds of other yummy things. Do you girls have something to wear besides your bathing suits?"

The Nakasone girls bounced off the bed. "Yes! We have party dresses."

Maile stayed on the bed. Once again, she crossed her arms as if trying to make herself as small as possible. "I don't have a party dress," she murmured. "Or any dress."

I stood. "Yes, you do. You can wear mine. See how short it is? It'll be a little long on you, but it will still look great. Give me a minute to make a phone call." I phoned Elle. "How's the reception going?"

"Like clockwork, except a bride is missing."

"She's with me. Can I ask a favor?"

"Sure."

I asked her to grab one of the colorful *pareos,* or tropical shawls, they sold in the gift shop. I'd pay for it before I left. I inquired if the hotel had any sewing kits.

"You mean like to fix a button or something?"

"Yes."

"I have a 'bridal emergency basket.' It's got everything. I'll bring it along. What's this for, Kat?"

I explained we were improvising the lack of a party dress for Maile.

"Got it. I'll be there in a flash. Oh, and the *pareo* is on the house. Your money's no good at the Hotel Hana."

Elle soon brought a cerulean blue *pareo* decorated with batik white seashells and swirls of fuchsia. She helped wrap it around me and tied it behind my neck so that it resembled a dress.

"Ta-da!" said Elle. "You look like you just stepped out of a Paul Gauguin painting."

Maile slipped into my silk gown. It hung too low on her chest, so Elle folded the shoulders over and used safety pins from the sewing kit to secure them.

"You're very handy with those pins," I said. "I can't see them at all."

She laughed. "Working with brides requires a plethora of unique skills."

"Check the mirror, Maile. You look very pretty," I told the girl.

The dress came nearly to her calves and was too generous around the middle, but the gorgeous fabric more than made up for the plain style. Windy took a couple of hair bows and offered them to Maile to complete her look.

After hugs of encouragement, the girls took off with Edith and Elle to find cake. Lei told me she had to go to the station to file her report and paperwork. "I'm calling Candace at CWS about Maile," Lei told me. "She will be so glad to hear the girl's okay."

"Perfect," I said. "I'm sure she'll take good care of Maile. As to where she should go tonight—maybe she can spend the night with the Nakasones. I can call their father and ask."

"Make it so," Lei said, and I laughed at the Star Trek quote.

I sat on the front porch chair. First, I called Joe, and he was fine with an extra kid for the night. Then I made a call to Doug Beachum, the UPS driver who'd first spotted the girl in the window.

"Hey, Doug," I said when his voicemail picked up. "Kat Smith here. I have some good news about the girl you saw in the hermit's window. She's been found alive and well. Thought you'd want to know."

Then I called Keone.

His phone also went to voicemail.

Our relationship had hit a rough patch, but I hoped it wasn't over yet. Was I wrong? Only one way to find out.

I left him a one-word message. "Banana?"

39

THE RECEPTION WAS WINDING down and most of the guests had gone home. I made one more round with the guest book and the plumy pen.

Aunt Fae had caught a ride with Red Hat friend Rita back to Ohia, and both had been overjoyed to hear about Maile's discovery. I wanted to stay until the end in case Keone showed up.

Suddenly my cell chimed. *Keone?* I dug around in my clutch and was disappointed when I saw it was just the landline number from our house in New Ohia. "Hey Auntie," I said. "Want an extra piece of cake or something?"

"Katherine, you are needed here at the house," Aunt Fae said.

Aunt Fae only called me by my full given name when I was in trouble. "What's going on? Is it Tiki? Is she okay?"

"I don't give a diddly damn about that silly cat of yours," she said. My hand froze holding the phone; my eyes widened in shock at her words as Auntie went on. "I need you to get *back* here. You hear me? *Back*. Now."

The line went dead. I had a feeling she wasn't alone because Aunt Fae never swore; she never even got close to it.

I told Elle that Aunt Fae was having a problem. I asked her if she'd make sure Maile and the Nakasone girls got home safely. Then I ran out to Sharkey, hopped in, and drove home like a ticking time bomb had hit the one-minute mark.

Something was very wrong.

I recalled Aunt Fae's message. "Get *back* here. Now." She'd emphasized the word, "back." It might mean nothing. But then again, it might mean she wanted me to come in around the "back" of the house.

As I whizzed past the development's fancy clubhouse, I noticed a mud-splattered vehicle parked outside. The clubhouse was closed on Sundays, and I was sure we'd locked it up tight when we'd done our caretaker duties yesterday afternoon. Why would a vehicle be parked there? Possibly so they could approach a house on foot...

I slowed as I approached our driveway, then parked halfway up. Because our house was on a slight rise, the white SUV would be out of sight from anyone peering outside.

I got out and edged up the driveway, sticking to where bushes hid my advance and provided cover. I wished I'd had my weapon, but it wasn't good manners to attend a wedding armed, so I'd left it safely tucked in my nightstand.

When I got within sight of the house, I spotted Tiki outside, scowling and licking her front paw in the driveway as if sharpening her claws.

What in the world was going on in there?

I crept around the house, staying on the south side which had fewer windows, and creeping along below the sight line. I had to tamp down a grim feeling of *déjà vu* as I recalled sneaking around the hermit's shack using the same tactic.

I reached the rear patio and slowly edged forward so I'd be able to peek inside. Nothing out of the ordinary was visible. I had my key out so I could unlock the slider. The kitty door insert had been pulled away and the door latch was in the "up" position, meaning it was already unlocked.

I slowed my breathing and narrowed my concentration, slipping out of my heels so I could move faster as I approached.

Whatever I did next was crucial. Aunt Fae was in trouble, and I was probably within fifty feet of her . . . *just as I'd been with Maile Ortiz, when I'd gone out to the hermit's shack that fateful day.* I listened at the door and heard scraping sounds coming from somewhere inside. I carefully pulled open the slider. An armed assailant might be aiming a weapon at me from inside, but when I'd backed off under similar circumstances, I'd been plagued by sleepless nights and an avalanche of regret.

Not this time.

I sprinted through the living room on light feet and heard muffled sounds coming from the kitchen area. I peered around the wall into that room and sucked in an involuntary gasp at what I saw.

40

AUNT FAE WAS TIED to a chair with bungee cords on her ankles and wrists. A dishtowel had been stuffed in her mouth, and a man was in the act of duct-taping it into place.

The gasp I'd given brought his gaze around to lock with mine. He was familiar, and not in a good way.

"How do you like it now?" he said. "Someone comin' to your home and messin' with your family?"

I said nothing.

"'Cuz of the likes of you, I had to give up my daughter. Twice. First, she gets messed up while I was in Iraq and I couldn't do nuthin' about it. Then I find her again and you show up and I know they'll take her away."

Hugh Dragoon was clearly unbalanced. I had to assess how armed he was; I couldn't see a weapon from my angle, but Auntie kept darting her widened eyes to the left. She was trying to signal me about something.

"You're all so stupid. I been watching you for a while now. Even came inside here. Found this here gun, but you didn't do nothing about it."

He lifted his arm with a grin that revealed bad teeth.

Now I saw the gun.

My gun.

"Oh, crud on a crouton," I whispered. There was always one round in the chamber, even if he hadn't found the extra ammo.

Aunt Fae stared at me, terrified. I locked eyes with her and jerked my head to the right, hoping she got the message. Then I leaped out from behind the wall, lunging at Dragoon with an earsplitting yell designed to throw off his focus.

Aunt Fae used her feet to shove her chair; it crashed to the floor, hopefully taking her out of the line of fire. I had one objective: the big hairy hand holding the weapon.

I body-slammed into Dragoon, catching his gun hand in both of mine and knocking it high. He seemed to stutter-step backward, still holding the weapon, then spun and sprinted for the front door.

I squatted beside Auntie and pulled the partially secured towel out of her mouth. "Are you injured?"

"No," she croaked, and ran her tongue around her lips in an effort to moisten them. "Don't let him get away. But be careful, remember he's got your gun."

Like I could forget! Dragoon was right. I'd been stupid not to lock it up after I noticed it had been moved after he broke in.

Dragoon had left the front door open in his getaway. I bolted after him. It felt good to stretch my legs to run as I pursued the target, even though the *pareo* flapped open and the rough driveway scraped my bare feet as if I was getting an overexuberant pedicure. The suspect had made it to the bend in the driveway so I couldn't see him, but I heard a distinctive yowl and then, a human cry of pain.

Tiki!

I made it over the rise in time to see my raccoon-sized mama cat clinging to the man's upper back like a bronc rider. She'd latched on, her one ear pinned back, her body's thick fur all a-bristle. All four of her feet were dug into Dragoon's flannel shirt as she sank her formidable claws into him. Her kinked tail was extended, stiff with rage, as she attempted to bite the back of his neck.

Dragoon yelled, windmilling his arms to dislodge her, and then spotted me. He fired a shot that whizzed by my left ear with surprising accuracy.

This guy obviously knew his way around a Glock. My *laulau* was thoroughly baked if he'd found the magazine that gave him fifteen more rounds.

Dragoon fired again.

This time, the weapon made an empty "*click.*" He hadn't found the ammo!

Dragoon tossed the gun and grabbed for the door handle of the SUV. Tiki took the opportunity to sink her teeth into his neck. He howled and reached around, trying to swat her away. I seized the moment to lift my *pareo* off and toss it over his head, enveloping him in a mass of bright blue fabric.

In the tangle of cloth and pissed-off cat, Dragoon tripped. On his way down, his head struck Sharkey's side with a hollow metallic *thump*, followed by a *thud* as he hit the asphalt.

His prone body lay still, the printed batik seashells on the *pareo* settling over him like a deflating parachute.

Tiki crawled out from under the fabric, hissing her displeasure with the entire situation. She streaked off into the bushes.

I stared down at the man, waiting to see if he moved. In my eagerness to apprehend Dragoon, I might have killed him.

Aunt Fae trotted to where I was standing, carrying her favorite weapon—the cast iron skillet. She dropped it beside the useless gun and glared at the man in the road. "Hope he's dead," she said.

I prodded the inert body at my feet with a bare toe. "He might be."

"So? He tied me up to use as a hostage. He wanted to kill you."

I had a lot of questions. I started with the first one. "How did you get free?"

"*Pfft*. Those bungee cords? Pathetic excuse for restraints. They stretch, you know."

At that moment, a loud jacked up purple truck roared up to join us—Pono's ride, Stanley. Right behind was Keone's green vehicle of similar make and model.

Pono jumped out of the driver's seat with a grin. "Now, here's a sight you don't see every day."

I glanced down—my lacy black bra and boy shorts were barely decent. "I needed to restrain the perp." I pointed to the discarded *pareo* covering the fallen man.

"Kat saved me from the hermit bomber!" Aunt Fae exclaimed. "He took me prisoner and tried to kill her."

Keone had slipped out of his truck. He carried one of his large beach towels. He draped it around me, covering me up.

"Oh, that's nice," I murmured into the warm terry cloth as Keone's arms tightened around me. Being wrapped up like this in his arms and towel felt so good. "Thanks."

"I don't call you 'Trouble,' for nothing," he whispered into my ear. "Are you okay?"

"Better than okay." I was beginning to shiver, though, with the aftereffects of adrenaline.

Pono squatted beside the immobile suspect and lifted the *pareo* from his face. He pressed two fingers against the man's neck.

"There's a pulse and he's breathing," he declared. "He's alive." He took out his phone and punched in 911, giving his badge number and calling for assistance.

I gazed down at Dragoon's pallid face. The good news was that there was no blood or other evidence of a skull fracture. The bad news was that the man was out cold and head wounds could be fatal without making a mess.

Now that the danger was over, I took a minute to examine the prone man at my feet. I squatted to lift the man's T-shirt away at the neckline, exposing wounds from Tiki's teeth that were definitely going to call for a tetanus shot.

There was a tattoo on the man's neck, a smudged blue diamond outlining the initials, "JAD." *Jennifer Ann Dragoon.*

I wished I could feel sorry for the man who'd experienced so much heartbreak, but I didn't. He'd passed it on to others in the worst ways.

41

LEI SHOWED up at the same time as the paramedics. "I was getting ready to drive back to Kahului when the call came in from Pono," she said.

The ambulance staff worked on Hugh Dragoon, then took him away with a whirl of lights as Pono and Lei conferred. She then bagged my gun, but after taking a photo of the skillet and weapon 'in situ,' allowed me to return the frying pan to the house "since it wasn't used."

Keone helped Auntie back to the living room; she was feeling the repercussions of extreme stress and had "gone wobbly on her pins" and asked to lie down. He and Pono settled her on the living room couch with a pillow behind her head; I smiled to see how much she was enjoying their attention and fussing.

I returned the skillet to the rack above the stove and put the kettle on for tea as Lei photographed the tipped-over chair and bungee cords in the dining area.

Lei returned to the living room and sat on the ottoman, facing Aunt Fae. "Are you up for giving us your statement?"

"Definitely. Soon as I have a cup of tea."

"Coming right up. Anyone else?" I asked.

Soon we were all noshing on banana bread and sipping from mugs. Once she'd had a few restorative sips, Aunt Fae filled us in on what happened when she'd come in the house and found the intruder.

"When I arrived after the wedding, Tiki was on the stoop, all agitated, and I heard noises coming from upstairs. The perp was in Kat's room," she said. "Going through her stuff. Like a ninny I confronted him before calling the police. If I had it to do over again, you can bet I'd have stayed outside and held my horses until help was on the way."

"Did he say why he'd come here?"

"The man was delusional. He seemed to think Kat had taken his daughter from him. He kept saying, "She took my family, so I'm taking hers." I wasn't very happy when he trussed me up like that, but I like to think he wasn't going to kill me. Seemed he was more intent on getting back at you, Kat."

"Was it his idea or yours to call me?" I asked.

"His. The man kept yammering on about needing to talk to you. He made me call you. Of course, I didn't want to, because I was afraid he'd do what he said he would—shoot you. But I thought if I was able to tip you off, at least you'd know something wasn't right. That's why I said what I did. I hope you'll forgive me for the bad language."

I got up and gave her a quick shoulder hug. "It was brilliant. I knew something was wrong and was able to sneak in the 'back' just as you warned me to."

I took over giving my statement of events. "This is good," Lei said at last, shutting off her recording app. "We're getting a clearer picture of Hugh Dragoon's activities and motivations since he staged his and Maile's deaths." She stood up. "Pono, let's get on the road. We still have a couple of hours of driving to go before we can call it a day."

Keone and I walked the detectives to the door and saw them off.

We turned to face each other, alone at last.

I tightened the towel around myself; I was reluctant to let it go for some reason. "Thanks again for this, Keone," I said. "I must've been in shock. I didn't even notice I was standing out in public nearly naked."

"Banana?"

"I thought I was the one who invoked our 'safe word.'"

He smiled. "Let's get your auntie settled upstairs, then we can talk."

"I can get myself to bed just fine, thank you very much," Auntie hollered from the living room. "But we need a real dinner first, and I want to kick that off with something stronger than tea."

The three of us ended up eating Auntie's special recipe beef stew, reheated, and having a generous glass of red wine apiece.

Keone lent Aunt Fae an arm to get upstairs after dinner; she claimed the wine had gone to her head. I followed them up.

Misty was already sitting on Auntie's bed with Tiki, who had slipped inside at some point. The cats seemed to know which of us might be in need of comfort, and tonight they had elected to stay with Aunt Fae.

I pointed at Tiki. "That's the real heroine of the hour," I told Auntie and Keone. "She almost took the perp down all by herself."

"Good Tiki. Beautiful Tiki," Auntie cooed. "You're our guardian angel." Tiki stuck out a hind leg and licked her nether regions, clearly in agreement with the praise.

I hopped in the shower, then changed into my striped flannel pajamas. I would send Keone a message that I wasn't up for getting busy in any form.

Keone grinned when he saw my outfit. "Where's Jessica Rabbit tonight?"

"We've got a few things to work out before she can come out to play," I said primly. "How about another glass of wine?"

We refilled and took seats on a pair of lounge chairs on the back patio just outside the sliding glass door. I didn't want to chance Aunt Fae listening in.

"Okay. Now. Where were you during the wedding?" I asked.

"It's a wild story."

"Sounds intriguing. We've got time." I stretched out my legs and crossed them at the ankle, taking a sip of my wine.

He leaned in. "First things first. How are you doing, really? That had to be crazy, having that guy shoot at you like that."

"I'm fine. Better than ever, actually, now that we know Maile's alive and we have some answers. Of course, I should've realized when my weapon was moved that night after the Red Hat get-together, that I needed to get a gun safe." I told him about finding Maile at the hotel and the events at the wedding. He listened as I fought back tears of joy and relief.

"Did it ever occur to you when Maile turned up alive that since the hermit spared her, he might not have killed himself either?" Keone cocked his head. His eyes were soft with concern in the low light.

"No. I had no idea he was the one doing weird things." I shivered. "Like pushing me outside the K & K office. He was probably the one to leave Barbara Long's braid on the steps and lock her in the shed. Now that was twisted." I took a sip of wine. "Your turn. Want to tell me why you missed the wedding?"

"I feel bad about that, especially when Pono told me about that dress you had on. But then, I got to see you minus the dress, so . . ." He smiled.

I waited. He still hadn't answered my question.

He set his glass down on the side table and turned to face me. "I had some excitement of my own this morning. I went to my mom's place before heading out for the wedding, and I found her passed out on the kitchen floor."

"Like, unconscious?" My voice squeaked like a fifteen-year-old boy who'd been given a wedgie. My mind flashed to discovering Artie collapsed in much the same way.

"Yes. Out cold. I panicked. Instead of calling for help, I picked her up myself and drove bat-out-of-hell style back to the airport. I commandeered the plane I'd just come in on and flew her to Kahu-lui. An ambulance met the plane and took us straight to Maui Memorial."

"What? Oh no! Is she okay?"

He shook his head. "I wasn't thinking straight, but it turns out what I did might've saved her life. Mom's had a stroke, and they got the bleeding stopped and stabilized her at the hospital much faster than anyone could've out here."

I set down my wineglass so hard its contents splashed onto the glass tabletop. "Why didn't you call me? Or at least text me. Remember how angry you were when I forgot to call you when I was in trouble a few months ago?"

"Slipper's on the other foot now, isn't it?" He shook his head. "I'm sorry. I was too distracted at first, then I wanted to get back here to see you in person after I got your 'banana' message."

"How's Ilima doing?"

"She's going to be okay. Eventually. She's lost mobility on the left side of her body, but she was conscious when I left. Lots of family are with her, keeping her company. The doctor says she should make a full recovery in time, with a lot of physical and other therapies."

"Poor Ilima. I'm so sorry. Pono told me that missing the wedding had something to do with your job."

"Yeah, well. About that." Mr. K picked up his glass and took a hearty swig. "Pacific Wings isn't pleased about me grabbing a plane of theirs for my emergency. I told the passengers who were booked on the outbound Kahului flight that they'd have to wait for the next one. I didn't have time to fool around with getting them boarded and dealing with their luggage. I may be facing criminal charges. Stealing an aircraft is a felony called 'aircraft hijacking.'"

"Yikes! No promotion, then?"

"Out of the question. I'm just hoping they won't charge me. I'll be lucky to keep the job at all."

A long, glum moment went by. We sat there, gazing into the

night. Light spilled from the windows and illuminated waving palm fronds in the backyard. Somewhere out in the tropical darkness, a frog *burrumphed*. I smelled Aunt Fae's gardenia blooming in its pot beside the slider and inhaled deeply.

"Would it be mean of me to smile that you're not leaving?" I said at last.

"Very mean."

I covered the lower half of my face with my hands. "Then I won't let you see it."

He leaned over. We kissed, a tentative connection that strengthened until I was in his arms on one of the loungers.

"These flannel pjs are sexy," he muttered, fiddling with the button at my throat. "They make me have to remember you this evening in just your bra and panties."

"Nice reframe."

"I better get home. I've got to face the music from my employer tomorrow morning, and I don't think it's gonna be a tune I want to hear."

"I really am sorry about your mom," I said.

I escorted him to the door, where Keone lingered for a moment. "Now that the little girl has been found, are you ready to begin thinking about *us*?"

"I've thought about *us* and concluded I've got some 'me' work to do."

"Sounds fair. Are you planning to call that psychologist whose name Sophie gave you?"

"I am. And hopefully, you won't be in jail while I'm doing therapy." I kissed Keone once more, and then closed the door gently but firmly behind him.

42

ELLE SHOWED up at our door early on Monday morning. "Seven a.m.?" I yawned, straightening my pin-striped pajamas. "What's the emergency?"

"That was quite the weekend, wasn't it?" she said. "Want to go for a run and get rid of some of the bad juju from all the drama?"

I'd healed up almost completely from my rib injury, so I was eager to show Elle I wasn't the weakling she'd encountered on our previous run, even though wine the night before as well as pursuing a perp barefoot had left me a little worse for wear. "Sounds good."

I changed and met her in the driveway a few minutes later. We ran hard and fast for almost ten minutes without saying anything. My head began to clear, and my body remembered it used to like running and began to loosen up.

Elle slowed at last. "You remember me mentioning my 'water thing?' Well, here's the story on that. When I was about four, I fell into the deep end of a swimming pool and nearly drowned. My brother, Navy, ran and got my mom. My family thinks it's funny that Navy saved his sister from a watery death. But since then, I've been terrified of water. I don't swim. Don't go out in boats. Don't even like to take baths. If it were up to me, I'd rather roll around in sand to get clean than take a shower. I'm like a chicken."

"Wow. I'm sorry. That must've caused some hassles now and again."

"It has, but like you, I figured out ways to hide it. So. Tell me about how you became uncomfortable with being touched."

I gave her a condensed version of my parents' fatal accident and the trauma of being ripped from the wreckage hours later.

"That's tough. But your Aunt Fae's been there for you ever since?"

We slowed to a walk, and I tried to hide my effort to catch my breath. "Yes. But I still struggle with getting closure on losing both of my parents at such a young age."

"I learned something when everything went sideways for me out at Schofield," Elle said. "Sometimes closure isn't the answer. Acceptance is."

I liked that. I didn't know how it might change my perspective, but it was a start. When we got home, I called Dr. Kinoshita, the psychologist Sophie had recommended.

That was also a start.

I took a shower and went to work wearing my personally created uniform of dark pants and mostly-clean white polo shirt. I was about to go in the back door, when Pua came hustling over from Artie and Opal's with two coffees in hand.

"I got you Elixir of Life," she said. "Figured you'd need one after yesterday. Wanted to save you the trip."

Pua looked like she'd stepped from a page of Hawaii Vogue. Okay, there isn't such a thing as Hawaii Vogue, but if there was, she'd be in it. Today, she wore a pale green loose- weave cardigan over a cream top with pink capri length pants made from some kind of slinky fabric that hung wrinkle-free. Kitten-heeled slip-ons decorated her tiny, pedicured feet. "Did you want to tell me all the stuff that happened this weekend?" Her eyes sparkled; she clearly relished the opportunity to gossip.

"Sure. You missed a lot being stuck out at your house with the flooding." I summed up the major items that had gone on. "Maile, that's the girl's name, said the hermit took her because his own daughter died and she was a replacement." I got the back door of the post office unlocked and we went inside. I took my coffee and toasted Pua with it. "Thanks for this. Let's get those doors open. I'm sure the whole town will be stopping in hoping for the latest scoop."

Sure enough, the day went by with nearly everyone in Ohia coming in to pick up mail and talk story about the wedding, the return of the little girl in the window, my miniscule dress, and the crazed hermit who abducted both Aunt Fae and possibly the girl's foster mom. We had our hands full shooing everyone out at four.

After bidding Pua aloha for the day, I went to the K & K office, changed into my swimsuit, and walked to the beach for a leisurely swim in Ohia Bay to detox from it all.

I couldn't help thinking of Elle's fear of water as I spotted a turtle bobbing in the waves nearby.

She'd never get to experience this.

Maybe we could both get better about our issues by helping each other.

I was at home waiting for Keone to call and let me know what had happened with Pacific Wings when Lei rang my cell. "I wanted to keep you in the loop about what's going on with Hugh Dragoon."

"Great. I'm sure much of what I've heard has been embellished by the coconut wireless."

Lei told me that fingerprint evidence put the hermit at the foster mom's house. "We matched his prints from the military. The Army isn't always cooperative with us, but this time we managed to convince them to send us his records. And get this, Dragoon was an explosives expert."

"Sounds right. That's how he knew how to detonate his place to smithereens and use the magnesium to raise the temperature of the fire to make sure there was no evidence left behind."

"Yes," she said. "Seems he stayed at Long's house after he put her in the shed. He said she owed him room and board since she'd treated him badly when he'd been placed with her as a foster kid. He's been charged with assault, kidnapping, burglary, and attempted murder. Of course, if Barbara Long succumbs to her injuries, he'll be charged with murder. Each of the charges he's now facing are felonies though, so if he's convicted, our hermit is going to be spending a good long time in prison."

"Anything else you can share?"

"According to the Army, Dragoon was discharged when his wife and young child died in a car accident while he was deployed to Iraq. He experienced medical issues which affected his job performance after that."

"Mental health issues?"

"I'm not at liberty to confirm or deny."

"Got it. Thanks, Lei."

I ended the call as the doorbell rang. I hurried downstairs and opened the door for Keone. He held a bottle of champagne in one hand and a bag of popped kettle corn in the other.

I smiled. "You come bearing gifts."

"I do." He waggled the bottle and jiggled the bag. "Maybe you and Aunt Fae are up for watching a movie tonight."

"Is the champagne to celebrate or commiserate?"

"Both. To celebrate you finding your lost girl and to commiserate me learning I've been written up for unauthorized use of company property. The promotion went to the girl pilot."

"*Woman* pilot."

"Yes. I'm sure she deserved it." He seemed unfazed.

"But you're still employed? Not being charged with felony aircraft hijacking?" I pressed.

"The other thing to celebrate. They're not happy I snatched a plane to get my mom to the hospital, but the owner understands that 'ohana comes first."

"There will be other promotions. To quote a motto from the twelve-step program, you got to take life one day at a time."

"That's the only way to go, especially with my mom needing so much care right now."

"Well, come on in, Mr. K, and let's crack open that bottle. We have a lot to be thankful for."

43

ONE MONTH LATER

Relaxing after a vigorous post-work swim at Ohia Bay, I leaned back on my elbows on my beach towel, enjoying the late afternoon sun on my body. The days were getting longer, and that meant more time for fun after the post office closed.

I watched a pair of 'iwa, enormous black frigate birds, as they wheeled and dove above the turquoise water, performing an elaborate dance. Were they courting? It seemed like they might be. Every flap of their wings was filled with purpose and grace.

I couldn't help thinking of Keone as I watched the seabirds' spiraling flight. We continued our own dance, and right now, the steps seemed to be in tandem.

Therapy with Dr. Kinoshita was going well. She had me practicing "touch desensitization" daily. Keone was my main helper for this. He now had permission to surprise me with hugs, kisses, back rubs and more; my job was to lean into whatever he came up with. I smiled, remembering a recent surprise he'd planned involving edible massage oil. He was definitely taking his part in the therapy seriously.

I had passed on many of the techniques I was learning to Elle. She had taken to meeting me at the beach, working up to actually touching the water. Maybe she would be able to get her toes wet today. We'd see how long she lasted.

Elle was the one who'd come up with a solution to what to do about Maile Ortiz's living situation. Elle L. Beane wasn't just a highly trained medical researcher and event planner, she was also something of a matchmaker.

"Maile's such a delight," Rita Farnsworth had said to Elle after she'd been introduced to Maile at Edith and Josie's reception. "She reminds me of my child at that age." Rita's daughter had died of cancer as a young woman and Rita mourned her loss, finding comfort in helping cats but still experiencing a void in her life.

"Yes, Maile's so sweet. And that's what makes it so horrible, what's happening to her." Elle had said. She sensed an opportunity was about to present itself as they watched Maile, Sandy and Windy dancing in their party dresses to the music the DJ played for the reception.

"What's happening to her?" Rita frowned.

"This poor kid who's survived so much will be heading back into the foster care system," said Elle. "And you know firsthand how that worked out for her before. What she needs is a place where she can be safe and secure, maybe even adopted someday."

"Sending her back to any old foster situation is unacceptable," said Rita, straightening her red hat and firming her lips. "I'm going to check into becoming a qualified foster parent."

Candace the social worker made sure Rita Farnsworth was fast-tracked into getting approved as a foster care provider, and Rita took Maile home from the Nakasones' house within a week of the girl being found at Hotel Hana.

Theirs was a match made in kitty heaven. "I love cats!" Maile exclaimed when she saw Rita's backyard cat sanctuary. "And you have lots and lots of them."

Maile and the Nakasone girls now went to the same school, and the three girls were inseparable—either spending the night at Rita's house in Hana or playing with Sandy and Windy's kittens at the Nakasone home in Ohia.

For Hugh Dragoon the outcome wasn't as upbeat. After his arrest for all the charges associated with the home invasion at Barbara Long's, the DA tacked on an arson charge for good measure. Dragoon pled guilty to all of it, seeming not to care what happened to himself now that he'd been captured. Maile had asked if she could visit her "dad" in prison when she went to see her mother on planned visits, so maybe that would have a positive effect on him.

They say some people are just too mean to die. That saying applied to Barbara Long. She was discharged and, according to the coconut wireless, sold her home and moved to Honolulu to get a fresh start. No one on Maui was sorry to see her go.

For the moment, everyone in our little part of the world was either well or on the mend. Artie had a new treadmill and was walking daily to strengthen his heart. Keone's mom Ilima was regaining her speech and mobility with ongoing physical therapy. Aunt Fae was trying a new medication that helped with the dizzy spells that had been worrying us.

As the sun dipped lower in the sky, casting long shadows across the sand of Ohia Bay, peace filled me. The air was filled with the salty tang of the sea, and the occasional cry of the 'iwa seemed to echo the rhythm of my own heartbeats—steady, content.

Elle finally arrived; her expression was tentative but determined. She rolled up her pant legs and took off her fancy running shoes and set them beside my towel. "I'm going in this time," she stated.

"You got this!" I said. "I'm right here to support you." I watched as my new friend approached the waterline. She paused at the edge, then took a step forward until the waves were lapping gently at her feet. After a moment, she took a deep breath and stepped in deeper, allowing the cool Pacific to wash over her ankles.

"This isn't so bad!" Elle's lovely face lit up with a mixture of surprise and delight. I couldn't help but cheer for her small victory. She kicked her feet; the waves splashed her and she giggled. "I have a new goal, Kat. A triathlon! I have to swim a mile in the ocean to participate."

"You can do whatever you decide to do, Elle. I believe in you," I said.

"Glad to see that Elle's making progress." Keone had arrived. I was expecting him but had been too distracted by Elle's antics to notice his approach. He tugged off his tee and, very deliberately and with a grin, stretched out beside me on the towel, his body touching mine all along one side.

I breathed out the desire to move away even as my abs crunched up and goosebumps rose all over. I closed my eyes and focused on the sensation of his warm skin against mine; *it was pleasant*. Nothing bad was happening. I liked him. No, *loved* him. Therefore it followed that I enjoyed the feeling of being physically close.

"Yeah, she's really trying. It's not easy, but she's getting better," I said, and I was speaking of my own progress too.

Elle told us she wanted to get in a run before she lost the light, and we waved goodbye as she picked up her shoes and left.

The evening sky turned into a brilliant array of oranges and purples that lit clouds moving gently along the horizon, a picturesque end to another day in our little part of paradise.

"We're lucky, you know," Keone murmured as we stood to leave. "*Maui no ka oi.*"

"Maui is the best," I translated, proud that I knew the saying. I felt the truth of Mr. K's words deep in my bones. "It's not perfect, but it's home, and filled with people who genuinely care about each other."

We walked back to our cars with the shush of the waves and rustle of palms a gentle background music.

As we drove to the house in New Ohia for dinner with Aunt Fae and the sunset faded behind us, I reveled in gratitude for everything—our community, our friends, our challenges, and our triumphs.

Each element was a thread in the tapestry of our lives, making up a patchwork of pain, joy, loss, and love. Like the *'iwa* birds, we were part of a dance that intertwined us, no matter the storms we faced.

44

Dear Readers,

I find myself reflecting on the journey we've embarked on together through the pages of this story. We're exploring the lives and loves of a close-knit community set in a wonderful place. Each character, even each "villain," is a testament to the many aspects of the human spirit.

I am deeply grateful that you chose to spend your time in the Paradise Crime World with characters who, I hope, have become as dear to you through these many books as they have to me.

I was excited when JoAnn Bassett, who writes the cozy mystery series *Islands of Aloha*, answered my call to co-author. I have always enjoyed sharing the creative process with other like-minded writers, and in the coming year you'll be seeing more of these shared stories in the Paradise Crime World.

If you've laughed, cried, or found a moment of peace or reflection while reading, then JoAnn and I have done our jobs as storytellers. So, if you enjoyed your time in Ohia, *please consider leaving a review on your preferred platform.* Reviews are more than just critiques; they are a bridge that connects writer, reader, and future reader. They help keep the characters alive, their stories resonating with new audiences. If you have a moment, please share your thoughts about *Pau Hana* and the *Paradise Crime Cozy Mysteries* with the world!

Thank you again for being a part of this journey. Readers like you transform the solitary act of writing into a beautiful, shared experience. Let's raise a "Pau Hana" drink to many more adventures together in the days to come.

Want to keep up with the next book in the series (because there will be more!) and be informed of specials and giveaways? Sign up for my newsletter HERE and get a free full-length mystery, TORCH GINGER, starring Lei Texeira, the original heroine who kicked off the Paradise Crime World!

Curious about Sophie Smithson? Download WIRED ROGUE, a Paradise Crime Thriller set on Hawaii, FREE. A great introduction story to get to know the CEO of Security Solutions and her complicated life and loves.

If you enjoyed this story and my voice on the page, you might also like my memoir FRECKLED: a Memoir of Growing up Wild in Hawaii, my personal (award-winning) account of life as a child growing up hippie in 1970s Kauai. (Spoiler alert: it's like the Glass Castle, but Hawaii.)

In case all that wasn't enough, here's a complete list of all of my 50+ books. Yes, I write a lot! And I hope you keep reading. *As long as you do, I'll be writing.*

With heartfelt gratitude and aloha,
Toby Neal

CO-AUTHOR'S NOTE
JoAnn Bassett

ALOHA TO TOBY NEAL'S readers!

I want to begin with a big *mahalo* to Toby for her support, encouragement, and always upbeat attitude while we were working on *"Pau Hana."*

It was my great pleasure to join her in creating this latest installment in the Paradise Crime Cozy Mystery series. It's a lot of fun to spend time in Ohia and Hana, Maui with Kat, Tiki, Keone, Auntie Fae and the rest, watching them work out the problems and circumstances they face in their little corner of paradise.

If you enjoyed this story and want to read another cozy mystery series portraying life in Hawaii, please take a peek at my I*slands of Aloha Mystery Series* and *Escape to Maui Series,* available in e-book in Kindle Unlimited and in paperback, too.

Here's a list of the *Islands of Aloha Cozy Mysteries* series books, available in KU:

"Maui Widow Waltz"
"Livin' Lahaina Loca"
"Lana'i of the Tiger"
"Kaua'i Me a River"
"O'ahu Lonesome Tonight?"
"I'm Kona Love You Forever"
"Moloka'i Lullaby"
"Hilo, Goodbye"
"Isle Be Seeing You"

AND THE *ESCAPE to Maui* series books:

"Mai Tai Butterfly"
"Lucky Beach"
"Cane Field Revival"

MAHALO FOR READING *PAU HANA*, Paradise Crime Cozy Mystery #5! If you enjoyed it, would you be so kind as to leave a review? We'd appreciate it so much.

A hui hou!

JoAnn Bassett

ABOUT THE AUTHORS

Toby Neal and JoAnn Bassett met in 2016 over a shared love of all things Hawaii. Their career paths were very different in life, but both ultimately found a home in writing.

You can find their social media with a simple search by name.